What they're saying about...

Stories for the Starving Romantic

"Wonderfully written collection of short stories."

"What an unusual and gratifying experience in reading."

"Great read. I looked forward to the end of the day so I could escape the news and get lost in one of these very entertaining and thoughtful stories. Give us more! We are all starving out here."

"In a world that often seems overwhelmed by bad news, fear and hopelessness, these small stories offered me a sweet, quiet, amusing escape time to lose myself each night before I fell asleep."

"What delightful stories..."

To Koko –
We are going to miss
you very much

Stories for the Hungry Romantic

Stories for the Hungry Romantic

by T J Moran

Carmel, California
August 2018

This is a work of fiction, a compilation of stories that the author thought would be good reading, particularly at bedtime but really any time. As noted in my first books, ***Stories for the Starving Romantic***, reading these tales is certainly better than reading mysteries or thrillers that might impinge on one''s peace of mind. And much better than watching television. There is no connection to any people, alive or otherwise, except as specifically stated.

Stories for the Hungry Romantic

Published by SetonPublishing.com.

ISBN-13: 978-0-9989605-8-6

Printed in the United States of America

Table of Contents

Stories for the Hungry Romantic

Publisher's Note

Bravo to Terry! Another delicious read.

Yes, he has quit his day job, or rather has significantly cut back his hours. A nationally-renowned pioneering cardiologist in the study of lipids, Terry has shifted his practice away from the hospital to a shared private office in Monterey.

Which means he will devote more time to his writing. Which is good news because he has two novels in the works.

But don't go anywhere. The stories in the following pages are a real pleasure. Romance is probably our most powerful feeling. That hunger for romance drives us, often beyond reason, as we reach for that ultimate connection ... love.

You picked up this book because you are on the path. Free your appetite. Revel in the romance. Find your love

Tony Seton

Dedication

This book is dedicated to my take-no-prisoners editor, fondly known as my wife, Lydia, and to our five wonderful (most of the time) children — Leah, Travis, Tyler, Parker, and Spencer.

Oh, and I can't forget the dog, Penguin.

Acknowledgments

After publication of ***Stories for the Starving Romantic***, I found that I really enjoyed writing light romantic stories with a twist ending. What was even more fun, was that sometimes even I didn't know in what direction the story would go. All writers know that at times their characters can take on a life of their own, and lead them to places they'd never anticipated. Well, in several of my stories that is exactly what happened, which made writing them even more enjoyable for me. So I hope that you will be entertained with this new group of short stories contained in ***Stories for the Hungry Romantic***.

As always there are more people involved in helping one write a book than you can ever thank. To everyone who has had even the slightest input into this book, I salute you and say, thank you very, very much.

There are, though, a few stand-outs that deserve mention. Once again Madeline DiMaggio — writer, writing instructor, good friend, and constant supporter — has had a huge hand in seeing this get to publication. I can't look at this book or the previous one without seeing her in the background directing and cheering me on. I won't say thank you because that's way too inadequate, and she already knows how much I appreciate her.

There is an old adage that you should never give your writing to family or friends for critique because they won't be honest in their comments. Someone forgot to tell that to my wife, Lydia. You might laugh, but it's her honest evaluation and editing that has taken these stories from a primitive scrawling to something which I am proud to publish. Without her, there would be no books.

And of course, no acknowledgment would be complete without a huge thank-you to my publisher, Tony Seton — a dynamo who makes publishing a book seamless and fun. The mimosas will continue at the Cypress Inn.

The Pool Hall

Looking at me now you might not know it.
I've had my moments, days in the sun
Moments I was second to none.

Moments by Emerson Drive

After parking their car, Mark Jennings led his daughter Melissa down Main Street to an open doorway, above which was a sign announcing Peter Pan Billiards. They descended the scuffed wooden stairs into a small dingy anteroom. The right side of the room was taken up by a glass enclosed barbershop with a single old fashioned barber chair, presently unoccupied. Its walls were plastered with faded black and white photos of boxers, football players, and numerous other athletes that Melissa couldn't identify. Off to her left was the entrance to a large dimly lit room from which the crack of pool balls could be heard.

"Why would you come here to get a haircut?" Melissa said with surprise, and a touch of disdain. "What, True Cuts is too modern for you?"

Her dad smiled. "Old dogs, old habits."

"Whatever that means," Melissa smirked and rolled her eyes. "So what am I supposed to do?" she asked looking around. "This place is a dive with a capital D."

At the entrance to the pool room was a glass counter topped with an antique cash register. The elderly clerk behind the counter had his shirt sleeves rolled up, and was reading the sports section. He glanced up over his reading glasses and silently nodded at Melissa's dad.

"You're on restriction and stuck with me all day, so live with it," Mark replied.

"So my punishment is a boring afternoon with a boring dad. This is bullshit."

The man behind the counter said calmly, "Watch your language, young lady."

Melissa turned and gazed at him, shocked that he'd interrupted their conversation, and even more surprised at her father's reply.

"Thanks, Eddie," Mark said to the man behind the counter. "Keep an eye on her, will you please?" Her dad pointed to several chairs scattered around the waiting area. "Grab a seat. I'll get this done as quickly as possible." With that he walked over to the barbershop, and climbed onto the chair. An older man with grey hair and wearing a white barber's coat, put his paper aside, and approached Mark.

"The usual?"

"That would be fine, Bill. How're your wife and kids these days?"

Melissa picked up a year old *People* magazine and leafed through the pages. It was all she could do not to scream. This was Saturday, her favorite day to hang with her friends. Instead she was grounded and stuck with her dull, predictable dad.

After a few moments, she tossed down the magazine, stood up, and walked over to the entrance to the pool room.

Eddie looked up from his sports section. He gave her a hard look, and then smiled. "Go on in, just don't interrupt the playing."

She stepped through the opening and paused to take it all in. It was a long rectangular room with a polished cement floor. Fifteen ancient looking billiard tables were set in three rows, with elongated, fluorescent lamps above each table, casting illumination just to the edges, leaving the players in shadow. A worn wooden bench lined the walls which Melissa assumed were for spectators to watch the games. She caught a hint of cigarette smoke and stale beer.

There were eight people standing around different tables, some of them bent over with pool cues lining up shots. A few looked over at her, and then back to their game. She noted that several were drinking beer. Conversations were in a hushed tone. There was no laughter, no cheering, just serious players concentrating on their games. The dress was causal, although several were in dress pants with rolled up shirt-sleeves, loosened ties, and suspenders.

Melissa climbed the single step up to the side wall bench, and eased herself down. She slowly glanced around the room, wondering what kind of people spent their Saturday morning in a dump like this. Once again she cursed her parents for putting her in this situation.

"May I join you?" The deep voice came from her right. She swung around, ready to fend off whoever was trying to hit on her, and stopped. The man was in his sixties, black, with an athletic build and shaved head. He had a commanding presence that was augmented by his dark suit, but mellowed by his easy smile, and the cup and saucer he was delicately holding.

"My name is Joseph, I'm the owner. You must be Melissa." He sat down, and took a sip from his cup. "I've known your father for a number of years, and he's often spoken of you."

Melissa half-smiled and said blandly, "Nice to meet you."

Joseph turned and slowly pursued the room. "We're a bit slow right now, but tonight things will be jumping." He turned back to her. "Are you a pool player?"

She shook her head. "I've never even seen a game of pool."

Joseph nodded. "You're not alone. Unfortunately, the game seems to be on the wane. It can't compete with the video games that occupy young people these days." He took another sip. "Yet it's a beautiful sport, and anyone can play." He gestured to one of the empty tables. "Would you like to try it? I'd be happy to show you how."

Melissa couldn't think of anything more unexciting. And besides, she didn't want to make a fool of herself in front of all these people, so she politely declined.

Joseph took another sip, and stared at her over his cup. "Your father has never brought you here before, and apparently on this occasion it's not to play pool..."

"I'm on restriction." She hesitated then explained. "I went out with a senior."

"Is that a problem?" Joseph said with a frown.

"I'm a sophomore, and the rule is I can't go out with anyone that's more than one grade ahead of me."

Joseph nodded and looked at her. "And you don't agree with this?"

"Of course not! Just because I'm sixteen, they're treating me like a child. I'm smart enough to pick my own dates."

"So you're here because your dad is keeping an eye on you?"

She leaned back against the bench. "Yep, just me and my good old dad."

There was a loud noise in the corner and both of them turned toward it. After a moment, Joseph said, "I have a story that might interest you."

She glanced toward the entrance but there was no sign of her father. How long does it take to get a simple haircut, she wondered? "Yeah, apparently I've got nothing but time."

Joseph smiled. "Well, it happened a number of years ago. It was a Thursday night, and things were fairly slow like it is now. A young man named Red came in with his girlfriend. I don't recall her name but let's call her Mary. As I remember Red was a senior in high school and Mary was a sophomore."

"Oh, I see where this is going."

"Red was the classic bad boy. Girls saw him as dynamic, exciting, and so mature compared to the boys their age. He had his own car and did what he wanted with no concern for authority of any kind. This combined with his smoking and drinking made him the young rebel that so many girls of Mary's her age were attracted to." Joseph held up his cup. "Forgive me for being a bad host. Would you like some tea?"

"No, I'm fine."

"Well, Mary had a very different background than Red. She came from a middle class family, followed all the rules, and attended church regularly. So stepping out with Red added excitement and danger to her mostly mundane existence."

"Let me assure you, my existence is anything but mundane," Melissa said. "It's my parents that live the monotonous life."

Joseph smiled. "Remember this is just a story, not a reflection on you." After a moment, he went on. "Well, Red had been in here a number of times and considered himself a fairly good pool player. He'd even won some money off lesser players."

"People bet on these games?"

"Well, it's not legal and we don't encourage it, but it happens fairly frequently."

Melissa glanced around but didn't see any money on the tables or changing hands.

"Red wanted to impress his girlfriend on what a cool guy he was, and he decided that winning money playing pool would do that." Joseph shook his head slightly. "Unfortunately, he picked the wrong night. The only player in here who would bet with him was a man named Nagel."

"He sounds creepy already."

"Nagel was as friendly as a tiger looking at you for lunch, and everyone knew not to get in a money game with him. Everyone that is except Red.

Red walked Mary over to a side wall bench and sat her down.

"I don't like this place, Red," she said quietly. "Let's go somewhere else."

"Oh, come on, Mary. This is my kind of place. Let me win some money and then we'll head out." He grinned at her. "This is going to be fun."

He smoothed back his long red hair, and walked out into the middle of the darkened room. "Anyone interested in a game of pool?" He held up a fistful of dollar bills as he said this.

Several people looked over and then went back to their games. "What, no one up to the challenge?"

He was turning away when a voice in the back of the room said, "Sure, I'll play with you, kid." And out of the shadows stepped a tall, burley man with a dark mustache. He had a leather case under his arm. "Pick a table," he said as sweetly as the wolf probably spoke to Red Riding Hood.

Red looked over at Mary and winked. "No, you pick it so there won't be any complaints later on."

Nagel grinned ever so slightly, and moved to a center table. "This looks good." From the case, he pulled out his pool cue which was in two parts. He screwed them together, and set the cue on the table.

Red moved to the wall, and picked a pool cue off the rack. He put it on the table and rolled it back and forth to make sure it was straight without curves. Glancing over at Nagel, he said, "I'm ready when you are. How about we play 8 ball?"

"Sounds good to me," Nagel replied and innocently added, "Say ten dollars a game?"

"What is 8 ball?" Melissa asked.

"It's a popular game. 8-Ball is played with the white cue ball and fifteen numbered balls, half of which are solid colors numbered 1-8, while the other balls, 9-15, are striped. One player must pocket balls of solid colors, while the other player must pocket the striped balls. The player who pockets their entire group and then legally pockets the 8-ball wins the game." He glanced at her.

"How do they decide which person plays solid and the other striped?"

"They rack the balls up in a triangle at the start of the game. One of the players then breaks that group of balls apart with the cue ball. The person who first sinks a ball gets his choice of solid or stripes. Once this selection occurs, he is not allowed to hit the other person's balls to get his balls into the pocket." He watched her for a moment and realized she understood. "So getting back to Red and Nagel."

Red pulled the balls out of the side and corner pockets and assembled them at the foot end of the table. Pulling a triangular-shaped rack from beneath the table, he placed it on top and loaded the 15 balls into it, keeping the 8 ball in the center of the group. Using the rack, he moved the balls to a marked point at that end of the table, and then lifted the rack off. The balls were tight in the shape of a triangle pointed toward the head of the table.

"Shall we lag for break?" Red asked.

"Just flip a coin," Nagle said.

"Okay." Red pulled a coin out. "Call it." As he flipped it in the air, Nagle said, "Heads."

They leaned over the coin when it hit the felt, and then Nagle looked up. "Looks like you break."

Red smiled over at Mary, confidence written boldly across his face. He set the cue ball down, lined it up with his pool cue, and then struck it hard with the tip of the cue. The balls flew apart, and a solid went into a corner pocket while the others scattered around the table.

After looking the table over, Red said, "I'll take solids." He then proceeded to knock first one then another solid into a pocket. On his third attempt, he hit a solid which bounced around the opening of the pocket but then came out.

"Nice shooting, kid," Nagle said as he stepped to the table and lined up his first shot. He sank a striped ball, but his next shot was way off. He looked over. "Say, what should I call you, kid?"

"You can call me winner in a few more minutes," Red said with a big smile. "But for now, the name's Red."

"Well, my name's Nagel."

Red grabbed a small cube of chalk and rubbed his pool cue tip with it so the tip wouldn't slip off the cue ball when he hit it. He then proceeded to knock one and then another solid ball into the pocket before losing his turn.

Nagel sank one of his stripes and then missed on his next attempt. Red stepped back and looked over the table. He had only two solids left, both close to pockets, while Nagel had five stripes spread all over the table. Red made his first shot, hitting the cue ball with rightward spin so it veered to the right after hitting the solid ball. This lined up his next shot perfectly, and he easily sank his last solid.

With a wink at Mary, he then sank the eight ball and the game was over.

"Man, you know how to play," Nagel said. "You some kind of hustler?"

"No, just a guy who likes to play pool. Shall we go again?"

This time Nagel did better and only had two balls on the table when Red finally sank the eight ball.

Nagel checked his watch. "I have to get going soon, but I want a chance to win back what I've lost. How about we up the stakes?"

Red smiled. "I'm in."

"How about a hundred dollars a game? Can you handle that?" Nagel said this with just a touch of sarcasm as if he knew that it was too rich for Red. And it was, but Red was riding high and he saw some easy money coming his way.

"Give me a second," he said, and walked over to Mary. "I need to borrow your prom dress money. I don't have that much myself."

"Red, do you know how long it took me to save that up?"

"Hey, I'll give the money right back. You saw me beat this guy twice, and I didn't even show him my best game."

"The lady's right. You shouldn't bet with this guy." Mary and Red turned toward the individual who'd interrupted them. He was tall, with a mop of dark hair, faded Levis, and a worn white shirt. In one hand, he held a large push broom.

"Hey, I know you," Red said. "I've seen you at our school. What are you doing here?"

"I work here before and after school, cleaning up and closing the place."

"Oh, yeah." He pointed to the broom. "You're the guy they call Push-broom." Red looked him up and down. "So when does a janitor start offering me advice?"

Pushbroom, who was a head taller than Red, stepped forward forcing Red to move back. He looked at Red and then Mary. "Nagel's a pool shark and comes here to win money. He's a much better player than you've seen. He's been holding back, trying to sucker you into this bigger bet."

"Well, I'm a pretty good player myself," Red said, "and I think I can beat him." He turned to Mary. "Trust me, baby. I can handle this."

Nagel yelled from the table. "Hey, Pushbroom, can you sweep up over here? My foot slipped on some crap on the floor."

The tall boy left them and walked over to the table. He used his large broom to sweep the surrounding area, grabbed the dust pan hooked on his belt, and then swept it up. "It looks pretty clean now, Mr. Nagel."

Nagel pulled a dollar out and gave it to him. Pulling him aside, Nagel said quietly, "Pushbroom, why don't you let Red make his own decisions?"

They both looked over to where Red was still arguing with Mary. Finally, she gave in and handed him the money from her purse. "If you lose this, Red, that's the last straw and we are done."

He kissed her on the cheek, and ambled back to Nagel. "Let's play."

Nagel stepped back from the table. "Why don't you break, Red?"

Red gave him a questioning look, shrugged his shoulders, and moved to the table. He racked the balls, set the cue ball in a spot he liked, and then hit it hard. The rack of balls broke apart, but none of the balls went into a pocket so Red's turn was over.

Nagel chalked his pool cue tip as he looked over the location of the balls.

"Didn't leave you much," Red said with a half-smile.

Nagel nodded slowly. "But you left me enough." He lined up a ball and sank it. "I'll take solids," he said. Then as methodically as a metronome, he began pocketing balls. One after another after another. In no time, he had cleared the table of solid balls, and was now lining up the eight ball. "I call eight in the corner pocket," he said. With a boom, the cue ball collided with the eight ball and drove it straight into the corner pocket.

Nagel set his pool cue on the table and held out his hand to Red. "I think you owe me one hundred dollars, son." Red slowly handed over the money, his face flushed with shame since he knew he'd been suckered. Several of the spectators moved away, shaking their heads at the stupidity of some people.

Over the sounds of the pool hall, someone could be heard sobbing. It was Mary.

Nagel elbowed Red and said, "You'd better attend to your girlfriend, kid."

With his head down, Red shuffled over to Mary. "I'm really sorry, Mary. I'll make it up to you, I promise."

"When, Red? The prom is in two weeks and you don't have any money." She wiped her eyes and stood up. "Take me home, now."

The two of them turned and started to walk out when a hand grabbed Mary's arm. "Don't leave yet, Miss." She swung around and it was Pushbroom. "I'll get your money back."

Mary realized she'd seen Pushbroom around school but had never paid him much attention. She thought he might be a junior, but for her he was just one of many faces in the crowd. And she'd cast her lot with Red, which now seemed pretty stupid. Mary looked at Pushbroom and shook her head. "Thank you, but he's not going to give it back."

"I wasn't planning on asking for it." There was a tone in his voice that gave Mary the confidence that it might be possible, but then she remembered how easily Nagel had beaten Red.

"No, you'll just lose your money. I can't ask you to do that."

"Let me worry about that" He gestured to the bench she'd just left. "Why don't you sit back down and let me see what I can do."

Red stepped between them. "If you've got money to play, then let me play him," he said. "He just got lucky. I can beat him."

Pushbroom leaned into Red. "If I ever see you in here with her again, I'll kick your ass." Red stepped back, turning a bit pale. "Now keep out of my way."

Nagel had put away his pool cue and was starting to leave when Pushbroom said, "How about a game, Mr. Nagel? I'd like to win this girl's money back for her."

Nagel laughed. "Pushbroom, you're a good kid and I salute your gallantry, but do you even play pool?

"I know which end of the stick to hit the ball with."

Nagel thought for a moment, then shook his head. "Tempting, but the management here wouldn't like it if I took your money."

"You're pretty confident, Mr. Nagel."

"Please, enough of the Mr. Nagel. It's just Nagel, and no I won't play with you."

Pushbroom yelled to Eddie at the entrance. "Say, Eddie, how much work money are you holding for me?"

Eddie popped open the cash register, and after a moment yelled back, "Two hundred and fifty dollars, Pushbroom." After a moment, he added, "Joseph's not going to be happy."

"Relax Eddie. I'll handle Joseph." He swung back to Nagel. "One game for a hundred dollars. So how about it?"

Nagel stared at him for a long moment, and then smiled. "Okay, kid, you're on. But don't say I didn't warn you." He opened his leather case, took out his pool cue parts, and screwed them together.

Pushbroom put his dust pan and broom in the corner. He then

walked to several of the different racks that held pool cues. After examining a number of them, he finally selected a pool cue and walked over to the table. "Let's play," he said.

"You're not going to roll it and make sure it's straight?"

Pushbroom shook his head. "I already know this cue is straight."

"Suit yourself. So what are we playing?"

"Straight pool. Call your shots. First one to 100."

"I don't want to interrupt again," Melissa said, "but what's straight pool?"

"That is one of the more popular tournament games. The shooter can shoot at any pool ball on the table. One point is scored for each ball pocketed. The goal is to reach a set number of points determined by agreement before the game. In professional competition, straight pool is usually played to 125 points. Straight pool is a call-pocket game, meaning the player must indicate the intended object ball and the pocket on every shot."

"But there are only 15 balls. So what happens when those are cleared off?"

"Actually, they leave one ball still on the table. They rack up the other 14 pocketed balls, putting them in the triangle configuration. The idea is for the shooter to then pocket the single ball that was left, but hit it in such a manner as to cause the cue ball to carom back, hit the racked balls, and spread them over the table. If you don't sink a ball, the next shooter takes over."

"Wow. How many balls can a good player sink during his turn?"

"Varies tremendously, but Willie Mosconi holds the record of pocketing 526 balls in a single turn."

"That's incredible," Melissa said.

"That's an extreme example. Most regular players sink 2 to maybe 5 balls during their turn. The professionals can pocket a lot more."

"You mentioned the term 'lag' for who breaks. What is a lag?"

"Each player selects a ball, and they shoot it off the wall or cushion at the other end of the table. The object is to rebound the ball and see how close they can bring it back to their end without touching their cushion. If you hit the cushion, you lose. The winner then gets to break."

"Shall we lag for serve?" Nagel said.

They each chose a ball, and then at the same time shot it toward the other end of the table. Nagel's bounced off the distant cushion and ended up a few inches from the cushion at his end. Pushbroom's ball came back and hit the near cushion.

"Not a good start for you, Pushbroom." As he spoke, Nagel chalked his pool cue tip. "I'll give you one more chance to back out." He grinned. "But of course, then you'd lose your opportunity to impress the young lady."

Pushbroom gestured toward the table. "I thought we were playing pool not welching on bets."

Nagel chuckled. "Just don't go crying to the management when I take your money." With that, he bent over, lined up his shot, and dropped a ball in the corner pocket. It was the start of a run of 8 balls being pocketed, before he missed. He stepped back, and waved his arm toward the table. "Let's see what you've got, kid."

Pushbroom had an easy shot into the corner pocket, but when the tip of his cue hit the ball, it slid off the side, and the cue ball missed everything.

"Nothing like a miscue to get you started," Nagel said with a laugh. "Try chalking your tip next time."

Red leaned into Mary. "This guy has no idea how to play pool."

Still staring at the game, Mary replied quietly, "What's the worst he can do? Lose like you?" She turned to Red. "He's risking his own savings to get a stranger's money back. Something I can't ever see you doing."

Nagel pocketed another five balls before his turn was over. The score was now 13 to 0.

After chalking his tip, Pushbroom moved around the table eyeing the two balls left. Choosing one, he leaned over and took the shot, sinking the ball.

"Good shot," Mary said, but when everyone turned to look at her, she realized that she'd overstepped proper pool room decorum.

Pushbroom, seemingly oblivious to the harsh stares Mary had generated, replied with a smile, "Thank you."

With one ball left, they racked up the other fourteen at the foot end of the table. Pushbroom picked up the cue ball, carefully placed it at the head end of the table, and hit it toward the ball standing alone. The lone ball popped into the corner pocket as the cue ball ricocheted into the triangle of balls, spreading them out across the table. Moving around the table, he carefully lined up on a ball close to a side pocket, but his shot went wide.

Red winced. "My grandmother could have made that shot." He grabbed Mary's arm. "Let's go. This is going to be a slaughter."

She pulled her arm away. "I'm staying until the end, and then I'm going to thank him for what he tried to do."

Nagel stood at the head of the table and slowly took in the location of each ball. When he'd finished, his grin spread across his entire face.

Mary involuntarily shuttered. "He's like a wolf looking down on a flock of sheep as he gets ready to devour them."

Once again Red stood up to leave, but Mary grabbed his arm and pulled him down.

"What do you think, Pushbroom," Nagel said. "Could you have given me a better leave?"

"Quit gloating and let's play," Pushbroom said with a touch of anger.

Nagel glanced over at him. "I warned you, Pushbroom." Nagel swept his arm around to include all the spectators that had gathered, and said to them, "Didn't I warn him not to play with me?" He raised his voice. "Hey, Eddie. You heard me warn the kid. You make sure that Joseph knows that. I don't want to be blackballed from here."

Eddie snickered. "Oh, you're not the one that's going to be in trouble, Mr. Nagel."

Mary leaned over to Red. "Why would Pushbroom be in trouble?"

Red shrugged his shoulders. "Probably not supposed to gamble with the customers."

She shook her head. "Nagel's twice his size even if they are the same height. I feel like I'm watching David and Goliath, only this time David's not going to do so well."

Red regarded her questioningly. "Who's David?"

Mary shook her head and let out a long sigh.

Nagel bent over the table, and the slaughter began. Ball after ball disappeared into the pockets. Pretty soon there was just one ball left, and the score was 26 to 2. They racked the balls again, and Nagel ran through them as easily as wind through a wheat field. Now the score was 40 to 2.

Nagel was leaning over to take a shot and then straightened up. "Hey, I have an idea, Pushbroom. Why don't we just call this game mine, and start a new one. You've still got money left to bet, and a new game would give you a chance to win since this game is in the bag."

Pushbroom glared at him for the longest time and finally nodded. "I do still have money left, but I don't want a new game. I want to bet it on this one."

"You want to add another one hundred and fifty on to this bet? Am I hearing you right?"

"You are."

Eddie yelled from his place at the counter. "Pushbroom, don't make this any worse than it already is."

Unable to help herself, Mary stood up and walked over to Pushbroom. "I can't thank you enough for what you've tried to do, but now it should end. I'm not going to let you lose all your money."

With the gentlest of smiles, Pushbroom escorted her back to her seat.

"Can I have that ribbon in your hair?" he asked.

For a moment, she was caught by surprise, but then she smiled back at him and untied her ribbon. "Of course."

Pushbroom moved back to the table. "So Nagel, is it a bet or not?"

Once again, Nagel spoke to all the spectators. "You all heard the bet. It's now two hundred and fifty on this game, not a new one." With that he turned and said to Pushbroom. "I have to give it to you, kid. You've got no smarts, but you've got balls. I'm almost sorry to take your money."

With that, Nagel took his next turn and put 9 balls into the pockets before he missed. The score was now 49 to 2.

"You know much about the knights of old, Nagel" Pushbroom asked. Nagel shook his head, wondering where this was going. "Well, in the old days, when a knight went into a tournament, he often wore the colors of the woman he admired, both for luck and to let her know he was doing this for her." With that he tied Mary's ribbon on the end of his pool cue.

"You got class, Pushbroom," Nagel said with a grin. "Just wish you had a game."

Pushbroom held up the end of the cue with the ribbon on it, pointed it toward Mary, and bowed. "For you, my lady."

Caught up in the moment, Mary stood and clapped. "Whether you win or lose, you will always be my shining knight, Pushbroom."

The crowd tapped the floor with their pool cues signaling their approval.

"Before I throw up all over the table, let's get back to the game," Nagel moaned.

"Ever watch the movie, *The Color of Money*, Nagel?" Pushbroom asked. "It's about pool hustlers."

"Can't say I have, kid."

"Well, Paul Newman is in this bar and notices a young Tom Cruise beating everyone in pool without even trying. Newman has never seen him before, and after a bit approaches Cruise's manager/girlfriend. He offers to play against Cruise for five hundred dollars a game. The manager looks Newman over and is thinking about it when Newman says she should turn the offer down. And then he gives her the reasons why." Pushbroom readjusted the ribbon on his cue and then stared at Nagel.

After a few moments, Nagel said, "Okay, I'll bite. What were the reasons?"

"Two of them. First, Newman was an unknown and they'd never seen him play so they didn't know who they were up against. Second, the bet was too high. Newman wouldn't have bet that much unless he knew he could beat Cruise." Pushbroom smiled. "Do those reasons sound familiar?"

Nagel laughed. "Movies ain't real life, Pushbroom. So let's get back to playing pool."

"Just remember those two reasons while we play," Pushbroom said. He then bent over the table and ran twenty balls before his turn ended. Now the score was 49 to 22.

It was a different Nagel that took his next turn. He'd gone silent, and his movements were cautious and careful. He dropped five balls and then lost his turn. Pushbroom was also quiet, but more like a surgeon waiting to complete his task rather than from nerves. With his next turn, Pushbroom sank eighteen balls before he missed a shot. The score was now 54 to 40.

Red leaned into Mary. "Maybe this guy can play."

Nagel had a nice run of six balls before his turn was over. Pushbroom moved to the table, chalked his cue, and then looked over at Nagel. "Tell you what, Nagel. I'll give you a break. You return the lady's one hundred dollars, and we call the game a tie. How about it?"

"You don't actually think you're going to win, do you?" Nagel said with a snort. "I'm just getting warmed up."

"You should have warmed up before we started, Nagel. Now is too late." Pushbroom moved to the other side of the table. There were four balls stuck in a group. "I call the 4 ball in the corner pocket."

With that, Pushbroom hit the 7 ball at the edge of the group and as they all bounced apart, the 4 ball went into the corner pocket.

By now, everyone in the pool hall had gathered around to watch the game. With this combination shot, they all tapped their pool cues on the floor.

Pushbroom slowly chalked his cue, starring at the table. "I grew up watching every movie I could find about pool. Memorized the lines in each of them." He paused for a moment. "I love this game so much, it's why I work here just to be near the action." He ran his hand over the felt on the table. "Did you ever see Paul Newman in *The Hustler*?"

"Yeah, long time ago. So what?"

"Remember the scene at the beginning of the movie when Newman is playing Minnesota Fats, supposedly the best player around. Newman's gone through hell to get this game against him."

"I have a vague recollection."

"Here Newman is playing the very best, and instead of being nervous, he smiles and asks Fats, 'I've got a hunch. I feel like it's me from here on. That ever happen to you, Fats, where all of a sudden you feel like you can't miss'?" Pushbroom looked at Nagel. "Well, I've got a hunch too." With that, he ran twenty-five balls, before Nagel finally got his turn. Nagel pocketed ten balls before he missed. Pushbroom took over and dropped another fifteen, making the score 70 to 81.

"Don't know where you got such luck, kid, but now it's my turn to kick ass." With that, Nagel put eleven balls in the pockets.

"We make our own luck, Nagel, and I've got more than enough for this game." Moving with precision, Pushbroom then knocked in nineteen straight balls, and the game was over. Score 81 to 100.

Nagel unscrewed his pool cue and packed it away in his leather case. He walked over to Pushbroom and stood staring at him. He slowly shook his head, and said, "You out hustled a hustler, kid." He fanned out a number of bills that added up to the money Pushbroom had won and gave it to him. Then he put out his hand, and they shook. Nagel said, "You play a hell of a game, Pushbroom. It was a pleasure watching you." With that, he turned and left.

Pushbroom walked over to Mary and handed her the two hundred and fifty dollars he'd won.

"That's too much," she said trying to give back the excess.

He pushed it away, and said, "The extra is for you to buy an even nicer dress, although you're so pretty it wouldn't matter what you wore. You'd still be the best looking girl in the room."

"Hey, I think some of that money should be mine," Red said stepping up to them.

"Get lost, Red," Pushbroom said, elbowing him out of the way.

Mary and Pushbroom stared at each other for several moments, and then she gave him a long hug. "Thank you so much. How can I ever repay you?"

Pushbroom gestured with his thumb at Red. "Just don't go with that jerk to the prom. Find some nice guy that will treat you right."

"Wow, that's a pretty cool story," Melissa said. After a moment, she added, "So did Pushbroom ever get in trouble for playing Nagel?"

"That's the funny part. Eddie told Pushbroom not to play, not because he might lose his money, but rather he knew that Pushbroom would beat Nagel." Joseph smiled as if remembering those past days. "Before he opened and after he closed the hall, Pushbroom would practice for hours by himself. He was a natural at the game. In fact, he became so good that I wouldn't let him play against the customers because it wouldn't be fair. That's what Eddie was trying to remind him."

"Pushbroom sounds like a really neat guy." Melissa looked at Joseph. "What happened to him?"

"Well, first we quit calling him Pushbroom. After that display, he was always called "Mr. P". Rumor has it that he and Mary went to the prom together, and were married a number of years later."

"That's so rad," Melissa said. "I hope someday a person like Pushbroom comes into my life."

Joseph smiled. "You never know."

Melissa's father walked up just then, rubbing his new haircut. "So are you ready to get out of this 'dive', honey?" He looked over at her older companion and winked. "So what lies have you been filling her with, Joseph?"

"Nothing but the truth, Mr. P. Nothing but the truth."

Shocked, Melissa glanced at Joseph and he answered her silent question with a nod.

Melissa slowly turned back to her father, who was now watching one of the games. "Dad," she said.

When he looked over, she starred at him and wondered how she'd been so blind. This was no dull, couch potato. This was a man with eyes bright with the passion of life. She easily saw him now as that high school boy saluting a distraught young girl with his ribbon tied pool cue.

After a moment, he raised his eyebrows. "What?" he asked with the beginnings of a smile.

She wanted to reach out and hug him but instead, trying to keep her voice steady, she said, "Dad, can we stay, and... and you teach me how to play pool?"

* * * * *

This story had several inspirations. When I was in college I spent time in Salt Lake City and played pool at the Peter Pan Billiards. It was an unforgettable place; the epitome of the shady pool hall your parents warned you against, and I loved it.

The other inspiration was a patient of mine. The first time I saw this older gentleman, he came shuffling into my office. Glancing warily around, he'd eased himself down on my exam table and let out a sigh of relief. I wondered briefly about his life and just assumed it had been as sedate and reserved as he was now. I took care of him for a number of years as his steps grew slower and his memory faltered. It wasn't until after he died and I read his obituary that I discovered that this quiet, unassuming individual had been a bomber pilot in World War II, had lead numerous hair-raising raids over Italy, and been awarded multiple medals, including the Distinguished Flying Cross.

I realized then how often we forget that the aged individuals we see in front of us have had long, full lives, and that they may have done things we couldn't imagine accomplishing. And then I thought of my own parents, and how little I truly knew of their lives when they were young. Their thoughts, their dreams, their adventures.

So next time you're in the presence of some older individual, remember they weren't always that way. They've had their moments, their days in the sun when they were second to none.

A Night at the B. V.

Overnight a lot can change

You can go from cloudy grey

To the morning brilliant blue

... It's all up to you"

One Breath, Michael Tomlinson

The wooden doors of the Buena Vista Café — known fondly by the locals as the BV — swung inward, allowing entry of a tall, slender woman wearing a long black coat. She paused to look over the scene, and as she did, Drago the bartender noticed her. He set down the coffee pot he'd been using to fill a line of 6-ounce coffee glasses on the bar. Quickly, he glanced around the room. All the tables were filled, but there were two open seats together at the bar. He gestured to Mike Hallor, one of the regulars, calling him over.

"Do me a favor and occupy one of those seats," Drago said. Hallor started to ask why but Drago cut him off. "Do it now!" Hallor took a seat, leaving the one next to him open.

The woman in the coat slowly walked down the length of the bar, all the while her eyes sweeping the Café. Drago caught her attention and pointed to the only empty bar stool. As she approached, Drago surreptitiously removed a small sign in front of the seat which read, "Reserved."

The San Francisco fog was so thick, it was hard to see from one street lamp to the next. Craig Collins pulled his collar up and leaned into the mist. As he turned down Hyde St, a cable car loudly slid by, the driver clanging his bell to warn those obscured by the fog that the big metal car was coming. One block down, at the corner of Beach and Hyde was Craig's destination, the BV. He was a regular there every Tuesday and Friday night, so much so, that the bartender and close friend, Drago, reserved a seat for him.

Craig placed his hand on the brass plate on one of the wooden doors and pushed it open. The place was packed ,with little if any standing room. The crowd was incredibly cosmopolitan. Some wore suits, some wore sweaters, and others were in sweat shirts. Women in designer dresses and expensive coats rubbed elbows with ladies wearing off-the-rack outfits from TJ Max. Craig pushed on in, apologizing to those he gently shouldered aside. He was half way into the café when he caught Drago's eye. The place was too raucous to speak, so Drago just nodded toward the back of the café. Craig thought Drago looked concerned but decided he was mistaken.

He continued on down to his usual seat at the bar only to pull up suddenly when he found it occupied. He turned to Drago to ask what happened, and then his attention snapped back to the woman in his place. At that same moment, she looked up at him.

Craig slowly shook his head and with a wide grin said in his best Bogie voice, "Of all the gin joints, in all the towns…"

"Hello, Craig," the woman replied with a low, husky voice.

"God, but you look good," he said. "This is a wonderful surprise."

Drago gestured to Hallor who rose up and offered his seat to Craig.

"Thanks, Mike," Craig said, dropping onto the seat. He waved Drago over. "We need some drinks. How about two glasses of champagne."

Drago offered his hand to the woman, and they shook. "Hello, Miss Helena."

The woman smiled. "I didn't think you'd remember me, Drago."

"You're not easy to forget," he replied. Stepping back, he looked at both of them. "It's nice to see the two of you together again."

"I have to agree," Craig said, as Drago moved off. "It is nice, and what a coincidence. These last few weeks you have been continuously on my mind." He smiled. "*The Phantom of the Opera* is in town. How about we have dinner at Alfred's and I take you to see it? I know how much you love it." Settling back, he stared at her for several moments. "I have forgotten how good I feel just being around you. My whole night has now changed for the better."

Drago set the drinks in front of them.

"A toast," Craig said as he raised his glass.

As Helena lifted her glass, Craig looked into her eyes. "To us," he said, and took a sip. He noticed that Helena put her's back down without drinking.

"What's the matter?" he said.

It was a moment before she spoke, and when she did it was with a touch of sadness. "I'm getting married."

Craig felt his insides drop out. "You're kidding, right?"

Helena slowly shook her head. "No, I'm serious." She reached over and covered Craig's hand. "I've been putting off telling you as long as I could because I didn't want to hurt you."

Craig tried to regain his composure, tried to manage the pain and the shock. He spoke the only thought that came to mind. "When?"

She searched his face as she replied, "Tomorrow." She waited for a reply but he remained silent. "It's at Sherman Gardens, in Santa Barbara, at 2 PM. A civil ceremony with a small guest list."

He remained silent while his face reflected the aguish he was feeling. Finally he looked over at her. "Why are you even bothering to tell me?"

"I didn't want you to hear it through the grapevine."

"Sounds like a song," he mumbled, still aching to the core. Looking down at her hand, he said, "I don't see an engagement ring."

"It's being sized."

Craig ran his hand through his hair, took a deep breath, and straightened himself up. He had to get through this with some semblance of pride. "So who is the lucky guy?"

"You don't know him. His name is Jack and he's a stockbroker."

Nodding slowly, Craig said, "How'd you meet him?"

"Blind date."

Drago walked over. "Will there be anything else?"

"She's getting married, Drago," Craig said, his voice cracking slightly.

"That's wonderful," Drago said with a grin which quickly faded when he saw Craig's pained expression. He discreetly moved away.

Craig said, "I should be wishing you happiness too, but all I feel is pain and loss."

"You had your chance," Helena said gently.

"Yes I did, and I think about that all the time."

Helena nodded. "Is that before or after you go out on a date?" She picked up her glass and drained half of it before setting it down.

"I don't blame you for being mad," he said. "I was an asshole, a fool, a jerk. Whatever. In fact there is nothing you can call me that I haven't already called myself."

They were silent for a moment, each staring into their drinks. Finally Helena spoke. "I'm still hurt over our breakup."

Craig reached over and touched her hand. "You know I love you."

"Let's not go there," she said moving her hand away.

After a swig of his drink, Craig said, "So you really love this guy?"

Helena turned and stared at him. "That's why people get married."

"This could just be, what's it called, a rebound relationship," he said. "And they never work out."

"We broke off our engagement two years ago so this has nothing to do with rebounding."

After a moment, Craig said slowly, "I always thought we were destined for marriage. That even if we were apart and dating other people, it was just a matter of time before we'd get back together." He turned toward her. "We were so good together. We loved the same things – whether it was sports, food, traveling, animals, or each other. There was a comfortableness being with you. A feeling we were complete and needed nothing more. I just couldn't imagine either of us finding someone else."

"I thought the same for a long time. And then I realized I needed to think about myself and move on with my life."

Craig finished his drink and set it down. He turned to her. "Unfortunately for me, I still believed we were destined for each other."

"Do you think you might have mentioned that some time over the last two years?"

"Didn't think I had to."

Helena shook her head. "Did you assume I'd never find anyone as good as you, or you thought that I'd just sit and wait for you to come back?"

"I believed that no matter what roads we took, what turns we made, what mistakes we created, that one day we'd be together."

Helena reached over and put her hand on Craig's. She gazed into his eyes for a long moment, and then shook her head as if she was trying to shake off a memory. Pulling a tissue from her purse, she dabbed her eyes and then stood up. "Excuse me I need to use the ladies room."

Craig grabbed his cocktail napkin, and wiped his own eyes. He'd not seen this coming, and he should have. He'd let her slip away and he only had himself to blame. His mind drifted back to when he'd first met her.

He'd been traveling around Europe, and elected to catch a train from Geneva up to Dusseldorf to visit friends. In the Geneva train station, he'd climbed onto the train with his backpack and gone in search of a seat. About halfway through the car, there were a set of two empty seats facing two others. He'd just set his pack on one of the seats, when a very attractive young woman about his age started to go around him in the aisle. She stopped and pointed at the seats across from his, saying something in French.

"Parlez-vous English?" he asked.

"Oh, yes," she replied. "Are those seats taken?"

He gestured to them. "They are empty so please take one." As he gestured to the seats, a young boy of 6 or 7 slid onto one of them. Craig tried to tell the boy to move. Instead, the boy said something back in German.

The young woman shrugged her shoulders. "He's telling you he is saving the seats for his parents."

Craig thought fleetingly of tossing him into the aisle, but realized that would not be the impression he wanted to make. The young woman smiled at him and when on down the aisle, finding a seat near the far end of the car. By the time Craig went to sit down, the boy's parents had arrived and taken their seats. Cursing his luck, Craig pulled out a book and started to read, periodically looking down the aisle where he could see the back of the young woman's head.

The train stopped several times but the young woman never moved. When the train pulled into Basel, she stood up and took her bag from the overhead rack. As she passed Craig, she gave him a warm smile.

Craig sat for thirty seconds and decided that he was in no rush; Dusseldorf would still be there tomorrow. Grabbing his backpack, he quickly exited the train. The station was a large barn like structure, and there were crowds of people moving to the various exits. He hastily glanced around, and then saw her just passing through one of the exits. He moved rapidly in her direction and finally caught up with her on the street.

"Hello," he said.

"Hello yourself," she replied with a faint accent.

"I don't want to be too forward, but can I buy you a drink or a cup of coffee?"

She stopped and looked him over. This was it, he thought, the make or break moment.

"Yes, that would be nice," she said after a short eternity.

Craig glanced around but didn't see anything inviting in the immediate area. He turned back to her. "Any suggestions?" he said.

She laughed. "Yes, there is a nice tavern just around the corner."

They made small talk as they walked toward the tavern. Her name was Helena, she lived in Basel, and worked for a clothing designer. She spoke four different languages, because her father had been in the U.S. diplomatic service and they'd moved a lot, but also because her mother was French and insisted on speaking it in the home.

Settling at a table, Craig glanced around. It was the classic Swiss tavern with detailed, beautifully carved wood beams, hand carved tables and chairs, and the ever present cuckoo clocks. The waitress was a big Bavarian women who could easily carry four steins of beer in each hand as she demonstrated several times. The place was quiet except for a group of five people in the corner speaking German who were loud and boisterous

"Those are southern Germans, probably from Bavaria," Helena said quietly.

"How do you know?"

"Those from the north are quiet, conservative, and cold. While those from southern Germany are open, easy going, like to party, and much louder. The northerners consider them fat, lazy beer drinkers."

"Now I understand the joke someone told me."

She looked at him, raising her eyebrows in question.

"The joke is a blonde moved from northern Germany to southern Germany and raised the collective IQ's of both locations."

Helena laughed. "It is very common for the northerners to make fun of the southerners." She glanced over at the party table. "We enjoy the southerners more since they are so friendly, even if a bit obnoxious."

Craig finished his beer and, noting hers was also empty, ordered another round.

"I assume you aren't married since you have no ring, and agreed to have a drink with me. What about a steady boyfriend?"

She shook her head. "Americans are always so forward."

"Aren't you actually an American?"

"Yes, but I have lived so long over here that I consider myself European. Here we are not so blunt with our questions."

Craig laughed. "But you are very blunt with your sexuality."

She eyed him. "Meaning what?"

"Topless on the beaches or around the pools. Premarital sex is common. Red light districts like the one in Amsterdam. Those kind of things."

"Why do Americans always bring their conversations around to sex? For us, it is no big deal. Who you are, and what you add to the world is of much greater importance than if you have sex with someone."

He held up his hands in surrender. "Okay. I admit it. I am a prude when it comes to sexual matters." He paused, "But I am becoming more liberated."

She eyed him speculatively, "How so?"

"I now go topless around the pools."

Helena chuckled.

They talked for another 2 hours, and finally the place started to close down. As they stepped out of the tavern, Craig hosted his backpack on his shoulders.

"So where are you staying tonight?" she asked.

Craig glanced around. "I hadn't really thought that far ahead. I just knew I wanted to meet you and so jumped off the train."

She laughed. "Well, I'm glad you did since I wanted to meet you."

"And why was that?"

"I thought you were handsome and seemed like a gentleman."

"A gentleman? You mean because I didn't throw that little kid out of the seat?"

She laughed. "Something like that, although I admit I wanted to give him a nudge myself."

They were quiet for a moment, enjoying the stillness of the night. Finally Craig spoke, "As you know, I'm a bit new around here. Any suggestions of where I might spend the night?"

She tilted her head in thought. "Well, there is the park, and it should be safe, although you never know. And two miles from here is a hostel, but be careful you don't get your stuff stolen."

"Boy, you make those choices sound so appealing."

"There is another place which is safer, and I doubt anything will be taken…"

"I like the sounds of this better."

"It's my apartment," she said with a laugh.

"You Europeans are so sexually forward."

"It has two separate bedrooms."

"Now you are sounding more like an American."

The overnight in Basel turned into a week. Helena took time off from work, and she and Craig were always on the move. If there was something to see, they saw it. Wineries, castles, museums. They made day trips to the surrounding area, occasionally staying the night in local hotels. Among his many fond memories was when they stayed in a small inn, and the owner told them their room was directly above the dining room. He politely asked if they could refrain from any 'personal antics' during the dinner hour since it might disturb the diners below. Another lasting memory was laying on the floor in Helena's apartment, a glass of wine perched on his chest, listening to Simon and Garfunkel while she worked in the kitchen. He remembered the sense of total peace and contentment he felt lying there.

Craig especially loved the mornings when they would stay in bed, Helena reading him the morning paper, while they snacked on fresh bread with jam, cheese, fruit, and tea. He felt like he'd been reborn and this was the life he was supposed to lead with the woman he was destined to be with.

At the end of that week, Craig was deeply in love. He had long ago blown off the Dusseldorf trip, yet now it was time for him to fly home and get back to work. But even with that deadline hanging over him, he refused to leave until Helena promised to see him in San Francisco in a month when she would be in town to push her company's new clothing line. She was their leading sales person.

When Helena got off the plane a month later, he was there and their relationship moved into high gear. Shortly thereafter, at her insistence, Helena's work transferred her to San Francisco where she promptly moved in with Craig.

"Sorry I took so long," Helena said as she resumed her seat.

"No problem. I was remembering how we met."

She smiled. "That was a magical week, wasn't it?"

Craig smiled. "That week was the greatest week of my life... followed by all the other wonderful weeks I've spent with you."

Helena searched his brown eyes. "You have never really explained why you broke off our engagement?"

He turned and stared at her. It was half a minute before he spoke. "I was afraid. Afraid I was moving too fast. Afraid I wasn't ready for marriage. Afraid, as the song goes, 'that in your eyes I might not see forever'."

"What do you mean?"

"That maybe everything was good now, but in time I'd lose you. That you'd tire of me and move on. You are a gorgeous woman and could have whomever you wanted."

"I wanted you. I thought I made that clear."

"Well, in a moment of insecurity and lack of confidence, I pushed you away, afraid to take that next step." He swivelled in his seat and put his arms around her, pulling her close. "Please don't marry this guy. You were meant to marry me. I panicked before, but now everything is clear."

She eased back from his embrace. "Suddenly it's clear that you want to marry me?" She paused and then put her hand on the side of his face. "No, you want me only because I'm getting married to someone else."

"There hasn't been a day that I haven't thought about you." He wiped his eyes. "Other women don't interest me because they're not you."

She took his hand. "Why have you waited so long to tell me this?"

"Bad timing, right?"

"Very bad."

He clasped her other hand. "I love you, Helena. Marry me… now… tonight!"

She pulled her hands away. "We haven't seen each other for months, and now you want to marry me… tonight? No, actions speak louder than words and I've seen nothing that would convince me that's what you really want."

She stood up and grabbed her purse. "I too believed we were meant for each other, but it's not to be."

Craig felt drained. His legs would barely support him as he stood. "I love you. Please don't get married tomorrow."

"I was hoping you might come to the wedding and wish me well." She leaned forward to give him a light kiss on the cheek, but he turned his head at the last moment so their lips met. It was a polite, friendly kiss at the start but then passion took over as he pulled her closer and wrapped his arms around her. Somewhere in the distant a person yelled, "Get a room," and Craig would have loved nothing better. The kiss slowly ended, but the emotions still ran high as they parted, both breathless.

Helena, in a voice husky with sentiment, said, "You definitely should not come to the wedding tomorrow." And then she turned and was out the door.

Craig was still staring into his empty glass when Drago came over.

"You okay?"

"No, I'm not. I know it won't help but I want to get very drunk tonight so that I don't wake up until after her wedding tomorrow."

"Helena is the one you always talk about, right?"

"Yeah, that's her." He pointed to the back of the bar. "Give me a double Jack Daniels on the rocks, and keep them coming."

"Do you still love her?"

"More than anything, but it's over."

"What did Yogi Berra say: 'It ain't over until it's over'."

Craig shook his head. "Let me tell you, it's over. So please, get me that drink."

After a number of double Jack's, Craig decided he wasn't drunk enough because he could still remember what was happening tomorrow. He was ordering his third double or was it his fourth, when someone slid onto the empty seat next to him. Craig glanced over. It was his roommate, Tom Henry.

"Heard the news, bro. Drago called me." He pointed at the empty glass in front of Craig. "That's not the answer."

Craig started to tear up. "I can't imagine living without her."

Drago walked over and stood in front of them. "Thank you, Tom. I was afraid this might get ugly, weepy, whatever."

"Helena and I talk every couple of months," Craig said, slurring his words, "and several times I nearly asked her to marry me." He shook his head. "But it never seemed to be the right time."

"Well, you sorry sack, maybe NOW is the right time," his roommate said.

"You don't understand," Craig replied. "She's getting married tomorrow at 2."

Tom put his arm around Craig's shoulder. "That means you have until then to win her back."

Craig looked at him like he was crazy, and at the same time realized he was blitzed.

"Remember our old basketball coach, Coach Rivera?" Tom said. "He use to tell us before each game, 'If you think you're beaten, you are'. So you need to get positive and I need to get you sober."

With that he eased Craig off his seat, and with his arm supporting him, helped him stagger out the door.

"Wake up, sleeping beauty," Tom said the next morning.

"Oh, God, I'm dying," Craig moaned. "Let me die in peace."

Tom yanked Craig's covers off, and then pulled him to a sitting position, swinging his legs over the side of the bed. "We are now going to try something very difficult," Tom said. "We are going to get you to walk."

"Leave me alone." Craig stared to slide back into bed.

Tom shook his head. "I was afraid of this so I have taken precautions." With that, he picked up a bucket of ice water and threw it on Craig. The result was instantaneous. Craig leaped up screaming obscenities as he wiped water off his face and hair. He looked wildly around, then yelled at Tom, "What the hell was that for?"

"We have a woman to woo. So you need to get dressed. Now!"

Craig sat down on the edge of the bed, putting his head in his hands. "Oh, shit. I had almost forgotten. Thanks for reminding me this is the day my life ends."

"You hit the shower, and I'll get the coffee ready. It's a four and a half hour drive to Santa Barbara so we have to get moving."

"It's no use," Craig said. "She's in love with this guy, Jack. She already said I was too late."

Tom slapped him on the side of the head. "I remember a guy with balls. A guy who wasn't afraid of anything. Now he's losing the most important thing in his life, and all he does is sit and make excuses."

Craig stared at the floor for a long moment and then looked up at

Tom. "So you think I have a chance?"

"We'll never know if you don't get your ass down to Santa Barbara. So let's get going."

Several Advil, a pot of coffee, a hot then cold shower, all mixed with self-recriminations, and Craig was ready to go. Tom pulled up in front of the apartment in his Volkswagen convertible. Hanging on to the railing, Craig slowly made his way down the front stairs and approached the car.

He gestured to the cold, damp fog swirling around them. "Do we really need to drive with the top down?"

"Fresh air equals sobriety and mental clarity. Two things you are going to need. So get in and let's get going."

Craig climbed in and glanced around the inside of the car. "Is this thing going to last all the way to Santa Barbara?" he said skeptically.

"This is a 1979 Volkswagen Karman Cabriolet, the last of its kind. It will get us where ever we want to go. So buckle up." With that, they sped off.

It was an hour outside of Santa Barbara when the car decided to act up. Tom pulled it over to the side of the road and parked it.

Craig checked his watch. "We only have an hour and a half before the wedding starts. I need to get there ASAP if I'm going to try and convince her not to get married."

"Hey, everything is going to be fine. The car does this every once and a while. Just needs to sit for a few minutes and catch its breath. We'll be there on time."

"Why the hell didn't we take my car instead of this ancient junk heap?"

"Because you were in no shape to drive. Just relax."

Twenty minutes later, they were back on the road. "We are cutting this very close," Craig said. "Do you know where we're going?"

"I googled the directions on my iPhone." Tom looked over. "You just concentrate on what you are going to say to Helena. You told me she wanted to see some action or some event to prove you loved her, not just words."

"Don't you think coming all this way will say something to her?"

Tom shrugged his shoulders. "Let's hope so."

"Well aren't you Mr. Encouragement? What happened to the 'if you think you're beaten you are' attitude?"

"Just make sure you are totally committed to getting her back. Whatever you need to do, do it!"

It was 10 minutes to 2 when they pulled up in front of Sherman Gardens. Craig saw a number of people entering the front of the small building, everyone nicely dressed. The wedding was about to commence.

Tom pointed to a side entrance. "Go in there and see if you can find her while I find a place to park. This is going to be tight, so hurry."

Craig leaped out and ran for the side door. He pulled it open and stepped in. He was in a hallway with several doors on one side. He moved from one door to the next, but each room was empty. As he moved down the hall, he realized it led onto the altar where the ceremony would be held.

"Where are you, Helena?" he mumbled under his breath. At that moment, he heard the music start to play. Shit, I'm too late, he thought as he walked to the end of the hall. There on the altar, just in front of him, stood the minister and a handsome man in a tuxedo, both focused on the aisle, apparently waiting for Helena to enter.

He remembered Tom's words. If you really want Helena, you have to be totally committed, and you have to show her not just tell her. With that, he took a deep breath, tried to calm his heart and shaking hands, and stepped out on the altar. He walked over to the man he assumed was Jack and tapped him on the shoulder. The man turned.

"Jack," Craig said, "I'm sorry to tell you but Helena loves me. She told me that last night. You need to call this off."

The man stared at him for a few moments, and then said, "You must be Craig."

At that instant, the music changed to the wedding march. Everyone stood as Helena, beautiful in a flowing white gown and veil, started down the aisle.

Craig was lost in her beauty when he realized that Jack was speaking to him. "Helena said you would show up, but I wasn't sure." He paused. "Thank God you did or I don't know what we would have done."

"What are you talking about?" Craig said.

At that moment, Tom stepped out on the altar and moved over to Craig. He leaned in. "Let me give you a quick list of the players. Old Jack here is a witness, I'm the best man, and you, buddy, are the groom. Congratulations."

Craig turned to look at Helena and saw her beaming smile. Off to one side, he caught Drago giving him a thumbs up sign. And as he looked around, he realized he knew just about everyone there.

Helena stepped up on the altar and put her arm through his. She smiled up at him. "I got tired of waiting. Hope you don't mind."

Everyone at the wedding agreed that this was the first time they'd ever seen the groom kiss the bride before the ceremony started.

* * * * *

Who hasn't seen ***The Graduate****? What a great movie. It was one of the classics for my generation. At the end, Benjamin interrupts the wedding and runs off with Elaine, his true love. So I thought that I would have Craig burst in on Helena's wedding, only when I got to that point, my characters changed the story and it turned out Craig was bursting in on his own wedding.*

Writing is so interesting. You think that the story will end one way, only to have the characters switch endings on you. I have heard writ-

ers talk about how characters can take over control of a story and it really is true. The characters say and do things you never intended, and they can lead the story in directions that you never contemplated. So now when I write a story, I have an ending in mind but I realize anything can happen as we approach that supposed ending and often does.

The Buena Vista Café is a wonderful place in San Francisco. I first went there in college and loved it. Since then, I have been back many times. My parents use to visit it whenever they were in town, and even bought a painting of the BV which now hangs in my house. I hope to use the BV in future stories since it is such a great location. In fact, it is where Irish coffee was first introduced in the United States in 1952.

The Everyday Miracle

He drove into our valley in the early fall, and forever altered my belief in miracles.

I had borrowed my older sister's car only to run out of gas ten miles out of town. Not my fault of course. My sister's so undependable. Doesn't even keep her gas tank full. And to make things worse, my cellphone battery was dead, probably her fault too. So here I stood, alongside the two-lane state highway, surrounded by rolling farm land, hitchhiking into town. Maybe not the best idea for a sixteen-year-old girl, but I can take care of myself.

Over the distant hill came a bright red Camry. As it got closer, I saw the driver was a relatively young guy. He slowed, braked, and pulled over. I strolled to the car and looked in, not being one to take chances. Yep, he was youngish all right, and cute too.

"Need a ride?" he asked, smiling at me.

"No, I was just holding my thumb up to dry my nails."

He smiled even more. "Where you headed?"

"Into town. I ran out of gas."

"Hop in." He paused. "And try not to get any polish on my upholstery."

I climbed in. Up close, he was more handsome then cute. Black hair that had escaped the clippers far too long, a rugged all-angles face, and laughing dark brown eyes.

"What's your name?" he asked, pulling back onto the highway.

"Lisa."

"Well, Lisa, it's probably not safe..."

"Skip the advice," I interrupted. "One dad is enough."

"Okay," he said with a soft chuckle. "Where should I drop you?"

"At the first gas station."

"You mean Johnson's 76?"

Now I really checked him out. On the right side of his face, he had a fine white scar extending from his forehead down to his mid cheek.

"You from around here?" I asked.

His answer was lost in the sound of a police siren. I glanced back and saw the sheriff's car behind us with flashing lights.

"There is nothing worse than red lights in your rear view mirror," I said.

"Oh, you've had a lot of experience with that?" he asked as we pulled over.

"More than I'd ever admit to my parents."

The sheriff walked up to the driver's window. "Tail light out on the right. Can I see your driver's license?"

"Sam? Sam Murphy?"

The sheriff leaned down and took a closer look at my driver. Sheriff Murphy is one big dude, with a Marine haircut, and a no-nonsense expression that kept even vicious dogs at bay.

"Do I know you?" he asked in his hoarse whisper that could reach across canyons.

"Brandon Smith. I'm in town for the reunion," Smith said, sticking his hand out the window.

Murphy's face, with its bored "I've seen it all" look came alive. His jaw muscles bulged, his eyes narrowed, and his skin went livid. Ignoring the outstretched hand, it was a moment before he spoke. "You've got balls showing your face in this town, Smith."

Smith pulled his arm back. For the first time the sheriff saw me.

"Lisa! What in God's name are you doing with this guy?"

"I ran out of gas and he offered me a ride," I said.

Murphy's voice vibrated with anger. "Lisa, get into my car." He saw my hesitation. "Now!"

I jumped out and turned back to my driver. "Thanks."

"You're welcome, Lisa. Maybe I'll see you in town."

Sitting behind the sheriff's bug-splattered window shield, I watched the two of them interact. The sheriff said something and Smith got out of his car. Grabbing Smith's shirt, the sheriff pulled him close until their faces were nearly touching. I could hear his booming indistinct voice and see the spittle flying with each word. He then pushed Smith back toward his car and gestured to the road, in the direction heading out of town.

For the first time I doubted myself in choosing traveling mates.

Getting back into the police cruiser, the sheriff turned to me. "Lisa that man is a scum ball and can't be trusted around a woman… of any age."

We pulled out on to the highway. Smith was still leaning against his car and as we passed him, I swear he winked at me.

"What's he done that's so bad?" I asked.

"It's not worth talking about. Just stay away from him."

As we drove on, I could see his jaw muscles clamping and unclamping as he tried to control his anger. Finally, he glanced over and gave a pathetic attempt at a smile. "How's your sister doing, Lisa?"

"Jenny?" Talk about a change in topics! "She's fine. People keep telling her she should run for town council. I think that would be crazy."

"Don't underestimate her; your sister is one bright lady. We could use new blood in the mayor's office."

In five minutes, we were at the 76 station.

"You going to need a ride back out to your car?" the sheriff asked.

"Naw. Mr. Johnson's son will drive me back."

I was walking away from the cruiser when Murphy's voice stopped me. "Lisa, tell your sister that Brandon Smith is in town, will you?"

I didn't see my sister until we sat down for dinner that night. As was our custom, we would pass the food around and load our plates before beginning any table talk. I waited for everyone to get their portions, but before I could speak Mom started the conversation.

"Jenny, dear. How was work? Anything new at city hall?"

"Same old, same old," she replied. My sister hadn't gotten my gift of gab and I had missed out on her looks. She was tall and willowy, with long dark hair and eyes to die for – coral blue. I bet she could turn heads in a cemetery.

"How about that promotion they were talking about giving you?" Dad asked.

Jenny had a mouth full of food so she just shrugged her shoulders.

"Hey, that reminds me," I said. "Jen, do you know someone named Brandon Smith?"

You'd have thought I crapped on the table. Jen started coughing and couldn't quit. Dad's face went through five expressions, none of them good. Mom gave me a look that made me glad I was out of reach.

It was a moment before Jenny stopped coughing. And then, in her most could-care-less voice, she asked, "Where did you hear that name, Lisa?"

"I was hitchhiking and he gave me a ride."

"He's in town?" my father asked. I realized that he was really pissed since he'd completely ignored the fact that I had broken his cardinal rule to never hitchhike.

"Yeah, he mentioned the high school reunion."

"Well, he has some nerve!" Mom said harshly.

"It's what I would expect from a lowlife like him," Dad replied. "He was never concerned about anyone except himself."

This was getting interesting. Better than the market check-out-line tabloids.

"Who is this guy? What, did he kill someone or something?" I asked staring at Jenny.

Before she could reply, Mom cut in. "All you need to know is to avoid him," she said. "Now, let's just change the subject." She pointed at my plate. "Start in on your dinner, young lady, now."

For the rest of the meal, we danced among a number of subjects but I could tell that everyone's mind was on Brandon Smith. Since that topic seemed to be taboo, I decided to approach another interesting subject.

"How are you and Dave doing?" I asked my sister. Dave Lowry was my sister's obnoxious husband. I called him "Mr. Sun" since he thought everything revolved around him. How my sister ended up marrying him was always a mystery... or a tragedy, depending on how you viewed it.

"We're fine," Jenny replied curtly.

"Then how come you're living here instead of with him?" I asked.

"There are some things that we need to resolve."

Mom joined in. "I haven't seen Dave around lately."

"He's been spending all his time at the junior college working with the basketball team. If he has another great year, the rumor is he could move up and become head coach at the University in Stratton."

"How can he have a better year?" Dad said. "His team won the junior college state championship last year."

"One good year is impressive, but two is great," Jenny said. "So they'll be watching him closely this year. There's even a scout coming to watch tomorrow night's alumni game."

Dad nodded. "No wonder he's so busy." He glanced at Mom and then back at Jen. "We hate seeing you and Dave living apart. Can't you work things out under the same roof?"

"Dad, we tried. Besides, I'm the one that suggested we needed time apart."

The next day at school, I was walking through the gym on the way to my P.E. class when I heard voices coming from the coach's office. Normally I'd have paid no attention, but this time I heard the name Brandon Smith. I moved toward the door.

"When did he get here?" The voice was Dave Lowry, my sister's mistake of a husband.

"He arrived last night and is staying with me." That was Coach O'Hara's voice. O'Hara has been the head basketball coach at our high school since God created the Earth. Rumor had it that he had been slated to become the Junior College basketball coach five years ago, but Dave had slipped in ahead of him.

"So the town's prodigal son has returned. What the hell for?" Lowry said.

"The high school reunion tonight," O'Hara said. "And he's going to play for my alumni team tomorrow night."

"I can't understand why the junior college administration thought that the alumni team needed a coach, nor why they chose you over my assistant," Lowry said.

"Hell, Dave. Pretty obvious to me. They wanted to see if I could fill your job if you went off to the University next year."

"Having Smith play isn't going to change the outcome." He paused. "Besides, it's a meaningless game."

"You don't have another game for two weeks. If you lose tomorrow night, that's all this town will be discussing for the next ten days," O'Hara said sarcastically. "And I don't think the University will be too impressed to hear you lost to a bunch of has-beens."

"You're still sore that I got the head coaching job at the junior college, aren't you? Well, get over it," Lowry said. "The truth is this is a young man's game... and you're old."

"Well, thanks, Dave," O'Hara said. "It's always good to feel appreciated."

"Go ahead, put on a show, and make yourself look good," he said, "but if you actually try and beat me, I will crush you."

I heard a chair slide and figured Lowry was standing to leave. "And if that happens," he said harshly, "kiss your hopes for junior college head coach good bye once I'm gone."

Ducking behind a row of lockers, I waited until he'd gone and then peeked into O'Hara's office. He was sitting at his desk staring at a book case filled with past trophies.

"Hi, Coach," I said.

"Hello yourself, Lisa," O'Hara replied swiveling his chair toward me. His small dark eyes peering at me through large, black rim glasses always made me think of an owl, and a plump one at that. "What brings you here?" he asked.

"A question." I paused. "Brandon Smith. Who is he?"

O'Hara's response was a long, long stare before he spoke. "He's a lot of things, but to me he's the greatest basketball player I ever coached." He pointed to a small picture on the wall behind me. Standing in his basketball uniform was a young Brandon Smith with long hair and a devil may care grin. "He should have gone straight from here to division one basketball but his grades were miserable. In fact, I think the only reason he graduated from high school was that his teachers couldn't face the idea of having him around for another year. Hellion, juvenile delinquent, misspent youth were some of the nicer things said about him."

O'Hara paused staring at the picture. "But on the court..." His face softened and a slight smile appeared. "That was a whole different story. When he stepped on the court, even his worst detractors stopped talking and paid attention."

"So what happened?"

O'Hara's eyes left the picture and came to rest on me. "Besides his bad grades, Brandon's mother was very ill. She was his only kin because his father died in Vietnam. He wanted to be near her, so he stayed and played at the Junior College. Shattered every record." He shook his head. "If you didn't have a ticket at least two weeks in advance, you couldn't get into his games. Not uncommon for people to drive hundreds of miles to watch him do his magic. The division one schools were drooling."

O'Hara's reminiscing smile faded and he became quiet.

"Where did he go?" I said, hoping to get his enthusiasm back.

"He finished junior college here, and then went to play for New York State University at Stony Brook. He was a standout and should have gone on to the pros, but his life took a detour." O'Hara ran his hands through his thinning, scraggly hair then stood up. "Well, Lisa. I've got work to do and I know you have a class somewhere."

"If he was that good, how come I don't see his jersey retired on the high school gym wall?" I asked.

"No one deserved it more. Let's just say my vote was overridden."

As a junior, we were allowed to leave the school campus for lunch. I was at my usual spot in Marge's sandwich shop when I saw her in the parking lot of the Yankee Clipper Hotel, She'd just gotten out of a dark blue Lexus and was walking toward the hotel entrance. Even with a hat and dark glasses, I recognized Kody Kyle, also known as KK, the model extraordinaire. At least that's how Hollywood advertised her. I watched her glide across the asphalt. That she could move like that, while pulling a wheeled suitcase, was mind blowing.

Here was one of my all-time idols just steps away. I threw my lunch in the trash and, as ladylike as possible, raced across the street.

She had already checked in and was getting into the elevator when I burst into the lobby. I jumped in with her just as the door slid closed.

Trying to be as casual as my quivering voice would allow, I said, "I loved you in *Cosmo*."

She'd been lost in thought and now glanced over. "Excuse me?"

"Your spread in *Cosmo*. OMG! And your interview in *Vogue*. Totally my favorite."

She smiled. "Thank you." Whereas I had been ogling her, now she was staring intently at me. Even with her eyes narrowed and her brow furrowed, she looked awesome. "What's your name?" she said.

"Lisa. Lisa McKnight."

She shook her head slightly. When the elevator door opened, she stepped out, and turned back. "How is your sister Jennifer? Still as pretty as ever?"

The door had closed before I had closed my mouth.

Since my phone was still dead, I borrowed the hotel's pay phone. I couldn't dial fast enough. The phone seemed to ring forever before my sister answered.

"Sis, why didn't you tell me that you and Kody Kyle knew each other?" I yelled.

"Who?"

"KK, the supermodel."

"I know who she is, Lisa, but I don't know her."

"Well, she knows you and what you look like."

"I've never met her, so there must be some mistake," she said. "And I have to go. I'm buried in work."

I knew there had to be more. Hanging up, I raced over to the library and plopped down in front of one of their ancient computers, kicking myself that I didn't have use of my smart phone. First, I googled Kody Kyle and, although there were over 1,000 sites, there was really nothing about her early life. Basically, she was from New York, both parents dead, and no siblings. Not a mention of any college.

Well, that was a dead end, so I typed in my next Google search- Brandon Smith. I thought it would be nothing but basketball statistics, but there was more. He'd apparently dropped out of college near the end of his senior year and joined the Army. He'd seen action in Desert Storm where he'd received a purple heart. The article explained that his scouting patrol had been attacked and several soldiers killed. Despite being injured, Brandon had carried a wounded comrade three miles to safety before collapsing. They had interviewed Brandon for the article, and one of his quotes caught my eye.

"After coming that close to death," he'd said, "I took a hard look at my life, my own mortality, and my future goals. I decided it was time for me to start giving back instead of just taking."

There was much more, but glancing up at the wall clock, I realized I would be late for class if I didn't get going. Walking out the door, I remembered that this evening I was working as a volunteer at the Starlight Room of the Yankee Clipper Hotel for the reunion.

That night the place to be was the Starlight Room. It was filled with over seventy-five graduates of Grand View High School now returned ten years later. The local three-piece getup of T-shirt, jeans, and a ball cap mingled with three-piece Brooks Brother suits. There were women who only read the Farmer's Almanac mixing with women wearing outfits straight from the fashion magazines. Despite this variety, the tone was loud and friendly. The phrases "I can't believe" alternated with "Do you remember?" over and over again, rising above the music supplied by a DJ.

The buffet table was my assignment. It was a way to pick up the community hours I needed toward graduation. Most people, though, were clustered around the bar, keeping the two bartenders jumping with drink orders. I saw Jenny yakking it up with three of her old classmates. Her girlfriends were dressed to the nines, but they looked downright dowdy next to Jenny.

I was bent over restocking the shrimp platter when the noise level dropped away. In the entryway stood a suit-clad Brandon Smith. Nonchalantly, he glanced around the room, seemingly oblivious to the effects of his presence, nodding to several people while his smile gradually widened. After a moment, several men walked up to him, and the ritual of hand shaking began. Slowly the room noise picked up and the festivities got back in gear.

Two wannabe fashion divas drifted to my end of the buffet table. I had my back to them, opening a jar of cocktail sauce.

"What is he doing here?" one hissed.

"And acting like nothing happened. As if it wasn't his fault."

They were quiet for a moment, and then the first one spoke. "You know I had a crush on him."

"You and every other girl."

"It could easily have been me instead of poor Melinda."

"I've had the same thought myself," her friend replied. "Although what he ever saw in her I'll never know. Chubby, pimple faced, and topped with that God-awful red hair."

"Well, there's no accounting for some men's taste in women," the other said as they moved away.

A few moments later, up stepped Janice Kelly, the organizer of the reunion and no slouch in the gossip department. While she was loading food on to her plate, I moved over and said, "Hi, Mrs. Kelly. Looks like a big success."

"Hi, Lisa. Yes, it's as good as I'd hoped."

It was time to cut bait and throw out my hook. With an exaggerated motion, I sweep the room with my eyes. "I don't see... Melinda."

"Who?"

"You know. Melinda?"

"Do you mean Melinda Crowder?" Kelly replied, her confusion obvious.

Hooked and now to net her. "Yeah, why isn't she here?"

"She was two years behind this class." Kelly glanced over her shoulder. "But she wouldn't be here anyway."

I leaned forward like a fellow conspirator, hoping to tempt her into revealing more. "Why's that?"

"I really shouldn't bring this up," she replied stiffly, which I knew meant she couldn't wait to tell me."

Bending toward me, her voice dropped to a whisper. "Brandon Smith got her pregnant the summer before her senior year. He was away at the University when she found out, and he never came back. Just deserted her."

"Not good," I said.

"Worse than not good. Her father was principal of the high school and a rigid champion against premarital sex." She took a sip of her wine. "She left a note about her condition and then disappeared."

"What happened to her?"

"At first, they thought she'd run away, but when they couldn't find her anywhere, the sheriff wondered if she might have jumped off the state highway bridge. So they searched the river and found a sweater caught up on a log. There was speculation it was her's, but the river had damaged it so much they weren't sure."

"Did they ever find her body?"

"No, but the river has a history of not giving up its bodies." She nodded toward Brandon Smith. "Everyone blamed him for her death. So you can see why we didn't invite him to the reunion. And yet here he is, showing no sense of shame. He gave Melinda no support. Just ignored her according to her note."

With a quick flick of her wrist, she finished her wine. "I'm surprised you haven't heard all this before, Lisa. Your sister and Smith were almost engaged when this happened."

I was speechless, unable to even respond to Kelly's goodbye. Poor Jenny, I thought. Why did she keep picking these losers? I glanced over and realized I wasn't the only one interested in Jenny. Brandon Smith was walking toward her. Although people kept up their chatter, every eye in the place was following him.

He strolled up behind Jenny and lightly touched her on the shoulder. Jenny twisted around, saw who it was, and turned away from him. Once again, he tapped her shoulder. This time she spun around and slapped him. The sound rocketed across the room stopping all conversation. I couldn't see Smith's face, but my sister's was filled with anger. Just as quickly, the anger changed to surprise as if she couldn't believe what she'd done.

Whereas every eye had been on them, now everybody was looking at anything but them. And it was for that reason that people quickly noticed the new addition to the party. Framed in the doorway stood Kody Kyle, arm in arm with an older, grey haired man in a black suit. A pathway cleared before them as they strolled across the room. Breathtakingly beautiful was how *Vogue* had described her, and she was all that and more. In one fluid motion, she was up on the platform with the DJ. He stood open mouthed as she spoke to him. Turning away, he shut off his disc player and then handed her the microphone. If I had dropped one of my plastic serving forks, it would have sounded like a cannon shot in the silence.

"Good evening," she said.

If possible, the silence deepened.

"Most of you know me as Kody Kyle," she said hesitantly, "but a long time ago, in another life, I was Melinda Crowder."

Whisperings, sudden intakes of breath, and a few "Oh, my God" broke the silence.

"This has been a day to right the wrongs my lies did to some very decent and innocent people." She momentarily looked down, before continuing. "During my three years here in high school, I was labeled as the ugly duckling and had no social life, in fact, no life at all. And if that wasn't enough, my parents kept pushing me for better grades. I realized the summer after my junior year that I had to get out of here. I needed to start fresh somewhere else." She surveyed the room, taking in all the up turned faces. Clearing her throat, she said, "My only excuse for what I did is that I was selfish and immature." Her voice caught, and then she continued. "I decided to run away to New York. I invented the pregnancy thinking it would turn my father against me and he wouldn't come searching for me."

She gestured to the man who had accompanied her, and who now wore a gentle smile. "Yet, as I found out earlier today, he would have stood by me even if the pregnancy had been real."

She brushed away several tears. "As for blaming Brandon Smith, he was just a symbol, an unlucky substitute for all the boys that mistreated me. And I wanted people to believe that the most sought after boy in town had found me desirable."

The DJ slid over and handed her a Kleenex. After wiping her eyes and dabbing her nose, she continued. "After a while, I felt so ashamed that I couldn't come back." She moved closer to the front of the platform. "That is until Brandon Smith tracked me down. For reasons I'll never understand, he accepted my apology. And he also convinced me that the best thing to do was to go home." She smiled down at her father. "And he was so right." Turning her gaze to the rest of the room, she continued, "So I ask you all to recognize the real victim of my deceit." She swept the room with her eyes, "Brandon, where are you? I think it's time for you to really come home."

It took the crowd several moments to come to grips with their shame for how they'd treated an innocent man. But once they did, everyone clamored for Brandon to get up on the stage. One small problem. He had disappeared.

The next day, Jenny called all over town but no one had seen him. Even Coach O'Hara denied knowing his whereabouts, but he did offer the fact that Brandon had promised to play in the junior college vs alumni game that night.

Although Jenny and I went to the game together, once inside we were quickly separated. The gym was filled to capacity and more. Not only were people stuffed into the bleachers, but they lined the walls around the court. The fire marshal had tried to clear some of them out, but as soon as he left, they flowed back in. This town lived for basketball and hadn't had a whiff of it since last spring, so it was no wonder that the place was jammed.

Having lost sight of Jenny, I watched the two teams warm up. The junior college squad ran their pre-game drills with precision, while the alumni team stood around haphazardly taking shots and talking. I recognized a few of the alumni from years past. Nowhere did I see Brandon Smith.

Even from my seat in the top row, I could feel the anticipation and the excitement bouncing off the gym walls. Questions flew around me. Would this year's junior college team be as good as last year's? Was that even possible? Could the alumni team put up any kind of game against the junior college team?

All at once the wait was over. They introduced the players on both teams, and then introduced the coaches. A striped-shirted referee tossed the ball in the air and the battle was on.

At first, the game was close with the alumni hitting some lucky three pointers. Gradually, the junior college team began to pull away as the alumni team started missing shots and turning the ball over. It was obvious that the alumni were way out of shape. O'Hara used all his time outs trying to give them a rest, but it wasn't nearly enough. By the end of the first half, the junior college team was ahead by twenty-two points.

During half-time, people around me began talking about leaving. Maybe grab a pizza and beer, or rent a movie. No one likes to watch a blow out and that's what this was becoming.

The junior college team came back out and started shooting around. Dave Lowry stood on the edge of the court laughing and joking with several of his players. I was still watching him when he stopped and shifted his focus to the other end of the court. Coming out of the locker room with the rest of the alumni team was Brandon Smith dressed to play.

There had been a slow but steady migration toward the exit. Now there was a sudden shift in the tide as people flowed back, jostling their way into the stands. The pulse of the crowd picked up. People were talking faster, more animated. Brandon Smith was on the court. Anything could happen. They'd all seen his magic before, and now they might all see it again.

I watched Brandon warm up, but to my dismay, none of his shots were going in. My concern must have been evident for the man next to me said, "Don't worry, honey. Smith's a money player. He only makes his shots when they count." He grinned. "Looks like we might have a game after all."

Well, it didn't seem like it when Brandon's first game shot was an air ball. His second shot bounced off the front of the rim, and his third attempt was no better. I could feel the crowd's excitement draining away. That is until he stole the ball, raced down the court, and dunked it. The place came alive and so did Brandon. After that, he was everywhere. Impossible passes, steals, blocks, rebounds. A regular one-man team. As the junior college squad double- and even triple-teamed him, his passes constantly found the open man for a score. And if they guarded him one on one, he was unstoppable. Three-point shots, drives and dunks. For a while it appeared their strategy was to foul him whenever he tried to shoot. But since he rarely missed a free throw, they quickly gave that up.

Lowry played his first team and pushed them hard, but still the alumni slowly gobbled up the junior college's lead. Under Brandon's leadership, the alumni gained confidence and strength. And if that wasn't enough, the crowd had gotten caught up in the alumni's struggle. The cheers rang out now when either side scored. With ten seconds left, the junior college team missed a shot which one of the alumni rebounded and then quickly called time out. I checked the score board. The alumni were behind — 74 to 72 — with five seconds to play.

In the huddle, Brandon and O'Hara appeared to be arguing. Finally, I saw Brandon nod, and the alumni headed back on the floor.

By now, everyone was on their feet, and the noise was deafening. The referee handed the ball to the one of the alumni players on the out of bounds line, and then blew his whistle. The game was on. Brandon made several feigns, got free, and they threw him the ball. With seconds left, he drove past two junior college players and pulled up at the three point line. Like a bird set free, he rose above the defenders and took his shot. The ball was on its downward arc as the final buzzer went off. It hit the back of the rim and bounced away. There were moans, sighs, and cheers depending on what side you had been rooting for.

People were so busy talking about the amazing ending that I think I was one of the few that saw Brandon look over at Coach O'Hara and turned his palms up, as if asking a question. At first Coach O'Hara shook his head, and then begrudgingly he smiled and gave him thumbs up.

It was forty minutes later and the gym was essentially empty except for my sister sitting in the first row bleachers. After all that had happened, I had no intention of missing any of the upcoming drama and, knowing Jenny, there was drama brewing. I slipped under the stands and crawled up to within a few feet of where she sat. She was still there when Brandon and Coach O'Hara came out of the locker room. Brandon had showered and was dressed in a suit. O'Hara was laughing at something Brandon had said when Jenny stepped in front of them. From my vantage point, I was close enough to hear their conversation.

"Can I talk to Bran for a moment, Coach?"

O'Hara glanced at Brandon, and then excused himself.

Jenny walked over to the ball cart and tossed Brandon one of the basketballs. She pointed to the spot where he had taken his last shot. "Move over there and take that shot again."

Brandon shrugged his shoulders, walked to the spot, and launched a shot. The ball missed everything.

"If you ever want to talk to me again, make that shot." She threw him another ball. This time he set the ball down, took off his coat, and rolled up his sleeves. With a quick look at her, he turned and took the shot. Nothing but net.

She threw him another ball. "Again."

This next shot barely touched the rim as it went through.

"I thought so," she said. She walked up to him. "You let Dave win, didn't you?" She paused. "Well, we don't need your pity. Dave can get the University job without your help."

"If your husband had lost tonight's game then it's possible he might have lost his chance to become coach at the University."

"And why should you care about my husband?"

"If he gets the University job, O'Hara will get a chance to coach the Junior College team. It's been his dream for years." He shook his head. "O'Hara was so stubborn that he was willing to throw that chance away just to beat your husband. Well, I wasn't."

Jenny tilted her head back, examining his face. "In all the years we dated, I never knew you to care about anyone but yourself. Or maybe your basketball."

He shrugged. "People change, Jen."

Glancing down at the floor, there was a short pause before she spoke. "I am so sorry about last night. I think it was the frustration of knowing what you and I might have had."

"You're forgiven," he said softly, as they stared into each other's eyes. After a long moment, Jenny glanced away.

Brandon continued to stare and then looked around the gym. "How many times have we stood together on this court after a game?"

"Too many, I'd say."

"Too little, I'd reply."

Jenny wrapped her arms around her waist. "All these years and now suddenly you're back. Why now? Why not before?"

"I did come back. The day before you got married. I had plans to carry you off."

"But?"

"You looked so happy that I didn't want to spoil it."

She shook her head. "Don't you know anything but basketball, Smith?" They stood caught in another silent stare, until Jenny bent closer. "Where did you get that scar?" she said, reaching up and gently touching it.

"Kuwait. I was involved in Dessert Storm."

"You went into the military?"

He nodded. "The day after you got married." He shrugged. "My means of coping or something."

Still touching his scar, Jenny said, "I'm sorry. It seems I indirectly caused that."

"Don't be. The military was the best thing to happen to me. And in a way, it brought me here."

They were silent for a while, and then Jen said, "I made a major mistake marrying Dave. We are getting divorced, but he asked me to wait until after he hears from the University. He was afraid a divorce might hurt his chances of being selected."

Brandon nodded slowly. "I'm sorry to hear that… but it was inevitable."

Jen gave him a questioning look. "Inevitable?"

"This will sound trite, but… I'm the guy you were meant to marry."

Jen half smiled, but it was a sad one. "I've had a lot of years to think about us, Bran, and what might have been. But I know now that it was all just wishful thinking, not reality." She shook her head. "I seem to be destined to pick ego-centric, selfish men. First you, and then Dave."

She put her hand up to silence his response. "As much as I wish we could, I need a man that cares more about us than about himself. That just isn't you, Bran."

He put his hands on her shoulders. "A lot has happened since I last saw you, Jen. Give me a chance to show you the man I've become."

She eased his hands off her shoulders. "I will always love you, Bran, but I can't afford to make another mistake. I'd love to believe you have changed, but that would mean I'd have to believe in miracles." Wiping away her tears, she stared up at him for an endless moment. When she finally spoke again, it was so soft I could barely hear her. "God, how I would love to still believe in miracles." And then she turned and walked out of the gym.

By the time I had stopped crying and wiping my own tears, Brandon had left.

The next morning was Sunday. When Jenny finally appeared, her eyes were red rimmed and I knew she had cried much of the night. I had even cried some myself. Jenny didn't speak all the way to church. Several times I thought I saw tears, but she turned away so quickly I wasn't sure. Walking up the church steps, I saw a group of people gathered around our minister. I heard them make comments about last night's game, and several wished the minister good luck on his upcoming vacation. Jenny remained silent through it all.

Finally, the minister came out on the altar and all went quiet. He stepped up to the pulpit and welcomed everyone.

"As you all know, my wife and I will be going on an extended leave, so I've asked my fill-in to give this morning's sermon. Please welcome him."

Out on the altar walked Brandon Smith.

The minister turned to the congregation. "The title of Pastor Smith's sermon will be 'Everyday miracles: They do exist'."

One look at Jenny's face and I knew she didn't need to hear the sermon. She was already a believer in miracles.

* * * * *

The idea for this story came from the opening line of Shane, which is the greatest western I have ever read. The line was, "He rode into our valley in the summer of '89." So I too wanted a character that would "ride" into the valley and change lives. Shane was written through the eyes of a young boy, so I decided to make my story through the eyes of a sixteen-year-old girl. Fortunately for me, my thirty-two year old daughter was around to make sure my young girl dialogue had some semblance of reality.

It's tough creating a story from just a single opening line, but fortunately various pieces gradually fell into place. How many of you remember the song, "Ode to Billie Joe"? It was about a teenage pregnancy, and the end result was, "And now Billie Joe McAllister (the father) jumped off the Tallahatchie Bridge." So in my story, there is the alleged pregnancy and the townspeople are left with the suggestion that Melinda Crowder (the supposed mother) may have jumped off a local bridge which is why she disappeared.

And who doesn't love when a prodigal son returns home, and we find that this previous bad guy has changed into a stand-up good guy?

Basketball has always been one of my favorite sports. Two of my kids went through college on basketball scholarships which is another reason for me to love the sport. I have always felt that the true integrity of an individual is reflected by how they play their sport, so the basketball game in this story gave me a chance to illustrate Brandon Smith's true character, and how far he'd come from his old life. It was fun to write about a game I love and add a down-to-the-wire finish. Which was also a new beginning.

The Gypsy Wind

A gypsy wind is a breeze that swirls and varies in speed and direction — as if it follows no rules or custom — just like Gypsies.

Gypsy wind, you fly wild and free,
Make me afraid you'll capture me.
Blow away my inhibitions, leave my heart exposed
And when you're gone, my life decomposed.

Bob Seger

There was something in the air that day — a scent, a warmth, a freedom. A few people would later claim it was a gypsy wind, but that didn't seem possible since it never blew this far north. Yet no one disagrees that there was definitely something different that day.

It started out as usual at the Harrington County Courthouse. Bill Fellows, the janitor, unlocked the tall wooden entrance doors at 7:00 a.m. sharp as he'd done for the last fifteen years. Pausing on the court threshold, he noticed the day was unseasonably warm, yet the air was exceedingly still. A slow smile spread across his face as he remembered the last time air had felt like this and what it had forewarned. My God, he thought, that was when I lived in New Orleans more than fifteen years ago. Could it be happening here?

"This could become a very interesting day," he said with a low chuckle, rubbing his hands together. "Yes, siree."

Instead of merely unlocking the big, oak doors, he purposely left one of them propped open, allegedly to let in fresh air or so he later claimed.

It was just a minor change in his daily routine, but it was the first in a series of events that would contribute to what happened that day.

Boise McPherson climbed down from his truck, scraped the mud off his boots on the running board, and then stared at his cowboy hat sitting in the passenger seat. Always a debate whether to wear it into court or not. He felt naked without it, but opted this time to leave it in the truck. It was already too hot, especially with no wind. Checking his tie in the side view mirror, he slicked back his brown hair and adjusted his suit jacket. Either it was shrinking or he was putting on weight.

"Hey, Boise," a male voice said. "What's the rush this morning?"

Boise turned and saw Jason Rowlands shuffling toward him. "Howdy, Jason. We're early so I can go over a few things with you before court starts."

"What more is there to cover?" Jason said.

They began ambling toward the courthouse. "Actually, not much," Boise said. "But I wanted to make sure you were sharp and ready if the judge asks you anything."

"After that mediation gathering, you said we were golden. Now you sound worried."

"Not worried, just cautious. Anything can happen in court so I want us prepared."

As they walked, Boise glanced over at Jason. He wasn't surprised that Jason had a dejected look. This whole thing had been a shock to him and he still hadn't adjusted to it.

"Are you sure this is what you want?" Boise said.

Jason kicked a pebble to the side. "It's what it is, so I'm not going to fight it."

"If you aren't going to fight it, why haven't you signed the papers?"

"Just haven't had time to read through all the legal ease."

"I can help you with that."

He kicked another pebble. "Before I sign anything, I want my dog back."

"Don't bullshit me, Jason. This isn't about the dog."

Jason halted and grabbed Boise's arm. "We've already talked about this. You just focus on getting me my dog."

Boise shook Jason's arm off and said, "I have watched you and Lisa since high school. I just wish some woman would look at me the way Lisa looks at you." He poked a finger into Jason's chest. "You are making a mistake."

Jason pushed his hand away, and turned toward the courthouse.

This day was starting out hot in more ways than one, Boise thought.

Bill Fellow stopped in his repairing of the door handle to the clerk's office to watch Elaine, the attractive grey haired lady behind the counter. She handled the customers smoothly and gently, smiling frequently, and never losing her cool. Today she wore a bright blue dress that seemed to augment her beauty, although, Bill felt, she didn't need anything to make her beautiful, which was one of the many reasons he'd married her. He thought back on the day they'd met, and fell in love. It had also been the day the gypsy wind had entered his life.

Lisa Rowland stood in front of her hotel and checked her watch once more. Susan Frazer, her lawyer, was cutting it close, but they had been up late last night preparing their arguments, and there really wasn't anything more they needed to do except appear in court.

After the mediation fiasco where she'd had a chance to see her previous lawyer in action or more accurately missing-in-action, she'd immediately called her sister-in-law, Susan, and asked her to take over the case. Susan Lee had married her brother — Joel Frazer, a very successful corporation lawyer — a number of years back and the two girls had become close friends. This had morphed into best friends when her brother had been killed in a small plane crash three years ago. Lisa had dropped everything and rushed to Susan's side. They had been inseparable for the next month while Susan attempted to cope with the loss of her husband and Lisa with the death of her brother. Since then, they spoke often and at least twice a year got together for a long weekend. So when Lisa called, Susan had no hesitation about flying out to help her.

A black Lincoln town car glided into the hotel entrance and as it came to a stop, the back window slid down, and through it Susan beckoned to Lisa.

As the car pulled out into traffic, Susan asked, "How are you doing?"

"I've had better days," Lisa said with a sigh.

Susan grabbed her hand. "Divorce is never easy and never pleasant. But most everyone gets through it."

"What about those who don't?"

"Don't think like that. We'll get you through this, and then I want you to come to San Francisco and stay for however long you need."

They nestled back against the black leather upholstery, and were silent. After a minute or so, Susan said, "What happened? I thought you two were perfect together." When Lisa didn't answer, she said, "Have you discussed marriage counseling with Jason?"

"After the things we said, there is no going back."

Susan reached into her briefcase, and pulled some papers out. "If that's truly the case, why haven't you signed these divorce papers?"

"Here, give them to me." Lisa grabbed the papers, pulled a pen from her purse, but then stopped and starred at the papers. After a few moments, she sighed and then scribbled her name across the bottom. "There, now they're signed," she said, shoving them back to Susan.

As Lisa turned away, Susan saw a tear streak down her cheek, but opted not to comment. Instead, she spoke to the driver. "Can you turn the air conditioner on? This day seems to be warming up."

Boise reached into his briefcase, and pulled out a banged up thermos along with two plastic mugs. "Here have some coffee. It's going to be a long morning."

Jason waved it aside. "I've already got enough adrenaline for both of us."

They were seated on a bench a short distance from the courthouse. Boise took a long swig of coffee and said, "I was notified yesterday that Lisa has a new lawyer named Susan Frazer. Do you know anything about her?"

"Yeah, she's Lisa's sister-in-law. Works for a big firm in San Francisco."

Boise nodded slowly. "Does she specialize in litigation?"

"No idea, but Lisa claims she is a rising star at the firm." Jason looked over. "Is that a problem?"

"Hopefully not."

They went on to discuss Jason's responses to any possible questions the judge might ask, and were just about finished when they saw Lisa and Susan look over at them before turning and entering the courthouse.

Boise choked on his coffee and spit it out. "Who is that with Lisa?" he said between coughing spells.

"That's Susan Frazer, Lisa's lawyer. She's the one I was telling you about."

It was a moment before Boise spoke. "Well, she use to be Susan Lee," he said slowly, "and I went to law school with her."

"You went to law school with Boise?" Lisa said, after the two of them were seated in the hall outside the courtroom.

"I saw the name McPherson as Jason's lawyer but I never connected the two, until I saw him."

Lisa stared at her and then said, "Is that going to be trouble?"

Shaking her head quickly, Susan said, "No. Not at all." She put her briefcase up on the bench next to her. "Where do you know him from?"

"We all grew up in Newton together. Jason and Boise were best friends in high school. They use to rodeo together."

"Rodeo?"

"Yeah. Jason and Boise did team roping."

"What's that?"

"It's two mounted riders chasing a steer. The first rider ropes the horns and then turns the steer so the second rider can rope the back legs and bring the steer down. Boise was the header, and Jason the heeler. They were really good at it."

"Interesting," Susan said.

"Jason dropped out of rodeo after high school, but Boise went on to become a saddle bronc rider. He got a scholarship to Colorado State University for that, and then did two years on the professional circuit in bronc riding and team roping." She moistened her lips with some lip gloss. "Some people thought he had a chance at cowboy of the year if he continued, but he quit and went to law school."

"Well that explains a lot."

"Such as?"

"I thought he was some kind of wanna-be cowboy, always wearing boots and Levis to class. Even saw him a few times with a cowboy hat. I thought he was a joke."

"Boise is no wanna-be, he's the real deal. He started working on his parents' ranch when he was in grade school. Use to help herd and brand the cattle."

Susan was quiet for a moment, and then said, "I heard his parents were poor, and he had to pay his own way through law school."

"Well, if owning the largest ranch in the county is poor then they're poor. As for paying his own way, Boise has always done that ever since he went to college. Some kind of pride thing."

Lisa watched Susan as she absorbed all of this, and then it hit her. "You two dated, didn't you?"

"Boise, is there something I need to worry about?" Jason waited for a response but Boise remained quiet. "You mentioned going to law school with Lisa's lawyer. How well did you know her?"

"She graduated second in the class."

"So where were you?"

"I was in the middle." Boise glanced over at him. "Don't get excited. I can handle this." He stood up. "Let's get going or we'll be late."

They walked over to the courthouse, entered, and went through the metal detector. Boise pointed to the right. "We're over there in Courtroom 3, that's the family court."

When they got to the entrance of Courtroom 3, Jason gestured to a sign. "They actually need a sign to tell people not to bring a gun, knife, or other weapons into the courtroom?"

"Family court is the most dangerous courtroom there is," Boise said. "Emotions run high, and anything can happen."

They opened the door and walked into the gallery. Boise pointed to some seats on the left and they sat down. "My favorite story is about a female attorney who was married to a family law judge in Louisiana. When she was changing offices, she took her outdated law books and stacked them below her husband's desk in the courtroom so if shooting broke out, he could dive down behind them." He smiled. "No one he worked with thought that was unusual."

Jason nudged Boise, and tilted his head toward the right side of the gallery. Up near the partition, which separated the gallery from the rest of the courtroom, sat Lisa and Susan.

"As your client, I have the right to hear about your relationship with my wife's lawyer," Jason said quietly, "so let's hear it."

Boise rubbed the lower half of his face and stared straight ahead.

"You tell me now or we cancel this whole thing."

"Okay, okay," Boise said after a moment. "There really isn't much to say. I asked her out once."

Jason snickered. "You think I'm a greenhorn, Boise. Your tone tells me there's a lot more, so give."

Judge William Borman adjusted his black robe and checked himself once more in the mirror. He loved his job as a family court judge. The chance to help couples settle their differences, guard children's rights, and put compassion into the court's rulings were very important to him. Usually, he couldn't wait to move from his chamber into the courtroom, but ever since he began working on his book — which detailed his experiences in the judicial system - the courtroom had taken second place to his writing. Basically when not sitting on the bench, his thoughts were consumed by the book. One more year ought to see it finished, he thought, and then would come the hard part. Finding an agent. He planned on reading everything he could about procuring an agent. Then once he had one, he would devote all his spare time to promoting the book.

He checked his watch. Time to get the show started, and most days it really was a show. As he moved down the hall, he noticed how warm it was. Well, my courtroom is air conditioned so it's not going to matter, he thought.

"All rise. Court is now in session with the honorable Judge William Borman residing."

Everyone stood up as the judge entered, and once he was seated, they all sat back down.

"Good morning," the judge said. "I'm sure you would all like to be somewhere else so I'll try to get through these cases as quickly as possible." He glanced around the gallery. "Before we start, are there any questions?" When no one spoke up, he said, "Okay, let's get started." He looked at the computer screen perched on the left side of his desk. "I call case number 3412, Eugene Langsted versus Mary

Langsted."

With that, court started and case after case was gradually called up. The morning dragged on until ten o'clock, when the judge declared the morning recess and had everyone clear the court. Boise and Jason strolled out and found a bench down the hall, while Lisa and Susan ended up on a bench across from the courtroom doorway.

Lorraine Borman, Judge Borman's wife, had had enough. Enough of waiting for her husband to come home from court, only to have him bury his face in his computer writing his book. Enough of cooking, cleaning, and washing his clothes only to have him practically ignore her. They use to be close, sharing everything, going on weekend get-aways, but no more. Ever since he'd come up with his book idea, he'd become a stranger. She was asleep by the time he came to bed, and when she woke up, he was already in his study working. After that, he had a quick shower, dressed, and was gone. Not even a kiss goodbye at the door.

Two years of this crap was enough, she had decided. Today was ultimatum day. It was either her or the book, but the two couldn't continue to exist under the same roof.

After finishing with her make-up, she walked out to the car. Her plan was to go to the courthouse and face him there. Tonight she'd either have her husband back or her life was going to take a sharp U-turn.

She slid into the car and noticed that she was already sweating, both from nervousness and the hot stagnant day.

Slowly at first, the beginnings of a breeze developed and then gradually became stronger. Bill Fellows was back on the courthouse steps and recognized it immediately. It was the gypsy wind — that warm, enticing, perfumed woman carrying scents from near and far. Folk lore had assigned many attributes to the gypsy wind: a loosening of one's romantic spirit, a yearning for things one had never dreamed of, and a freedom of action that could be problematic if not controlled.

Although he hadn't felt it since his days in New Orleans, there was no denying its identity. After all, he thought, what other wind could make you want to expose your soul and free your emotions with just a touch?

He'd been, as they say, 'free-wheeling and fantasy free' until the day he met the gypsy wind. Next thing he knew, he was running to the marriage altar with a smile on his face. Yeah, no one had to convince him of the power of the gypsy wind.

And as Bill stood in the doorway, the gypsy wind once again blew around him and assailed his senses. Without hesitation, he opened the other courthouse door and then went down into the basement to make further adjustments.

The wind strengthened as it blew through both open courthouse doors, sneaking around corners, sliding under tables and benches, and engulfing everyone in its path.

"That courtroom is so stuffy, they need to open some windows," Lisa said, fanning herself with her hand. "Thank God they left the front doors open."

Both she and Susan were relaxing on a hallway bench, enjoying the gentle wind that had started to come through the courthouse entrance and swirl around them.

"I wonder where he got that suit. He looks good in it," Lisa said out of the blue.

"What?" Susan said. She turned and saw that Lisa was staring down the hall at Jason.

"I remember the first time I noticed him in high school," she said. "He was mucking out a horse stall and I thought he looked so cute in his dirty Levis, rolled up sleeves, and straw cowboy hat."

"Lisa, focus!" Susan said sternly. "We've got a case to win."

"I know, but for some reason I'm thinking about the good times I had with Jason." She put her hands up in a questioning gesture, and looked around. "How did I end up here?"

Susan stared at her, wondering what was going on. Smoothing back a tendril of hair the breeze had blown loose, Susan glanced down the hall at Jason and surprisingly had the same thought. Jason did look good in his dark grey suit. And then she studied Boise and decided he actually was a very handsome man. And a real cowboy to boot.

"That's all?" Jason said. "You asked her out once? So what happened?"

Boise took a deep breath and let it out slowly. "We went out and after that, she wouldn't go out with me again."

"Why? What happened?"

"Our first and only date was a disaster. Enough said."

Jason studied Boise's face, and then said, "Do you still have feelings for her?"

"Yeah, I do. I feel that she is a stuck up, pampered rich girl, who will fit right in with a large law firm where it's dog eat dog to get to the top." He glared at Jason. "Let's change the topic."

"Well, before we move on, let me correct a misconception. Susan was not a pampered rich kid. Her parents were barely scratching out a living in San Francisco when she went off to law school. She got by with school loans and summer jobs."

"Okay, maybe I misjudged her, at least the rich kid part." After a moment, he said, "But she was so stand-offish, almost like she was too good to be there."

"She was never like that around us. If anything she was shy and reserved." He stared at Boise. "Maybe you just mistook that for being snobbish."

Boise slowly nodded. "I may have been off the mark about her."

Jason was about to reply when he felt the soothing touch of the gypsy wind enfold him. "That breeze sure feels nice," he said. Tilting back his head, he sniffed the air. "I'm not sure what that smell is but it definitely reminds me of Lisa." Peering down the hallway, he saw Lisa and Susan get up. "Lord, she does look pretty today."

Boise shook his head. "Remember why you're here. The dog."

"Yeah, I remember, but it was Lisa that helped me pick it out." He leaned back against the bench, still fixated on Lisa. "Now, every time I look at the dog, I think of her." He turned toward Boise who just shook his head.

For some reason the air-conditioner was on the fritz, so Judge Borman had opened the windows in his chamber, only to discover that a wind had arisen. It felt so pleasant coming through the window, he just wanted to sit and enjoy it. The breeze seem to carry memories he hadn't thought about for years. As the air swirled around him, he recollected the first time he'd met Lorraine, how beautiful she'd looked at their wedding, and the incredibly romantic honeymoon they'd shared in San Diego. He tried to visualize their last vacation, and to his surprise, realized it was more than four years ago. How could that be, he wondered? But he knew the answer. Work and his book. When he wasn't working, he was slaving over his computer, trying to complete the book. Lorraine had been supportive, but lately he wasn't so sure.

This morning at breakfast, for example, she'd been curt with him, and hadn't bothered to make him a lunch which wasn't like her. He thought about all the things she'd done for him during the years, and realized how little he'd contributed in return.

He stepped to the window and sucked in more of that delicious, warm wind. God, it felt good to be alive, he said to himself. Glancing over to his desk top, suddenly all thoughts of his book were gone, and he found himself focusing on the picture of Lorraine which sat on the corner, and he wondered why he didn't notice it more often.

As he left his chambers, he began whistling softly, something he hadn't done in years. Passing Bill Fellows in the hall, he gave him a wink.

Bill Fellow had to suppress a grin. He couldn't remember the last time he'd seen the judge in such a good mood, but he wasn't surprised. This is how it started when the gypsy wind blew. People changed. Their real feelings bubbled up and over, spilling onto to those around them.

Lisa and Susan wandered back into court since it was about to start back up.

"You never told me. Did you and Boise date?" Lisa said quietly.

"I wouldn't call it dating."

"Well, what would you call it?"

"A real mismatch." Susan said no more, so Lisa jabbed her in the ribs. "All right, spit it out."

Susan finally said. "We had one regrettable date." She shook her head thinking about it. "He picked me up in a rusty, battered truck. It was hell climbing in with high heels, and then I had to sit on some dirty, old blanket that covered the front seat cover."

"Uh-oh."

"We'd only gone a couple of miles when the truck broke down. He spent twenty minutes tinkering under the hood before he called AAA, and they ended up towing it to the nearest garage." She glanced at Lisa. "If you can believe it, he was going to have us hitchhike into town. Fortunately, I called a cab and got us a ride."

Lisa started to laugh.

"We ended up at some hole in the wall bar. Needless to say, the food was barely edible. And just to top off the night, when it came time to pay the bill — "

"Boise had left his wallet in the truck," Lisa said cutting in, while trying to keep her laughter down.

Susan swung toward her. "How did you know that?"

"Did you piss someone off just before he asked you out?"

She shrugged. "A couple of guys tried to ask me out and I turned them down. Maybe I was a bit harsh. Why?"

"Why did you even go out with Boise when you thought he was this phony 'urban cowboy'?"

"I don't know. I guess it was for laughs or just to see what made him tick."

"Well, Boise gave you the Newton Shuffle. It's something the guys started in high school as a payback when some girl crapped on a friend."

"The Newton Shuffle?"

"Oh, yeah. Invite the girl out for a nice dinner. Get some shitty old car and then have it breakdown shortly after you pick them up. You were lucky. Sometimes the guy asks the date to help him under the hood, and she ends up covered in grease. Dinner is at some low life bar with terrible food, and then they discover they left their wallet back in the car. It's the date from hell."

"But why me?"

"Like I said, you must have really upset one of his friends, so it was payback time."

"But then he had the nerve to try and ask me out again."

"What?"

"I didn't even bother to answer him."

"Something's not right. If a guy gives you the Newton Shuffle, he has no intention of ever asking you out again." Lisa glanced around. "Lord, it's hot in here. What happened to the air conditioning? We need that breeze back."

"Please remain seated. Court again in session."

Judge William Borman took his seat and as he settled in, he realized how warm the courtroom had become. Apparently, it wasn't just the air conditioning in his chambers that had failed.

"Bailiff, contact Bill Fellows and have him open some windows in here while he's fixing the air conditioner." The judge then turned toward the gallery. "Please feel free to talk until we get this handled."

Everyone settled back and quiet conversations broke out amongst the gallery.

Susan swivelled around, facing Lisa. "I know you signed the divorce papers, but in the hall you sounded like you might be having second thoughts."

With a shake of her head, Lisa responded, "I don't know what came over me. I want this done so I can move on."

Susan took a sideways glance at Boise, and had almost the same thought. What made me think he was handsome? He's a jerk and the sooner I'm out of here the better.

The janitor, an older grey haired man with a bushy mustache, came into the court with a long pole. He spoke to the bailiff, and they shared a quick laugh as he set up.

The windows were placed high up on the walls so the janitor used a pole to unlatch each one and pull them open. Almost immediately, a draft of air could be felt throughout the room. It had a comforting touch, and it seemed like everyone leaned back and sighed.

While waiting, Judge Borman had been thinking about his book, jotting down notes about corrections and ideas. He was wiping moisture from his forehead, when he felt the lulling breeze that was slowly circling the courtroom. As if it was the most natural thing, he stopped scribbling memos about his book and began listing possible vacation destinations for him and Lorraine. He was so caught up in the planning, that it wasn't until the bailiff cleared his throat several times that he realized all the windows were open and Bill Fellows, the janitor, had left the room.

"Ladies and gentlemen," Judge Borman said pushing his notes aside, "Court is now back in session." Squinting at his computer screen, he called out, "Case 3428, Lisa Rowland vs Jason Rowland."

The four of them moved up past the gallery bar and into the courtroom proper. Just the other side of the gallery partition was a long wooden table with four chairs facing the bench and small microphones in front of each chair. Susan and Lisa took the two chairs to the right side of the table in front of a placard reading "Petitioner," while Boise and Jason grabbed the ones on the left in front of the placard, "Respondent."

Judge Borman was reading their file, when the courtroom door opened with a loud squeak. He looked up, and was shocked. It was Lorraine. She hadn't been in his court for ages.

Lorraine glanced around and found a seat in the back left section of the gallery. She had tried to enter quietly but the door had other ideas. Once seated, she looked up at the bench and saw her husband staring at her with a question on his face.

Well, he's going to have a lot more questions when I get through talking with him, she thought as she scrutinized the gallery. During the drive over, in her air conditioned car, she had become more and more upset about the last three years. Once out of the car, she had hurried into the courthouse. She was mulling over the harsh realities she was going to throw at him, when a puff of wind blew over the back of her neck and across her shoulders. It felt so good that her anger seemed to fade and she had the most unexpected thought: Bill's hair looks good long. It makes him appear adventuresome, sexy.

Judge Borman tried to re-focus on the case, but finding Lorraine in the courtroom had thrown him off balance. A gust fluttered some of his papers and he straighten them, but his attention was pulled back to Lorraine. How had he been so lucky to marry that wonderful woman, he pondered. Reluctantly, he turned and inspected the four people in front of him. "My understanding is that this hearing is about custody of a dog, and all other aspects of the divorce have been settled. Am I right?"

Both Susan and Boise stood to answer the judge.

"That is correct, your honor," Susan said. "In fact, my client signed her divorce papers this morning." She gestured toward Jason. "We are just waiting for his signature, and the divorce will be final."

The judge turned toward Boise. "Mr. McPherson, is there a reason that your client hasn't signed the divorce papers yet?"

Boise shook his head. "We'll have that done by the end of the day, your honor."

"Good. Now as to the custody of the dog, what is the problem," the Judge said, turning toward Susan.

Jason stood up. "It's my dog and she won't give it back. That's the problem!"

"Please sit down, Mr. Rowland. The custom here is that you are silent unless I specifically ask you a question."

"I thought you were, Judge."

"No, I was speaking to your lawyers." He nodded at Susan. "As the petitioner, the court will hear from Ms. Frazer first."

"My client wants physical custody of the dog. She is the one that originally purchased the dog, has fed and groomed it over the years, takes it to the veterinarian, and spends the majority of the day with the dog. So it only seems appropriate she should have custody of the animal."

"Who has the dog now?"

"My client. She is feeding the dog, taking it for walks, and generally caring for it as she has done over the last four years."

The Judge nodded thoughtfully. "Will she allow visitation rights?"

"Only if it's through a third party at a specified location away from her home."

Lisa reached over and tapped Susan. They conferred quietly for a moment. Susan shook her head several times and it was clear they were in conflict. Finally, Susan straightened back up.

"My client now says that Mr. Rowland can pick the dog up at her house, and there is no need for a third party."

The Judge turned to Boise. "Mr. McPherson, what does your client want?"

"He feels he is entitled to physical custody of the dog, and will grant visitation rights to Mrs. Rowland."

"And the basis for his claim of custody?"

"It's true that Mrs. Rowland feeds and cares for the dog, but that is because my client works all day, and she is at home. On the weekends, he takes the dog everywhere, including hunting, hiking, and running. During the week days, he plays with the dog when he gets home, the dog sleeps on his side of the bed, lays in his lap when watching TV, and generally hangs with him rather than Mrs. Rowland."

Jason tapped Boise on the leg and whispered something to him. "And my client reminds me that Mrs. Rowland gave him the dog as a gift."

The Judge focused back to Susan and Lisa. "Mrs. Rowland, please remain seated and use the microphone in front of you to answer." He cleared his throat. "Since the separation, has the dog exhibited any signs of depression? Is he sleeping less, eating less, losing interest in activities, or things like that?"

Lisa pushed her skirt down which the wind had lifted, and pulled the microphone closer. She looked over at Jason and blurted out. "No your honor, the dog hasn't… but I sure have."

Susan swung around toward her, and whispered, "What did you say?"

As if on cue, a gust of wind rustled Boise's hair and scattered Susan's notes onto the floor. Boise quickly moved to help pick up the papers. As he handed several sheets to her, their hands touched and a shock of static electricity passed between them. They both immediately jerked back.

Boise smiled, and before he could catch himself, said, "I'm sorry about how that date turned out."

Susan glared at him, and said coldly, "You mean that Newton Shuffle?"

Boise frowned and was about to respond when Judge Borman said firmly, "Councilors, can we please get back to the case at hand?"

Susan and Boise moved back to their respective locations.

"As you know, courts are now considering the best interest of the pets in determining who gets custody of them. We can award custody, shared custody, visitation rights, and even alimony payments to the owners," Judge Borman said. "My job is to try and consider which of these is best for the pet." He nodded toward Lisa. "Have you anything more to add that would help me in that decision?"

"Give us a moment, your honor," Susan said as she sat down and conferred with Lisa.

Boise couldn't believe he had apologized to her. Where had that come from?

Lisa and Susan conferred for several minutes, and it was obvious they were not in agreement. Finally Susan stood up and addressed the court.

"Your Honor, my client wants to make a statement."

The Judge nodded toward Lisa. "Go ahead, Mrs. Rowland."

"Your Honor, I wanted to make a comment to Mr. Rowland about visitation rights. He can come and visit Fluffy anytime he wants, and stay as long as he wants." She paused and glanced at Jason. "Fluffy misses him terribly."

"That's very generous of you, Mrs. Rowland." The Judge turned toward Boise and Jason. "Have you anything to add, Mr. Rowland?"

Jason leaned forward, almost touching the microphone, his eyes fixed on Lisa. "I have not been the same since leaving Fluffy. I'm depressed and have no energy to do anything. I don't want to go on like this. I need to visit Fluffy as often as possible, and stay as long as possible."

The Judge smiled. "Well, that makes my decision so much easier regarding who gets custody of Fluffy."

Boise stood and faced the bench. "Before you go on, your Honor, I need to correct a misunderstanding. The dog's name is not Fluffy, it's Penny."

"Then who is Fluffy?" the Judge asked.

"Fluffy is the nickname Jason calls his wife."

"Well, this does change things, doesn't it?" the Judge said a few moments later, after the court had quieted down, and he had his smile under control. "My ruling is that we put Fluffy back with her mate, and see how things go. As for custody of Penny, for now, let's leave her with Mrs. Rowland."

The four of them walked out together through the courtroom doors. As soon as they were in the hall, Lisa and Jason embraced, each telling the other how much they missed them, and saying they never want to go through anything like this again.

Boise moved over to Susan. "Can I talk to you?"

She raised her eyebrows. "Do we have something to discuss?" she asked stiffly.

Boise didn't know what was pushing him, but he said, "Yeah, our one and only date."

"You mean the Newton Shuffle?"

"I totally and completely apologize for that."

"But why did you do it?"

"My roommate at law school told me he tried to date you and you treated him like dirt. He asked me if I'd do a Newton Shuffle on you as payback." He opened his hands in a pleading gesture. "We were in the middle of our date when I knew something was wrong. You were way too nice to have done the things he described."

"Why would he do that?"

Boise shrugged his shoulders. "It was payback for a prank I pulled on him. His goal was to embarrass the crap out of me... which he did. But by time I realized what he'd done, it was too late."

"Too late?"

"I'd already left my wallet in the car and we were on our way to dinner."

"You could have changed restaurants."

He found himself being distracted by her dark brown eyes. Focus, he thought, giving himself a mental head slap. "I did change. The one we went to was supposed to be good...but I found out later that the chef was out sick, and his replacement, if you recall, was not quite up to par."

"That is an understatement," she snickered. "I had to pay for one of the worst meals I've ever tried to digest."

"Again, I'm sorry."

"Why didn't you tell me this during the date?"

"I was too embarrassed. I looked like a fool even when I tried to correct things." He straightened up and took a deep breath. "So I want to officially apologize, and ask you for another chance."

She felt the wind curling around her legs, and half-smiled. "Did you ever hear the story about the snowball in hell?" At least that is what she intended to say, instead what came out was, "That might be fun."

Bill Fellows' wife, Elaine, glared at him as they stood in the courthouse hallway. "I heard there was a problem with the air conditioner in Family Court today."

Bill nodded. "Yeah, it went on the blink, but it's up and running now."

She jabbed her finger in his chest. "You turned it off, didn't you?" When he made no response, she said, "I know it was you." She shook her head. "It was because of that crazy belief of yours, wasn't it?"

"Now honey, it's not crazy. The gypsy wind does exist, and it is magical. It brought us together, didn't it?"

"What brought us together was love and the fact I chased your ass. Our relationship had nothing to do with the weather." She paused, staring at him. "And why would you turn it off only to the Family Court if you thought that stupid wind of yours could help someone?"

Bill gestured down the hall to his right. "Those people down there in Traffic Court and Criminal Court are here because they committed a crime. The only crime the people in Family Court have committed is falling in love. And now they're here tangled up in divorce and custody fights. They need all the comfort and compassion they can get. So if my gypsy wind can offer them anything, I wanted to give it a chance."

"Why Bill, that is so sweet," Elaine said with a half-smile which quickly faded. "When we get home, I am throwing out your Bob Seger CDs. I know that's where you got all this crap about the gypsy wind." She pointed a finger at him. "And furthermore, don't you ever turn off the air conditioner again."

Over her shoulder, Bill saw Lisa and Jason walking past, arms around each other, smiling and hugging. Behind them came Boise and Susan. He heard Boise say, "I'll be in San Francisco next Saturday. So it's a date?"

"Only if we take my car," Susan replied, "and I want to see you have a wallet before you get in."

They both laughed as they passed by.

Down the hall, he saw the side door to Judge Borman's chamber open, and his wife step out, her face glowing with happiness.

Bill looked back down at his wife, who was still ranting and raving, smiled widely and wrapped his arms around her. "You're right, honey. It's just a plain old wind. Nothing magical about it."

* * * * *

Guess I'll need to throw my Bob Seger CDs away also since one of his songs was the inspiration for this story. I wanted a gypsy wind that would change people's attitudes, open them up to compassion and love, and generally expose their human side.

Making the case a fight over custody of the dog allowed the story to be less argumentative and more fun. The idea of making Fluffy the wife's nickname, and not the dog's name, was an unexpected twist when I was writing the courtroom conversation. It got me smiling so I left it in.

Pitting a high-priced, big city corporation lawyer against a small town, single firm attorney made the tale more exciting, and then I got the idea that they had gone to law school together, even dated once, which further raised the interest level.

Do Boise and Susan eventually end up together? A big city girl with a small town cowboy? Well, as a hungry romantic myself, the answer is of course – YES!

The Apprentice

"So you're my new replacement?" Jose Gonzales asked the young man standing in front of him.

"Well, since you've worked this job for so long, it was decided that retirement from here was in order," replied Matt Dane, not repeating the real reasons for shelving this old fossil. In truth, the powers-that-be felt Gonzales could not handle the job. He had become too involved, too attached, and too kind-hearted. Matt Dane had no such problem. In his training, he had been meticulous in his duties. Compassion, personal feelings - none of these had interfered with him completing his assignments. His utter callousness, for lack of a better word, was the very quality that had earned him the right to replace Gonzales, and given him his nickname, "Mr. Ruthless."

Matt held his arms out, examining his green uniform. "Why do we wear these stupid things?"

Jose shrugged. "The hospital did a study. Patients often associate white with pain and suffering. They view black as frightening, too terminal. The color they chose as most soothing, most relaxing was light green. Perfect for our maintenance man uniforms. The hospital wants us to blend, to be able to slip in and out of a patient's room almost unnoticed." Jose pointed at Matt's overalls. "You missed a button."

Matt glanced down. "Are you serious?"

"How you dress is a reflection of how you perform your job."

"Look, Jose. I don't need instructions or your help. I'm fully trained to handle anything and everything. In fact, you might pick up a few pointers from me if you ever work again." He looked down the hospital corridor. "So what am I scheduled for today?"

Jose stared at him for a moment, shook his head, and then glanced down at the work sheet. "Your first assignment today is in Room 2403. The toilet needs work."

"Room 2403 needs a flush?" Matt laughed, oblivious to Jose's sudden harsh glance. "Is the patient expecting us?"

Jose hesitated. "Well... he asked for us."

Matt grabbed the tool chest off the utility cart. He half nodded at Jose and turned to go.

"Matt," Jose said.

"Yeah?"

"We are in no rush. Your next assignment isn't for several hours, so take your time." Jose paused. "You might learn something."

Matt made no reply, except to turn and head toward Room 2403. He shook his head in disgust as he walked. Jose's comments – missed a button; take your time, you might learn something – all confirmed that this old fart had lost sight of the purpose, the goal, of this job. No wonder they were replacing him.

Arriving at Room 2403, Matt knocked on the half-opened door, and then entered.

"Who the hell are you?" a gravelly voice barked at him.

So much for soothing green, Matt thought. "Hi. Come to fix your toilet."

The man in bed looked terrible. Greasy, gray hair sticking out at all angles, several days of whiskers, sallow skin, and an emaciated figure. But what Matt noticed most were the man's eyes. They registered no interest, no energy, and no emotion. They were the eyes of the dying.

Yet with a shave, a wash, some normal skin color, and a few pounds of home cooking on the man's frame, Matt could easily see him as a commanding figure.

"Fix it and get the hell out of here," the man growled, turning his attention back to the window.

Matt quickly surveyed the single-occupant room. Above the patient, he saw a monitoring device. A green line moved across the screen registering the patient's heartbeat. On the other side of the bed stood an IV pole with several bags of fluid. One was a viscous white substance. Matt knew that fluid. They were feeding him intravenously. Apparently the man wasn't consuming enough calories on his own.

"I'll just be a few minutes, sir," Matt answered. What a jerk, he decided, stepping into the bathroom, and then he remembered Jose's comment about first impressions. "Well, my first impression is that when he dies, no one is going to miss this crotchety old man," Matt said to himself.

Matt set a few tools on the bathroom counter and checked his watch. He saw no reason to drag this out. His decision was interrupted by a new voice in the room.

"Hi, Jack. I got a call from your nurse and came over. How are you feeling today?" The voice had a quiet, soft, calming quality.

"Carolyn, you have to stop wasting your time here with me, Go back to your kids. They're the ones that need you."

He heard a light laugh from Carolyn. "Jack, you know they aren't kids anymore. Mike is nineteen and Jenny's almost twenty-four."

Gravel voice responded, "You know what I mean. Just let me die in peace!"

"You have to stop thinking like that. Your doctor told me there's a real chance you could get better… if you tried."

"Get better for what?" There was no humor in Jack's voice. "Better to go home to an empty house? Better to sit and look at pictures of Bill while I suck down scotch and remind myself of how I killed him?"

In the silence that followed, Matt concluded that Jack definitely was ready to die.

"Bill's death wasn't your fault," Carolyn replied softly. "Don't you remember our talk the other day?"

"I've been so drugged up, I don't remember anything," Jack nearly shouted. "But I do remember Bill died because of me. If I hadn't fallen asleep at the wheel, Bill would still be with us. With you and the kids."

"His spirit will always be with us, Jack."

"How can you stand to look at the man who killed your husband, killed his only son?" His voice dropped to a whisper. "I can't even stand to look at me."

The room was quiet so long that Matt thought the woman might have left, and then she spoke.

"If it wasn't for you, there never would have been a Bill. I'd never have had the chance to meet him, to love him, to have his children. Mike and Jenny wouldn't exist except for you." The softness in her voice disappeared. "Your decision to die, to let this illness defeat you, is not what Bill would have wanted." She paused. "We've shed enough tears, lost enough sleep, and shouldered enough blame. It's time to move on. Get past this."

Again a long quiet.

Jack's voice was so low that Matt had to strain to make out the words. "When Bill first introduced you to us, I could see in your eyes and hear in your voice how much you loved him. I told him right then that he must not let you get away. You were a treasure that few men experience. And through all the years that followed, I've never changed that opinion." A violent coughing spasm cut off the rest of his words.

"Jack! Are you okay? Should I call for the nurse?"

The coughing gradually subsided and Matt heard Jack spit something out.

"No need for a nurse," Jack said catching his breath. "Nothing she can do. And there's nothing you can do either. I appreciate your concern, but I really have nothing left to live for. No reason to go on. Shirley's long dead and now Bill's gone. My only companions left are guilt and depression."

"That's not true. You have me, but more importantly, you have your grandchildren."

"They don't really care about an old man like me. I'm just someone to be polite around."

"They are who you make them. Be a part of their lives and they will be a part of yours," she countered. "You can help shape who they will become."

"It's way too late, Carolyn," he said, his voice dropping to almost a whisper. "I don't have the energy left."

Once again, silence prevailed. Matt found himself siding with Jack. No wife, no son, and just an empty existence waiting at home. It was time for him to let go. Time to check out.

The woman spoke again, her voice almost pleading. "At least talk to Jenny. She's outside. I haven't told her your decision to die. She still thinks she has a grandfather."

"Carolyn, I don't want her to remember me like this," he said firmly.

"Don't even think of turning her away," Carolyn said, her voice rising. "She flew home this week from college, in the middle of her post-graduate examinations, just to be with you."

"Okay, I'll see her," he said after a few beats, "but it's not going to change anything."

"I don't expect it to." Carolyn paused. "But leave her some fantasies about you. Don't tell her you've given up and are waiting to die."

Matt heard her leave the room and then a new voice. This one also female, but younger, more energetic. "Hi, grandpa."

"Hi, yourself," Jack replied. Matt detected a change in the old man's voice. It was softer, almost caressing.

"You look more like your mother every day," Jack said.

"Is that a compliment, grandpa?" Jenny replied with an impish tone.

"The highest I can give you."

"You are going to get better, aren't you? I overheard mom speaking to your doctor. He said if you tried real hard you could beat this."

The old man had another coughing spell but it resolved quickly. In almost a whisper, he said, "I'm doing the best I can, but sometimes old men and pneumonia aren't the best companions."

"Grandpa, you have to get well," she said, her voice breaking.

"Jenny. Jenny. Don't be crying over an old relic like me."

"You don't understand. I haven't even told mom yet. Scott asked me to marry him."

"That's wonderful," Jack replied. "I always liked him." He paused. "So what's the problem?"

"With Dad gone, I thought that when I got married you would be the one to walk me down the aisle. So you have to get better."

In the quiet, Matt heard a quick intake of breath and realized it was his own.

"Grandpa, I didn't mean to make you cry," Jenny said.

"Oh, Jenny," the old man replied, his voice nearly cracking. "You've touched my heart and my soul in a way you will never know." Suddenly, he laughed. Not the earlier sarcastic guffaw, but instead a rich, robust sound. "By God, Jenny, I am going to get well. You can count on it. I will be at your side. Nothing could make me prouder or happier."

Then they were both laughing and crying.

"I love you, grandpa."

"I love you too, honey. Now let an old man get some sleep if he's going to get well. Oh, ask your mom if she's free, would she come by and see me tomorrow?

"Okay, see you soon, grandpa."

It was a moment, and then a voice came over the bedside speaker. "Hello. Did you need something, Mr. Bayworth?"

"Yes. Please find my nurse. Tell her to get rid of this damn white crap they've been pouring in my veins. I want some real food!"

"Are you sure you're okay, Mr. Bayworth?"

"Miss, this is the best I've felt in a long time. Now please find my nurse."

Matt placed the tools in his tool chest. It was time for him to do his job. Time to complete his rounds, yet he felt a constriction in his chest and hesitancy in his movements that he had never felt before. With almost a sigh, he picked up the tool chest and stepped into the patient's room.

The old man was holding a picture in his hand and smiling. He looked up. "Gosh, I forgot you were still here. Sorry about my rudeness earlier, I..." He stopped in mid-sentence seeing something in Matt's expression, in his deadly stare. The old man's face went pale and then he began to cough. It was a harsh, body rattling sound. Each explosive cough followed by another, so close he couldn't catch his breath. He began to go white, then blue. Frantically he groped for his nurse call button. It slipped off the bed onto the floor at Matt's feet. The old man looked up at Matt, his eyes wide and pleading, then he collapsed back on the bed, no longer coughing, no longer breathing.

Matt stood over him, remembering how the old man had been willing death to come to him. He had been ready to embrace it. Now death was here, and yet Matt felt strangely dissatisfied. He bent over and picked up the picture that had fluttered out of Jack's hand. It was that of a pretty young girl, her face lit with a beautiful smile. At the bottom was the inscription, "I love you, grandpa. Jenny."

This is my job, yet why do I feel so conflicted. He's just an old man, and old people die every day, Matt told himself. Once more he glanced at the picture, and after a long moment tossed it on the bed. "Ah, hell!" he muttered. Quickly, he picked up the nurse call button and pressed it. Rolling the old man flat on his back, he struck him hard in the center of his chest. Immediately, Jack began to cough and sputter, his eyes opening wide with fright.

Matt turned and walked out, nearly colliding in the hallway with two nurses rushing toward the room.

Jose was still standing next to his utility cart.

"Well," he asked, a bit anxiously.

"He's still alive," Matt grumbled.

Jose smiled. "So Mr. Ruthless had a heart?"

Matt glanced up, frowning. "In training, we just approached the individual, gave them the death stare, and they died. It was so easy. No decisions. No weighing of our actions. Just simple and straight forward." He shook his head. "I never had a complication like this."

Jose put his hand on Matt's shoulder. "How did it feel to let him live?"

"That's the scary part," Matt said slowly. "It felt good, and it felt right."

"Don't beat yourself up because you discovered compassion in your soul," Jose said.

Matt shook his head. "Death and compassion. Seems like an unlikely pair." After a bit, he said. "I'm going to ask our supervisor if you could stay on a while longer. Help me learn the job a little better." He looked sheepishly at Jose. "That is, if you don't mind."

It was several hours later and Matt had left for his next assignment, not nearly as cocky nor as cold-hearted. Jose walked into Room 2403.

Jack looked up from his soup. "Were we successful?"

"You're still alive and I get to keep my job for a while longer. I'd call that success."

Jack pushed his tray away. "Now, before you snap your fingers or whatever it is you do to erase my memory of you, I have a few things to say."

Jose leaned against the wall. "I thought you might."

"Thank God you overheard my conversation with Carolyn and Jenny the other day," Jack said, "and had the sense to realize I didn't want to die."

"I make it a practice to know my assignments before its time to act.

Unfortunately, my superiors replaced me with someone else who was to carry out your death. I have no control over your fate once you're not my assignment."

"That was brilliant to tell Carolyn and Jenny that I couldn't remember our previous conversation and asked them to repeat it, which allowed your replacement to hear it." Jack sighed and shook his head. "I was pretty worried he might still carry out the original plan."

Jose grinned. "Didn't I tell you that even death has a conscience? Although, sometimes it needs a little guidance."

* * * * *

This story started with the idea that Room 2403 was somehow magical, and instead of people dying when they were in that room, their lives were changed for the better. As the story evolved, death became a person instead of a concept, and who better for that role than a maintenance man since they move around a hospital essentially unnoticed. And then the final piece was added – death had a conscience. So instead of the room causing the effect, it was death making the decisions, and these could be altered by circumstances.

There is no question that a person's attitude can affect the course of their illness in a hospital, especially in the elderly. Jack, the patient in this story, is typical of many older individuals who when faced with a serious medical problem develop the perception, real or imagined, that they have nothing to live for and therefore put up little if any fight. Jack is an example of how family can sometimes make a huge difference in a patient's outcome. Keep that in mind the next time a family member or good friend is in the hospital.

Waiting for Superman

Yeah, he's still coming, just a little bit late

Got stuck at the Laundromat washing his cape.

Waiting for Superman, Daughtry

Ann Robbins stared at the FedEx package on the bar and then glanced at the clock. The three men were due in the next ten minutes. When they arrived, her written instructions had been clear. She was to serve them whatever they wanted, and then once they were settled at the bar, she was to play the DVD that was in the package. That was simple. It was the last instruction that was a bit more involved and yet so intriguing – "Carefully monitor and report the comments of the three individuals as they watch the DVD."

It was only 4:20 pm, and normally the bar didn't open until 5 pm, but the money in the package had been more than enough to entice Ann to open the bar early, but as instructed, just for the three men.

Once again, she rechecked the DVD player and made sure it was displaying properly on the large screen TV at the end of the bar. She wanted to play at least part of the DVD just to make sure everything was set and it functioned properly, but the instructions had been very clear. It was to be played only once, and just for those three men. Afraid that playing it more than once might damage the disc, she'd opted to follow the instructions.

Glancing up at the clock, she noted it was now 4:30 pm. At that same instant, there was a knock on the front door. Ann wiped her hands, and went to unlock it. The two gentlemen standing at the door where a contrast in appearance.

The first was short and thin, dressed in a gray pinstriped suit with a bright red bow tie. Below his tortoise-shell glasses, a wide smile appeared on an otherwise formal countenance.

"We were told to look for the beautiful bartender, so you must be Ann. Hello. I'm Henry Jackson," he said, offering his hand, and nodding toward the man next to him. "And this is Bubba Bronson."

Bubba was a large man with broad shoulders and a spreading gut. "Howdy, Miss," he said with a slight southern twang as he tipped his Stetson. Ruddy-faced with dark blond hair, a brownish mustache, dressed in Levis and a black sports jacket, he was an imposing figure, made more so by his rugged good looks. There was a gaudy college ring on the hand he'd used to tip his hat.

"Nice to meet you both," she said. "Please come in."

Entering the bar, Henry glanced around and said, "Typical. Bean is late."

Ann pointed toward the end of the bar where she had three stools grouped together. "I have seats for you over there," she said moving behind the bar.

"What would you like to drink?" she asked once they were settled on their stools.

Bubba laughed. "Well, the letter said whatever we wanted, so how about a glass of your best bourbon?"

"Would Pappy Van Winkle be good enough?" Ann said straight-faced.

Bubba's eyes widened, and he let out a yell. "Now you're talking, little lady."

"Your host thought you might prefer that and provided us with a bottle." She turned to Jackson. "What would you like?"

"Martini up," he said with a smile.

At that moment, there was a pounding on the door.

"That'll be Bean," Bubba said, stepping off his stool and holding up a hand to stop Ann. "Go ahead and finish. I'll let him in."

Ann was working the martini shaker with an eye on the entrance, when through it passed a tall, gangly man in shorts, a sweat shirt, and high-top basketball shoes.

Jackson gestured to the new comer. "Ann, this is Bean. Coaches for the junior college basketball team. Seems we have pulled him away from practice."

"No shit, Sherlock," Bean said glancing around. "If it wasn't for the money, I'd never have come." He removed the whistle he had on a lanyard around his neck, and put it in his pocket. "My assistant is covering for me, so..." he said looking at the liquor choices behind the bar. "How about a Jack Daniels on the rocks?"

"You might want to rethink that Bean. They have Pappy," Bubba said holding up his glass.

"Well, God damn, coming here might just be worth it," Bean said. "Make it a double of that holy water."

As Ann set up his drink, she heard the three talking behind her.

"So old BM sent you guys the same letter," Jackson said, glancing at the other two, "promising five hundred dollars if you came here and watched his DVD?"

"Why would he invite the three of us?" Bubba said. "Other than being in the same fraternity house, we had nothing in common."

Placing a napkin down, Ann set Bean's drink in front of him.

Bean took a sip from the glass, let out a long "ahhhhh," and then set it back on the bar. "Now that is how bourbon is supposed to taste." He looked at his two companions and slowly shook his head. "You both know what we have in common. We were the ones in the house that gave BM the most shit. The one's that constantly harassed him for four years." He gazed at Jackson and then Bubba. "What we have in common is that he hates us." He picked his glass back up, and stared at it as he swirled its contents. "So I'm not sure why he's being so generous."

"We only hazed him for his own good," Jackson said. "All he ever did was study and go to class. We wanted him to get involved with sports, come to the fraternity parties, enjoy life." He shook his head. "I can't even remember seeing him with a girl."

"Oh, I saw him several times with girls, but it was usually in the library," Bubba said.

"As if I'd ever believe that," Bean said.

"What? That he might have a date?"

"No, that you were ever in a library," Bean said with a snicker.

Bubba stared at him for a moment, then said, "I don't remember you getting an invitation to Phi Beta Kappa."

"Gentlemen, let's get back to the here and now," Jackson interjected.

"Face it," Bean said, shaking his head. "He didn't belong in the fraternity. I'm not sure why we ever let him join."

Bubba snorted. "He got in because he was a legacy."

The three of them fell silent and sipped on their drinks.

Ann had been doing busy work nearby so she could hear their conversation. She stepped over. "Anyone need a refill?" Both Bubba and Bean nodded. "I couldn't help overhearing your comments. Who is BM?"

There was a pause, and then Jackson spoke. "His name is Bill Meyer, hence the BM reference, although often it was used in a derogatory sense." Looking at Ann, he shrugged his shoulders, trying to negate the immaturity of the whole thing.

"And what is a legacy?" Ann asked.

Bubba explained as she filled his glass. "A legacy is someone whose father has been a member of the house. Their sons are automatically invited to join." He paused, and then thoughtfully said, "Although truth be told, I think the only reason BM joined was to please his father."

Staring into his drink, Bean added, "His other nickname was Mr. Someday." He half smiled. "Whenever we tried to get him excited about something he might consider doing, he'd pass it off with the comment that he'd get to it someday." He looked over at Ann. "Yet we all knew that someday was never coming."

Jackson finished the last of his drink and set the glass down. "Well, Ann, why don't you play that DVD we were invited here to watch."

Ann wiped her hands on a bar towel, and then went to the DVD player. She pressed the play button, and then stood back looking up at the bar TV screen.

At first it was just fuzzy grey, and then suddenly it was in focus, and there was a man standing there. He was dressed in a Hawaiian shirt, jeans, and flip-flops. His causal look was topped off with light brown hair worn long.

The figure on the screen moved closer, and smiled. "Hello from Bill Meyer, a voice from the past. I hope all three of you were able to make this presentation. I'm sure you are wondering why I asked you to this gathering. Please be patient. The reason will become apparent," he said.

Ann noticed his blue eyes and pleasant, young face. There was a hint of softness, an air of living comfortably, in his look and demeanor. Yet there was also a determination and a hardness in his voice.

Bean raised his glass. "Here's to you, BM. Let's just hope this is short and to the point."

"Oh, yes, during college you constantly harassed me, made fun of me, and generally made my life a living hell. But I hold no grudge, in fact, you three are what made me who I am today," he said with a half-smile. "Gene Hackman once stated that the difference between a coward and a hero is one step to the side instead of one step forward. In college I had other agendas so I took one step to the side, but since graduation, I have taken one step forward and these are the results."

"I am getting bored already," Bean said, leaning back in his stool.

"Bean, I'm sure you're itching to leave, but you won't get your money if you do, so take a deep breath and relax."

Bill moved to a movie screen set up next to him.

"I was frequently referred to as Mr. Someday in college. Well, today is that someday." He gestured to the screen with his hand. "I believe the saying is 'One picture is worth a thousand words.' So let's watch some pictures."

The camera honed in on the screen next to him. There was now a movie playing on it, showing Bill on a bridge, with long ropes being attached to his ankles.

"He's going to bungee jump. I've done that a number of times. Lots of fun," Bubba said.

'Hey, that's no big deal," Bean said faking a yawn.

"Cut the guy some slack," Jackson said.

"Did you mean that pun?" Bubba said with a laugh. "Actually, it is a big deal for a guy who never did any sports."

On screen, Bill moved to the edge of the bridge then out on to a platform. He waved at the camera and gave a thumbs up. Turning away, and without pause, he leaped out into space. There was no scream or yell, just his silent figure falling and falling. Just when it seemed like it would never end, he was suddenly jerked up as the ropes came to their full length.

"Impressive. He's finally coming out of his shell," Jackson said.

"He did good," Bubba said in agreement. "I think I screamed the whole way down my first time."

Bean twisted his stool away from the TV and looked out over the empty barroom. "Got to keep telling myself that I'm making money watching this crap," he said, stifling another yawn.

The next shot was of a group of people loading onto a small prop airplane. The last one climbing in, turned to the camera, and gave a thumbs up. It was Bill. As the camera pulled back, the letters on the side of the place were visible: Hilltop Jump School.

"Now he's going ski diving. A bit more adventuresome," Jackson said.

"Hell, I've been up six times," Bubba said. "Loved the exhilaration of falling through space."

The next camera view was inside the plane. People were seated on either side of the fuselage. At the front on the right was a large open door with what appeared to be the instructor standing next to it. He began slowly shouting out numbers, and one by one the jumpers came forward. He checked their parachute pack, gave them a pat on the back, and then as each would jump, he filmed them going through the open door. The last figure forward was Bill, wearing a helmet and goggles. He spoke briefly to the instructor, turned and smiled toward the camera in the back of the plane.

"Is he wearing a parachute?" Jackson said sharply.

"Holy cow," Bubba yelled. "He doesn't have one."

Bean swivelled around and saw Bill step to the opening and jump.

"What the hell?" Bean said. "Hey, Bubba, how many times have you done that?"

The camera in the plane showed the instructor immediately following Bill out the plane, still holding a small camera in one hand. In the distance, Bill could be seen shooting down like a rocket with his arms at his side to gain speed. It was clear that the instructor was now doing the filming.

Ann couldn't take her eyes off the screen.

Bill was moving out of sight of the camera, he was falling so fast. He appeared to be angling toward another figure that had his arms and legs splayed out, and was dropping a lot slower. In the far distance, the camera caught Bill now extending his arms and legs trying to slow his fall as he neared the other figure. The two figures then appeared to merge. As the camera got closer, they could now see that Bill was getting into a harness that was attached to the other individual. In the far distance, the ground was now coming into focus.

Suddenly the camera was jerked away from the two ski-divers as the instructor apparently pulled his rip cord and his chute opened. A few seconds later, Bill and his now attached buddy popped their common chute. The camera watched as they pulled up and then slowly drifted down, finally hitting the ground. Soon after, the instructor was on the ground. He quickly angled the camera over to show Bill unhooking himself from his companion. Stepping out of the harness, Bill turned, flipped his goggles up, and gave the camera a big thumbs up.

No one spoke, but as the shock of what they'd just witnessed slowly dissipated, Bubba quietly said, "Do you know how hard it is to catch and hook up with someone who went out the door before you?"

"Are you talking about your experience with women who went out the fraternity door before you?" Bean teased.

"Seems old BM has grown some balls," Jackson said in awe.

Ann was stunned that someone would go to this length to prove himself. But as much as she disagreed with the risks he was taking, she was impressed with his fearlessness.

The scene now showed a helicopter landing on snow and the side door opening. The rotor wash caused the powered snow to swirl up and partially obscure the copter's side door. The first person out, dressed in a ski outfit with goggles pushed up on his forehead, was Bill. He had skis in one hand, and poles in the other. Quickly, he moved away from the helicopter and then dropped his skis on the ground. With a practiced motion, he snapped his boots into the skis, pulled his goggles down, and turning to the camera, he gave his signature thumbs up sign.

"Didn't know he'd ever been in snow, much less skied," Jackson remarked.

"I've helicopter skied a few times," said Bubba. "Lot of fun. They take you to some open slopes with deep powder and it's a gentle ride down."

Jackson turned to Ann. "Bubba is our resident jock. He has tried or done just about every sport you can think of."

The camera pulled back and then up, making it apparent that it was on a drone. As it continued to ascend, it showed Bill and the helicopter on the top of a snowed covered peak with near vertical slopes and crevices angling down from the top, amidst numerous exposed rock outcroppings.

"No way," said Jackson. "Even extreme skiers wouldn't attempt that."

"I always knew there was something wrong with this guy," Bubba said shaking his head.

"What? You never did this either, Bubba?" Bean asked.

At that moment, Bill poled himself off the top and immediately plunged into a steep chute, almost free-falling it was so sheer, making quick, short turns as he flew down the shaft, dodging the rocks on either side. It was so steep that his skis rarely even made contact with the snow. At one point, the chute abruptly ended on a ledge and he flew out into the air, dropping at least twenty feet before he touched ground, and then he continued on down the near vertical slope. This whole time he kept up tight controlled turns, never losing his form.

"Holy crap," said Bubba. "Our mild mannered Clark Kent has changed into Superman!"

Ann had been intensely watching the video, but with that last comment she glanced to the back wall of the bar. Her focus was on a small picture of Superman she'd pinned there long ago. She stared thoughtfully at it for a moment and then turned back to the screen. She had to admit she'd never known anyone that would be comfortable on top of a peak like that, much less ski down it. Watching this guy, Bill, she couldn't believe his sense of adventure, and the excitement he generated. It was then that she realized she had met him before because he definitely looked familiar.

As he dropped lower and lower, the terrain began to flatten out. He charged off another ledge, dropped at least fifteen feet, hit the powder below, and then seemed to take a tumble, disappearing into the white hillside. Almost immediately, though, he reappeared out of a cloud of snow, regained his balance, and continued plunging down the slope, now making wide smooth turns in the deep powder. The drone dropped lower and lower, getting closer to the skier. With the snow becoming more packed, and the terrain almost flat, the skier did a sharp turn, spraying snow up at the camera, and then pulled to a stop. Wiping the snow off his face, and lifting the goggles, Bill smiled at them, and once again gave his thumbs up greeting.

"If I wasn't seeing this, I'd never believe it," Jackson said.

"Who is this guy?" Bubba said. "What's happened to him?"

Bean shook his head and held up his empty glass. "I'll need another to watch any more of this." Everyone laughed easing the tension in the room.

Ann was filling Bean's empty glass, when there was a group intake of breath. She turned back to the screen.

The scene had shifted, and now it was an ocean setting. In the foreground was a sandy beach, while in the distance, there were huge crashing waves. Occasionally a surfer could be seen racing across the face of one of them. The waves were at least three times taller than the surfer.

"That's Pipeline," Bubba said. "It's on the north shore of Oahu. The waves can be huge, and, if you fall, there are coral heads scattered just below the surface."

As if to make the point, a broken surf board washed up on the sand. The camera shifted to a scene further down the beach, where a young man in trunks was being helped out of the water. His face was a mask of blood. The camera slowly panned from him out to the huge explosive waves in the distance.

"I've been there a few times in the past, but never surfed it. Way too much for me," Bubba said. He was silent for a moment, his face a question, and then he burst out, "Oh, my God, that's not Pipeline, that's Outside Pipeline. It only breaks when the waves are humongous."

The camera angled back toward the beach, and there was Bill in red trunks, wearing a bright blue t-shirt, and holding a surfboard under his arm. He grinned at the camera, gave a "hang loose" sign with his hand, and then entered the water. As he started paddling out, the camera once again shifted to the waves. This time the lens magnification was increased, and now the waves filled the screen. The surf was even bigger than before with the waves four times the size of the surfing figures.

The scene ended and when it started again, a small figure could be seen paddling at the top of a gigantic wave. He caught it and dropped down the enormous face. As he streaked across this huge wall, they could see he was wearing red trunks and a blue shirt. It was Bill.

"Do it," Bubba roared, "Ride that mother!"

"Come on, buddy, you can make it," Bean shouted, his eyes glued to the screen.

"Incredible," Jackson said. "Absolutely incredible."

Bill was angling across the thirty-foot face when the wave started to break behind him. The white water was like a huge avalanche rolling down the face, trying to catch and bury him. He angled up the wave and then dropped back down, trying to pick up speed to stay out of reach of the angry white monster chasing him. For a while, the up and down motion on the face kept him in front of the foam giant that was slowly catching up. At the last minute, he angled hard back up the face and exploded out over the top, crashing down behind the crashing wave as it continued on past him.

"What a stud," Bubba said, slapping his hand down on the bar.

"I don't even deserve to hold his jock," Bean said, taking a large gulp of his drink. "Unbelievable."

"Bill has not only emerged from his shell, he's demolished it," Jackson said. "I wouldn't be surprised to see a Nike swoosh on his clothes, and find out they're sponsoring him."

Ann just shook her head, and said, "The guy is amazing. I can't believe you had to push him to go to fraternity parties. He must have had girls falling all over him."

The three men turned as one and stared at her. Finally Bubba spoke. "In college he was very smart, but not an athlete. And he definitely was lacking in the dating game."

"You mean he wasn't as 'swave and deboner' as you?" Bean said with a smirk.

"Well, I have had some social success if I do say so myself," Bubba replied, sitting up straighter on the stool and flashing his wedding ring.

Bean was about to reply when the film shifted to a new location.

The screen now showed a two-door Mercedes sports car pull up in front of a mansion, and a parking attendant moving to open the door. Out stepped Bill who smiled at the camera, as he adjusted his suit and tie.

"I've never seen him in a suit," Jackson said. "He cuts quite a figure."

The camera followed Bill in through a high arched doorway and toward a crowd of people. As he got closer to the group, it becomes apparent that it was a party in full swing. Bill grabbed a glass of champagne off a passing tray and turned toward someone on his left. The camera swung to his point of view and it was George Lucas.

"Bill, I'm so glad you could make it," Lucas said, offering him his hand.

"You know I never miss your parties, George," Bill replied as they shook.

A voice off camera cried, "Bill!"

Bill and the camera turned to the right, and there was Taylor Swift striding past. She called out, "I want to karaoke with you later. No excuses this time."

As the camera swung back, George Clooney and Brad Pitt came up to join Lucas. Clooney stuck his index finger in Bill's chest. "I want a chance to win my money back," he said "so don't even think of miss-

ing next week's poker game."

"George, it's become embarrassing taking your money," Bill said with mock regret. "Save it for the twins."

Pitt laughed and slapped Clooney on the back. "Give it up, George. It's time to stop making him rich."

Lucas hooked his arm into Bill's and pulled him away. As they moved off, Lucas was heard to say, "I want to discuss an idea I have for a new movie. See what you think."

The movie on the screen went dark as the camera pulled back to show Bill standing next to screen. He glanced down for a moment, and then looked back up at the camera. "Thank you, guys, And I really mean it. You made me the man I am today."

The DVD playing on the bar TV slowly faded to black.

The three men were silent, each lost in his thoughts. Bubba broke the stillness. "We were too quick to judge." He glanced around at his friends, his hands opened in a plea for agreement. "But who could have guessed what lay beneath this guy's quiet facade."

Bean stood up, and finished his drink. "I should have given him a chance to show what he was really made of." He slowly nodded his head. "I'd have been proud to call him my friend."

Ann dropped the FedEx container on the bar. She reached inside and pulled out three slips of paper. "I have a check for $500 for each of you, as per my instructions." She handed one to each of them.

Jackson stared at his for a long moment, looked at the other two, and back at Ann. "I am embarrassed and disappointed. I had a chance to get to know a fascinating, courageous individual and I blew it." He ripped the check up, and Bubba and Bean quickly followed suite.

"It was a pleasure meeting you, Ann," Jackson said, standing up.

Bubba leaned over the bar and offered his hand. "No more judging acquaintances at face value. So long, Ann."

"Sounds trite, but the analogy of a book and its cover is what I'll remember," said Bean as he dropped his torn check pieces on the bar. "Thanks for everything, Ann."

With that, the three of them walked out the door.

Ann was cleaning glasses when twenty minutes later the door opened. The individual in the doorway was backlit by the sun, wearing a baseball cap and dark glasses. Once he'd settled onto a bar stool, Ann walked over and dropped a napkin in front of him. She was about to ask for his order when it hit her.

"You're him, aren't you?" she said excitedly. "Mr. Someday, BM or whatever."

"Yeah, I am," Bill said, pulling off the cap and glasses.

"I almost didn't recognize you without your cape," she said with a grin.

He tilted his head at her. "Cape?"

"Those guys were calling you Superman, so I figured..."

Bill laughed. "Sorry to disappoint but... I sent it out to be dry cleaned."

After a beat, she said, "You look very familiar."

"I use to come in here for drinks."

"That's where I know you. But then you disappeared."

"Good memory." He looked around the bar. "Can I get a cold Corona from you?"

"Oh, I'm sorry." She smiled at him. "Coming right up."

When she returned, Bill had unzipped his jacket, and was settling back in the stool.

She set the beer down, and he said, "How long have you been working here?"

"Almost 5 years now." She shrugged her shoulders. "What can I say? The owner is my cousin, and the work is easy."

"No judgement call here," he replied, taking a sip of his drink.

Ann wiped the bar down, and then looked up. "Actually, I'm going to college during the day trying to get a master's in art history. I hope to someday become a curator at an art museum."

Bill put his drink down. "I'm impressed."

"Oh, it's going to happen, believe me."

"I have no doubts," he replied.

Neither spoke for a moment, and then Ann said, "Speaking of accomplishments, your DVD was pretty incredible."

Bill stared down into his beer and made no reply. She was about to step away when he looked up at her. "As I remember, you were waiting for Superman."

"What?" Ann said with raised her eyebrows. "Who told you that?"

"One of the bartenders. He told me you were waiting for some hero to come along and carry you away. The description he gave was the guy had to be adventuresome, exciting, and romantic." Shifting his position on the stool, Bill continued. "And you told him that you'd never find that kind of guy hanging out in a bar like this."

"Oh, come on, how many people ever meet the love of their life in a bar?"

"Well, he advised me, not to waste my time trying to ask you out." He glanced around behind her. "Do you still have that picture of Superman pinned up back there?"

Ann laughed. "I tell the drunks that's who I'm waiting for, and usually they get the point."

"But that's the kind of guy you're looking for?"

"Well, if some good-looking guy came and carried me away, I wouldn't protest."

Ann moved to change the focus of the conversation.

"After your friends' comments, what you did on that video was a complete surprise." She gestured toward him with one hand. "And now you socialize with the Hollywood crowd. Wow."

"I can imagine what was said before the DVD," Bill said, running his hand through his hair, "but what did they say afterwards?"

"They were shocked and," she paused and then added, "and so was I."

"So even some guy who looks like Mr. Milquetoast can turn into a Superman?" he asked with a wry grin.

She smiled. "I never thought you looked like Milquetoast. In fact, I thought you were kind of cute."

"Not the impression I got sitting at this bar."

"What? Did you expect me to woo you as I took orders and mixed drinks?

They were quiet for a bit, and then Ann remarked, "I am still surprised at the risks you took just to stick it to these guys. You could have been killed doing the things you did. Was it worth it?"

"I don't know, but I'll find out soon."

"And how's that?" she said, and then remembered. "Oh, you mean my feedback on what they said."

"No, that's not it," he replied, looking at her over his beer. "It's the answer to a question I have for you."

"A question?" she asked, obviously perplexed. "What question?"

"How about a date?" he said quietly.

She gazed at him for a long moment and then said, "Hollywood parties, skiing incredible peaks, surfing mountains, jumping out of a plane without a parachute." She laughed and shook her head. "I don't think I could keep up with you."

"So now I'm too much of a Superman?" he said.

"I don't know what you are, but you're not what I thought," she said.

The two of them stared at each other, and then Bill broke the silence. "What if I told you that I was a CPA who worked for George Lucas, and that I saved him an enormous amount of money? So much so, that he offered to reward me anyway I wanted."

"Okay," Ann said, not sure where this was going.

"Everything you heard about me in college was true. But everything you saw in the movie, and I do mean everything, was faked compliments of Lucasfilm Production Company." He paused, watching her expression. "That was the reward I asked for."

"You're kidding, right?"

Bill shook his head.

"That whole charade was just payback to those fraternity guys?" Ann said.

"No, that was never the end goal."

"Then what was?"

"It was to get your attention. I've wanted to go out with you for the longest time, but you never noticed me."

"Hey, I just told you I thought you were attractive so I must have noticed you."

"No, you were too intent looking for your Mr. Superman, so I figured I had to become that person. At least long enough to catch your eye."

She stared at him, a half smile playing on her lips. "So you didn't jump out of a plane without a parachute?"

"Oh, I did that... but the plane was on the ground and I jumped onto a mattress. Even sprained my ankle doing it."

Ann had a full smile. "That huge wave in Hawaii. That wasn't you?"

"Oh, I did paddle out... about twenty feet from the shore and nearly drown in the white water. The guy you saw on the wave was a stunt-double."

It was a long moment before she spoke again. "And you don't leap tall buildings at a single bound?"

"Sorry. I have trouble stepping over sleeping dogs."

Ann laughed. "And you don't wear a cape or spandex outfit?"

Bill shook his head slowly.

Ann paused for a moment, seeming lost in thought, and then said, "Well, that's good since it would have been hell for me getting an outfit that would go with yours if we went out."

It was a while later when Bill emerged from the bar. Glancing around, he saw Bean leaning on a car, and Bubba and Jackson relaxing on a bench. They all stood up expectantly as he approached.

Bean was the first to speak. "Well, were we successful? Did you get the date?"

Bill glanced around at each of them, his face a solemn mask. And then he broke into a huge grin and flashed them his now trademark thumbs up sign.

* * * * *

This story originally was going to be titled "Mr. Someday" with the idea that the lead man, Bill, was always pushing off adventures by saying he would do them some other day. In that story, he was going to show up with a bogus movie to shame the ex-fraternity brothers who had been so hard on him and that was it.

That plan died when I heard Daughtry's song, Waiting for Superman. The goal of the story changed. It became Bill's attempt to woo the pretty girl waiting for her superman to show up. In a sense, Bill's willingness to try such an outlandish attempt to win a date made him pretty super in her eyes.

Even with the change in direction of the story, the three friends were still going to be cast as bad guys. But as I explained the tale to my wife, all of a sudden I liked the twist that they were actually close friends and were in cahoots with Bill getting a date. Once again, it was a case of the characters telling me what role they wanted to play, and not the role I had chosen for them.

The Game of the Gods

It was another typical early morning in paradise. In a cloudless azure sky, a dazzling tropical sun was just rising over green craggy mountains. Yet, even at this early hour, Waikiki was already up and about. Its streets were crowded with joggers, tourists, surfers, and retired transplanted mainlanders. A causal glance would have passed over the entire mix without pause except today was the third Thursday of the month. Today the quick glance would have paused on the tall, older man with the koa wood walking stick. Dark skin, long white hair, smiling countenance, wearing an exotic floral Hawaiian shirt above ivory colored trousers and sandaled feet.

Exactly what caught one's attention wasn't clear. Maybe it was his athletic stride or his colorful outfit; whatever, people took notice. He would smile at some, nod at others, or clap a few on the shoulder as he passed. Some unseen force seemed to part the sea of humanity, opening the way for him as he strode down Kalakaua Avenue.

If this colorful Patrician garnered attention, it was nothing compared to the figure two blocks away heading toward him. Medium height, dressed entirely in black, with coal black hair combed straight back above a pale face. Intense black eyes glared above a pencil thin mustache and goatee. His air of menace was enhanced by the tattoo on his left arm. A coiled snake encircled his bicep, extending down onto the forearm ending in a malevolent head with barred fangs. His aura of danger permeated everything in front of him such that people rushed to get out of his path.

On the sidewalk, at the edge of the beach, stood an open sided wooden-

roofed structure which covered three worn picnic benches. Painted on the top of each of the tables was the black and white pattern of a chessboard. It was in front of one of these tables that the Patrician and the black Menace came face to face.

They nodded to each other and the black Menace flashed gleaming white teeth. He gestured toward the center table.

"Shall we?"

The Patrician smiled and it lit up his face. "I've been looking forward to this."

"Not as much as I have," the Menace replied.

They moved to the table, settling in opposite each other on the benches. The Patrician produced a small wooden box from which he poured chess pieces onto the table. As if it was a given, each knew which color pieces they would be playing with. The Patrician pushed the black pieces across to his opponent while keeping the white ones. Neither spoke as they set up the table.

"What are the stakes?" the Patrician asked.

"A soul," replied the Menace.

"Whose?"

The Menace leaned back while starring at his fingernails. "Let's make it someone sworn to be honest, say a New York police officer. How about Michael Gallo?"

The Patrician paused a moment then nodded. "The usual rules? Players have freedom of choice, but we can try to influence those choices."

"Exactly. So let the game begin," the Menace said.

After a moment, the Patrician picked up a white knight, which briefly changed into a white shirt, and moved it forward into harm's way.

Dressed in a long sleeve, white shirt, Mike Gallo said, "Sure, we'll get right on it, Lieutenant," and hung up the phone. He shifted his attention back to the pictures on his cluttered desk. The sounds of the other detectives in the New York City squad room faded away as he studied the two framed photographs.

In one, a beautiful young woman with shoulder length golden hair sat in the driver's seat of a dark blue Mercedes convertible, her head thrown back in laughter, exposing movie star teeth. A closer inspection picked up the opulent ruby necklace, the fawn skin driving gloves, and the elegant picnic basket on the passenger seat. Gallo remembered that day. It sat prominently in his memory bank, filed under moments that make life worth living. Things seemed so simple then. Just he and Elizabeth on a wonderful, carefree date.

He glanced at the other picture. His second generation Calabria parents and thirty of his closest relatives gathered around a younger Gallo dressed in the dark blues he wore that day when he'd graduated from the Police Academy. Another moment he'd stored away. Yet the two pictures were like the ends of a spectrum. Elizabeth with her wealth, her global life style, and her nothing-is-unaffordable attitude. While at the other end, simple people bowed with responsibilities, unpaid bills, long hours, and limited education. On a whim, Elizabeth might fly to Paris for dinner. His Italian family did nothing on a whim. A big night was having the same relatives over, eating the same pasta dishes, drinking the same dago red, and repeating the same boring conversations about their aches and pains, who died, and who got married. True, the laughter flowed, but it seemed so stagnant whereas Elizabeth's life was a constant whirl of travel, parties, and excitement.

Gallo knew he had to make a choice on where he wanted to fit into this continuum. Yet, as attractive as Elizabeth's world appeared, there was a lack of reality, of honesty, of substance in the people she associated with, and the things that she did. As much as he might try to escape his background, sometimes homemade pasta, cheap wine, and laughter with family was priceless. Hell, he was starting to sound like a Visa card commercial.

The Menace lifted his black knight. As he set it in its new position, the piece changed colors and briefly became a dark plaid. He reset the chess clock, and then leaned back with a satisfied smile. "Your move," he said.

"Hey, Mike," called out one of the detectives, wearing a dark plaid suit. "When are we going to meet this new girlfriend of yours? Why don't you bring her to the department party?"

Gallo glanced over at the speaker and nearly laughed out loud. Are you kidding? he thought. Elizabeth hangs with princes, world shakers, and celebrities. Desk sergeants, file clerks, burned out detectives, and narcs were not something she could even imagine, much less party with.

"I'm not sure if she's free," Gallo said.

"Well, you better ask her soon. It's tomorrow night."

Pulling his suit coat off the chair, Gallo slipped it on over his shoulder holster, made an adjustment to his tie, and left the room.

Moving with a quick stride down the hall, he went through the double doors and into the waiting area of the mid-Manhattan precinct station. The desk sergeant in charge looked over from his counter.

"What's up, Mike?"

"I'm looking for my partner."

"I saw him go out front just a few minutes ago," he replied before turning back to the elderly couple standing in front of him.

Gallo moved toward the entrance door.

The Patrician put his hand on a pawn, hesitated, then reached over and held the clock button down, freezing the time. "I'm feeling lucky today. How about we play for two instead of one?"

"Two souls it is," the Menace said softly. "Who did you have in mind?"

"Another policeman. Patrick Leary."

"So you knew I've been watching him," the Menace replied. "Fine. Let's add him to the winnings."

The Patrician took his hand off the clock and instead of moving his pawn, moved his rook. When he set it down, it briefly glowed purple.

As Gallo crossed the room, a hand reached up and grabbed his sleeve. He glanced down, surprised to see an older woman in a bright purple dress with long grey hair and piercing brown eyes staring up at him.

Grabbing his hand, she turned it palm up.

He gently tried to extract it but she held it tight. "I read palms," she said. "Your future is spread in front of me." Her eyes roamed the creases and ridges of his hand. Suddenly she glanced up, her eyes wide.

"Green," she whispered. "If you value your soul, beware of green."

"Hey, Marie," the desk sergeant yelled. "Leave my detectives alone or I'll put you back in the holding cell until your lawyer arrives."

The old woman let go of the detective's hand and turned from him. Gallo watched her shuffle away. She went over and sat in a chair against the wall, carefully avoiding his gaze.

Walking outside, Gallo couldn't shake a sudden sense of foreboding. A powerful unease that the palm reader had planted in his mind. He'd never believed in such things, but his mother and sister had regularly visited the moga — the Italian word for witch — that lived on their street. Through the years, he'd had to listen to their insistence on the accuracy of her predictions. He shook his head, hoping to shake loose the whole episode. He looked up and down the street for his partner, Patrick Leary. Gallo saw him sitting in an unmarked police car.

The Menace grabbed a pawn, smiled briefly at the Patrician, and moved it two spaces forward. As he set it down, the piece changed to a cellphone, then back to its original shape.

Walking toward the police vehicle, Gallo noticed that Leary was on his cellphone. No surprise there, Gallo thought. Leary was always on the phone, either checking that all was well at "Luck of the Irish," the bar he owned, or arguing with one of his many girlfriends. At fifty-five, he continually fell into dead-end relationships which he laboriously discussed with Gallo and anyone else who would be forced to listen. An Irish philosopher who used sarcasm and wit to make his point, a recovering alcoholic who loved the inside of a bar, and a very street-wise detective. This all added up to never having a dull work shift for Gallo when he was with Leary.

Seeing Gallo, Leary raised his hand and waved him over.

As Gallo approached, Leary closed his phone.

"We need to roll," Gallo said. "Shoplifting case."

"Since when do we cover shoplifting?"

"When it involves $10,000 in diamonds."

Leary raised his eyebrows. "Where?"

"Tiffany's on Fifth."

The Patrician slowly and purposely slid another pawn forward and hit the clock. Once again, as the piece touched the board, it changed colors, briefly radiating a dark brown.

As they entered the store, the first thing Gallo's eyes fell on was not the numerous display cases filled with diamonds, rubies, and sapphires, glittering in the artificial light. No, his attention was immediately riveted to the corner, where a woman in a chocolate brown sweater sat with a security guard standing over her.

She was in her late twenties, with auburn hair spilling down the back of her tight fitting sweater. As they moved toward her, she looked up and stared straight at Gallo. Her eyes caused him to stop in his tracks. They were dark green.

Leary pulled his badge out and held it up. "Detectives Leary and Gallo," he said to the security guard. "I assume this is the suspect?"

"Yeah, this is her. And I'm Lyle Johnson. I did twenty-one years on the job in the Bronx before I retired." He gestured to the woman. "Not much of a suspect, more like a perp since we caught her leaving the store with a $10,000 dollar necklace in her pocket."

The girl moved her gaze from Gallo to Leary. "This is just a simple mistake," she said calmly. "But if it's not corrected quickly, I will sue this place for every penny it can scratch up."

Leary moved to her side. "I'm Detective Leary, and the man with his mouth open is my partner Detective Gallo. You are?"

"Carly Davis."

Gallo stepped forward, still flushed from Leary's comment. "And what's your version of what happened, Ms. Davis?"

She swung her eyes back to Gallo, fixing on his polished, black loafers then slowly lifting her gaze, casually taking in his dark pin-striped suit, his power red tie, and then finally holding her eyes on his. She saw a squared jaw man with a face that just missed being handsome due to the scar on his left temple and his bent, broken nose.

Gallo flushed realizing this was the same once over he had given her.

Davis leaned back in her chair and turned to Leary. "I was looking at various items in the store, rings, bracelets, and necklaces, whatever. I must have accidently put the diamond necklace in my pocket when I picked something else up. Just a simple moment of forgetfulness."

Gallo found it hard to pay attention. Her eyes were mesmerizing even when she wasn't looking at him.

Leary turned to Johnson. "What did you see?"

"Oh, she's partially right. She handled a lot of items. Pushed them around on the glass top of the display cases, lifting one then the other." Johnson smiled. "She was smooth though. I never saw her palm the necklace, but I knew she did. I grabbed her just as she stepped out the door. The necklace was in her inside coat pocket." He pointed at a coat draped over the back of Davis' chair. "Hard to think that putting it in there was a moment of forgetfulness."

Leary nodded then stepped aside to make a phone call. Gallo watched him go then swung back to Davis.

"Is it Miss or Mrs. Davis?" Gallo asked, pulling his pocket notebook out.

The green eyes were on him again, measuring, appraising. "It's Ms. Davis."

Well, I guess I didn't make the cut on that evaluation, Gallo thought. "Do you live in the area, Ms. Davis?"

"No, I live in Greenwich Village. A studio apartment."

"Occupation?"

She paused a moment. "Security consultant. Freelance."

"And you make enough to be shopping in a place like this?"

"Yes, I make enough to shop here," she said, and then pointed at his suit, "but not enough to buy an outfit like that. I didn't know cops earned that kind of money."

Leary closed his cellphone and returned to the group. "I think you described this as just a simple mistake, Ms. Davis?"

"Do I look like a thief?"

Gallo decided she looked more like the girl of his dreams, except for one thing. Her green eyes. He couldn't get the moga's warning out of his mind.

Leary smiled at her. "No, you don't look like a thief. In fact, I am sure the other two times you were arrested for shoplifting you didn't look like a thief either."

Six years on the force and you'd think I'd learn, Gallo thought, mentally kicking himself.

Davis picked her coat up and put it on. "Let's get this done," she said.

Leary handcuffed her and the security guard led them to the door.

The Menace's eyes floated over the chessboard. He liked what he saw, very much. Time to set things up. He slid the black bishop diagonally across the open board. As it moved, the piece transiently assumed a blond color.

As the trio passed through the door and onto the sidewalk, a voice called, "Michael!"

Gallo glanced over. Emerging from the back seat of a black Lincoln town car was Elizabeth. She looked gorgeous with her blond hair piled high, and her athletic figure poured into a black clinging dress.

Gallo heard Leary's low wolf whistle followed by, "Mikey, me lad, don't let that get away."

"Excuse me a minute, Pat," Gallo said.

"Can you make it fast, Mikey," Davis hissed. "I really don't want to stand out here in handcuffs any longer than I have to."

"Elizabeth!" Gallo said, walking toward her. "What are you doing here?"

He reached to hug her but she put her hands up. "Careful! It took the stylist almost three hours to get my hair just right." She looked him over. "Don't you look nice? I should get you several more of these suits."

He hesitated for a moment. "Where are you heading?"

"I am having lunch with the mayor and a few close friends. I had no jewelry to match this outfit, so I thought I'd stop here and grab something." She glanced at her watch. "Oh, I'm going to be late."

"Wait a second, Elizabeth." Gallo knew Leary and Davis were taking this whole exchange in so he lowered his voice. "Saturday night the precinct is having a big send off for the chief. I want you to come and meet my friends."

"Oh, Michael. How sweet." She wrinkled her brow. "You know I'd love to meet your pals, but this Saturday just isn't good for me. I have a better idea. Why don't you go by yourself and we can get together later. Say around 11pm at the Plaza Oak Bar? Then my place after that?"

"Are you ever going to find the time to meet my friends?"

She ran her hand down his cheek. "Michael, of course I will. Just not this Saturday."

Gallo nodded. "Yeah, right."

She gave him a peck on the cheek. "Cheer up. I'll make it up to you Saturday night."

Before he could blink, she was off. Slowly, he walked over to Leary and Davis.

"Please tell me that's not your girlfriend?" Davis asked.

"That's none of your business."

Mimicking Elizabeth's voice, Davis said, "I'm having lunch with the mayor." She laughed and turned to Gallo. "I guess you did earn that suit after all."

There was only five seconds left on the timer when the Patrician lifted his bishop and moved it diagonally five spaces across. It changed into a jail door then back to a plastic piece.

"Let's go, we're taking you to jail." Gallo said grabbing her arm. They walked over to the unmarked police car. Gallo opened the back door, but Davis pulled away from him and turned to Leary.

"Hey, can we cut a deal here?" she asked.

Leary snickered. "Yeah, hop in the car without a struggle and I'll tell the DA you were very cooperative."

"How about instead of a simple shoplifting arrest, I could lead you to a large stash of coke…" she paused, "and two hundred thousand dollars in drug money?"

Gallo and Leary exchanged looks.

Leary leaned up against the car. "Now that could definitely get you something."

"I thought it might," Davis said. "A couple of days ago, I overheard this guy talking with his roommate about their 'stash' and how they were going to launder their earnings."

"And what the hell was your involvement that you know these guys so well?" Gallo said forcibly.

"I slept with the guy. Okay?" She saw Gallo's expression. "You of all people shouldn't be judging bedroom companions."

"Screw you," Gallo replied.

Leary chuckled. "Attitude is your middle name, lass."

Gallo pulled Leary aside. "Pat, let's take her down to the station now. We book her, and then work out the details."

The Menace sneered. "You really have no idea where this is going, do you?"

Resting his hand on his knight, the Menace moved it two spaces forward and one to the left. There was a brief flash as the piece evolved into a hand, then back to a knight.

Leary pushed Gallo's hand away. "No, we aren't taking her to the station."

"Are you nuts? We book her and that's that."

"Not this time, Mikey," Leary said adamantly. "If we take her down to the station now, she cuts a deal with the DA, they turn it over to the narc squad, and the narcs take all the credit."

"That's the way the game is played, Pat."

"This time I want all the credit on our record!"

"What's come over you?" Gallo said. "This isn't right and you know it." He pointed at Davis. "You don't really trust her do you?"

"It's a chance I'm willing to take. So are you with me or not?"

Gallo shook his head in resignation. "We're partners, Pat, so we stick together. But something doesn't feel right about this."

"What's not right? If she's telling the truth, we get a collar for shop-lifting and credit for a drug bust."

"She has malocchio, the evil eye."

"What are you babbling about?"

Gallo hesitated, realizing he'd already said too much, but now he was stuck. He told the warning the moga had given him about green.

After he finished, there was a brief pause before Leary spoke. "I'm just going to pretend I didn't hear that. Much less hear it from a cop who is supposed to cover my back." He elbowed Gallo aside and approached Davis.

"Show us where the drugs and the money are, and we'll see what we can do," Leary said.

"No. I want more than a 'we'll see,'" Davis said. "I want some kind of guarantee."

Leary spread his hands out. "On the grave of my dear dead mother, I give you my word that we'll definitely try to get you a deal."

"I don't want Irish malarkey about your mother's grave. She's probably sitting shit-faced in some bar right now."

"Oh, my God, Mikey. She's met my wee, sweet mother."

Davis pointed at Gallo. "I want his word."

Leary glanced at Gallo.

"Yeah, you have it," Gallo said begrudgingly.

Davis inspected his face, and then with a look of what seemed to be disappointment, nodded her acceptance. Ten minutes later, they were pulling up in front of a fire hydrant in the lower east side of Manhattan. The street was lined with overhanging trees and old four story brownstone houses.

Davis nodded toward a house three buildings over. "That's the place. An apartment on the third floor."

Leary was reaching for his door handle when Gallo put a hand on his shoulder. "Pat, let me call in for a search warrant."

"Good idea," Leary said. "Why don't you do that while I check this place out?"

"I have a key to the apartment," Davis said from the back seat.

Leary twisted around. "And where did you get that, darlin?"

"The guy I've been dating gave me a key."

"Now that is malarkey," Leary said.

"Okay. So I lifted it and made a copy. What's the difference?"

Leary snorted and climbed out of the car.

"We're not going anywhere unless you take these cuffs off," Davis yelled.

"If we let you go, it will be after we see what's in the apartment," Leary replied.

Three flights up an uneven, rickety stairway brought them to apartment 3C.

"So where's this key?" Leary asked.

Davis moved to the start of the next flight of stairs and pulled a key from under the carpet on the first step.

Gallo stepped between the two of them. "I thought we were just going to 'check' things out."

"Hey, she has a key and she is letting us in, so no problem," Leary replied.

"Pat, what's going on? You're sweating. Your hands are shaking. This isn't you."

Pushing Gallo aside, Leary pointed at the door with his gun. "Okay, sweetheart. Knock on the door and see if your boyfriend is at home." He glanced at Gallo. "If he lets her in, he's letting us in since we are with her."

Davis studied them both for a moment then moved to the door.

Gallo shook his head as he eased his gun out.

After the tenth knock, it was obvious no one was home. Leary told her to unlock the door, and move back. As the door opened, Leary stepped in, telling Gallo to watch her while he checked the apartment. A few minutes later, he was back.

"Place is as empty as an Irish whiskey bottle on St. Pat's Day." He glanced at Davis. "So where is it?"

Davis walked into the apartment, nervously looking around. "You sure no one is here?"

"Very sure," Leary replied closing the door.

The Patrician fingered one, then another, and finally a third piece. Slowly, he moved a pawn forward. It briefly assumed the shape of a paperback book then became a pawn again.

The Menace shook his head in disgust.

Davis led them back into a large cluttered bedroom. There were clothes strewn across the floor, mixed with empty pizza boxes, beer cans, and paperback books. She pointed to the closet on the other side of the room. "It's on the top shelf of that closet."

"Sorry, pops," the Menace laughed, "but you don't seem to be up to your usual standard of play today." With an evil grin, he pushed his castle across the board to the last row of the Patrician's side. For a few seconds it resembled a suitcase. "Check," the Menace said hitting the timer.

Leary opened the door, looked up, and pulled down a large, battered, suitcase. He laid it on the bed and opened the latches. As he swung the top open, Gallo and Davis moved to his side.

There was a collective gasp.

One side of the case was bulging with rubber band bound stacks of hundred dollar bills. The other side was filled with plastic sacks of white powder.

"That is one load of money," Gallo said in awe.

Leary stared for a long time before speaking. "All my life I've searched for the end of the rainbow. And now here it is in an old suitcase."

"Gentlemen," Davis said pulling their attention away from the suitcase, "Why don't we make a little change in our deal?" She regarded each of them. "No one knows that I have this key. No one knows we have been here. You let me go. I walk out of here and never look back. You do whatever you want with the drugs and the money… if you get my drift."

Leary spent a long moment staring at her and then smiled. "Looks, attitude, and brains. What a combination." Leary swung to his partner. "What say you, Mikey?"

Gallo stared at the suitcase and then slowly turned to Leary. "So that's what this whole thing has been about. Why you acted so strange. Why you ignored everything I said."

Leary remained silent.

"There never was going to be a search warrant. The DA was never going to hear about this, was he?"

Leary sat down on the bed. "Remember that call I was on when you came out of the precinct? It was my bank. They're going to foreclose on my bar." Leary struck the bed with the flat of his hand. "Eleven years I have been making those payments." He slapped the bed harder. "Now I'm two months short and the bastards are going to take my bar away."

"How did you get behind?" Gallo asked.

"I loaned the money to my sister. She's hit some hard times." He spread his hands out to Gallo. "I have been going out of my mind trying to figure out what to do. I tell you, Mike, this is like a gift from heaven."

The Patrician looked across the board at the Menace. "Giving him the idea this is 'a gift from heaven' is so low. Why it's even below your standards."

The Menace put his hands together in prayer and bowed his head. "Forgive me, Father, for I have sinned." He looked up. "Now, let's get back to the game. I think you are in check."

Gallo contemplated the suitcase, all the while shaking his head. "This isn't the way, Pat."

"Hey, this could be good for you too. You'd have the money to really court Elizabeth. And once you married her, you would be set for life. She is one beautiful woman, Mike."

"Too late, Pat. We're over and done."

"What are you talking about, man? She's promised to fulfill your dreams Saturday night."

"I guess I saw her today for what she really is. Completely superficial. No, I want someone that thinks being together is all that matters, and would jump at a chance to meet my friends." Gallo noticed Davis staring at him with a surprised look. "You got a problem with that?"

"Yeah, I can't believe a man can see past the superficial, especially her superficials."

Gallo found himself once again lost in those green depths as they locked eyes.

Leary's voice pulled them back to the present. "Mike, how many times have you told me you want to live in a nice place, buy a car that doesn't live in the repair shop? Hell, you could even buy your own suits." He held his arms out toward the suitcase. "It's a win-win situation for both of us."

Gallo gazed intently at the money. Finally, he pulled his eyes away and turned to Leary. "How many years have we been on the force, Pat?" He paused. "Does that stand for nothing?

"Lad, I really need this."

"Hell, I could use it too. But do you think it's going to stop here?"

"Don't get all high and mighty with me. You had no trouble accepting that free case of champagne from Charlie Wurtz."

"That was a gift."

"No, it was a bribe to keep a closer watch on his restaurant," Pat said angrily. "I don't just need this; I've got to have it."

Davis walked over to the suitcase inspecting its contents. "What's the debate here? I'm sure this can't be the first time you guys have had a chance to grab a little free money on the job. Doesn't every cop?"

"Shut your mouth, lass," Pat said.

Davis turned from the suitcase, lifting her cuffed hands in surrender. "Do what you want with it. Turn it in, keep it, burn it, I don't care. But just let me go."

Leary stood up and walked over to her. He grabbed her arms and opened the handcuffs. "We cover mid-Manhattan. I never want to see your face in that part of town again. Not for any reason. Got it?"

Yanking her arm away, Davis said, "Real clear." She walked to the doorway and turned back. "I hope you both get what you deserve."

Gallo's voice stopped her before she left the room. "Davis, one question. Are you wearing green contacts?"

Davis snickered. "The only thing green in this room is the money. You want it, you take it." She stepped through the door and was gone.

Five minutes later, Gallo and Leary walked out the door of apartment 3C. Leary was carrying the suitcase.

The Menace watched the timer tick down. It was just a matter of minutes and he'd have the Patrician in checkmate. Then why was he smiling?

The Patrician brought his knight back, blocking access to the king. As the knight settled into place, it became a police badge, and then back to being a knight.

"Stop where you are and put up your hands," a deep voice boomed. "Internal Affairs. You are under arrest."

Gallo and Leary stared wide eyed at the three men approaching them with guns drawn. One man was holding up a badge and behind him came Carly Davis. She stepped forward as they cuffed Gallo and Leary. Flashing her badge, she said, "I'm also with Internal Affairs."

"So that's what you meant by 'security consultant'?" Gallo said.

Davis nodded. "There was a rumor that someone in your station house was dirty." She looked them both up and down. "And now it looks like we've found them."

"So this whole thing," Leary said, "was a set up to entrap us."

"Oh, here comes the entrapment argument," one of the Internal Affairs agents moaned.

"No," Gallo said. "You caught us fair and square. Let's just get this over as quick as possible."

"Oh, this isn't going to be over quickly," the Internal Affairs agent said sarcastically. "Not unless you think five to ten years in jail is quick." He pushed Leary and Gallo toward the stairwell, while one of the other agents picked up the suitcase.

The Menace slid his castle along the back row and took out the knight. One more move and he'd have the Patrician's king in checkmate. The castle flickered briefly as handcuffs.

They led Gallo and Leary into their own station house to be booked. At the sight of two of their best detectives in handcuffs, all sound ceased in the booking area. Gallo was pissed. He knew this debasement was Internal Affairs' not so subtle warning regarding what happens to cops that go bad.

The Patrician moved his pawn to the last square at the end of the board. He calmly informed the Menace. "I'm promoting my pawn to a queen."

For a moment, the Menace froze. He'd been so intent on his planned approach that he'd ignored the pawn, a piece that has been called "the soul of chess."

"And by the way… checkmate," the Patrician said.

As the Internal Affairs agents explained to the booking sergeant what was happening, Gallo found himself standing next to Davis. He whispered to her. "Do you have any plans for Saturday night? I thought you might want to go to a party with me."

Davis shook her head in wonder. "Well, you do have the brass ones, don't you?" She turned to face him. "To tell you the truth, I had hoped that we had made a mistake and you were going to walk away from this." She paused, a momentary longing in her eyes.

Leary spoke up very loudly. "Exactly what are we being arrested for?"

Hal, the Internal Affairs agent apparently in charge, said, "Stealing money and drugs from a crime scene."

Leary looked over at Gallo. "Did we steal drugs or money?"

Gallo shook his head. "But we did take a suitcase that didn't belong to us."

The other Internal Affairs agent picked up the suitcase and dropped it on the desk. Hal flipped open the top. The case was filled with paperback books. No drugs. No money.

"What the hell," Hal yelled. He glared at the other agent.

Leary's voice rose above theirs. "So let me get this straight. We are being arrested for stealing a suitcase filled with paperbacks? Is that the charge?"

"You son of a bitch," Hal yelled at Leary. "Where is the money? Where are the drugs?"

"Don't know what you're talking about, "Leary replied. "They're not in the suitcase. So I guess they must still be in that apartment."

The Menace stared down at the board then swept the chess pieces off the table with his arm. "God damn it! Those souls were mine!"

"Lucifer, how many times do I have to tell you not to use my name in vain," the Patrician replied with a wide smile.

Davis started to chuckle. She turned to Gallo. "So you talked him out of it?"

"A fortune teller told me today that green was going to decide my fate." He pointed to her eyes. "All along I was focusing on your green eyes. But when you left the room, I took your parting comment to heart."

"'The only thing that was green was the money'. That comment?" she asked.

"Yep. I told Leary that the money was cursed, and we needed to leave it alone." Gallo paused for a moment. "And it didn't hurt that I offered to loan him the money he needed."

"That was a nice fake with the suitcase." She said, leaning back against the counter. "How did you know it was a sting operation?"

"I wasn't sure, but I wanted to separate ourselves from the drugs and the money so there was no chance we might be connected."

"What made you suspicious?"

"You never fit as a thief."

"No, there must have been more," Davis said.

"It was your face. When it looked like we might take the money, there was a disappointment which didn't fit." Gallo pointed to Leary. "You saw him at a bad time. Neither of us has ever stolen anything on the job. That's not who we are, or ever will be."

Davis stared up at him for a long time. When she spoke there was a smile in her voice. "The fortune teller was right. You should be careful around green." A pause. "I don't have plans for Saturday evening… and my eyes really are green."

The Menace ran his hands through his hair, and then smoothed down his goatee. He gestured to the chess pieces scattered all about. "Sorry about that." He half smiled. "Patience is not one of my virtues."

The Patrician slowly shook his head. "Lucifer, you don't have virtues."

"Whatever." He flashed an evil grin. "So what do we play for next time? How about a natural disaster, like an earthquake, or a tsunami?" Suddenly, he held up his hands. "No wait. Let's play for my favorite," he said raising his eyebrows, "global warming."

* * * * *

Chess is considered the game of the Gods, at least by many chess fanatics. So I thought how much fun would it be to have the "Gods" actually play it, and of course they would play for souls. As for using Waikiki as the site for the game, there actually are several tables along the beach, set under thatched roofs, with chess boards painted on the table tops. People sit and play there all day.

And where else could you place a police-based story but in the Big Apple where so many of the police procedural movies and TV shows are shot.

<u>*The Midas Touch*</u>

In Greek mythology, King Midas is remembered for his ability to turn everything he touched into gold. This came to be called the Midas touch.

Zack sat back in the waiting room chair and starred at the astrological chart on the wall. He couldn't believe it had only been four days since the witch had put a curse on him.

Four days previously, the morning had started out so innocently. Zack's mother, Gloria, was in the hospital recovering from a hysterectomy and he'd gone to visit her.

"How are you, Mom?" he'd asked, giving her a kiss on the cheek.

"I'm okay," his mother said, "but I would be much better if you were coming to visit me with a wife."

"Mom, we've been down this road before."

"Your younger brother already has two beautiful children." She threw her hands up. "Am I asking too much of the same from you?"

"Can I get married first?" he said with a half-smile.

"Always the jokester," she said shaking her head. "What's the problem that you can't find a wife? You're handsome, smart, and have a good job. What more can a woman want?"

"That's not the problem, Mom."

She starred at him for a long moment, and then slowly nodded.

"Zack, it's okay. Mrs. Ramone's son is gay and we've talked a lot about how I would handle it if you came out of the bathroom."

"Mom, the phrase is out of the closet," he said. "And you know I'm not gay."

"It's Owen, isn't it?" she said, continuing on. "He's your... significant other."

"Owen's not gay either. Remember he's engaged to Jenny."

"Oh, right." She paused for a long moment, and then said, "But if you're not gay, and I would be fine with it if you are, what is the problem with finding a wife?"

"I just haven't found the right woman. Is that so hard to understand?"

His mother turned away and stared at the wall. Zack knew from long experience that this was her silent way of telling him she strongly disagreed. Only this time, she broke off the wall-stare fairly quickly, and turned to him with a knowing smile.

"It's time for your mother to get involved, and I know just the girl."

"As if you haven't already been involved?"

"No, this time I have just the right girl for you. I've know her mother for years."

"Mom, I've got to get going. I promised Owen I'd meet him, and I'm already late."

"She's my nurse and she is wonderful."

Zack patted her hand. "That's great, mom. I'm sure she's a nice girl just like all the other one's you've introduced me to that never lasted past the first date, if that long." He kissed her on the cheek, and promised to visit her the next day.

He caught up with Owen, his best friend, at the sports bar where they went every Saturday during football season to watch the college teams play on the multiple large screen TVs. After several pitchers of beer, the conversation had shifted from the games to Zack's visit with his mother.

"She's at it again, only this time worse," Zack said, dejectedly. "She's just had major surgery, yet that's all she can talk about."

Owen lifted his beer in a toast. "To getting a wife and family." He laughed as he saw Zack cringe.

"Some friend you are," Zack said. "I can't get anyone to understand that I'm not meant for marriage."

"Spoken like a guy who hasn't met the right girl yet."

"Owen, you know I've looked. She's just not out there."

"Maybe you're looking in the wrong places." He gestured to their surroundings. "I hate to break it to you, but sports bars aren't the best place to find a potential wife."

Zack turned to Owen. "How is it that you only dated a few women and yet you found someone?"

"No, she found me, otherwise I'd still be drowning in the dating pool."

They sat and watched the games for a while, sipping their beers.

"My God," said Owen gesturing at one of the TVs. "That cheerleader is gorgeous. Oh, to be back in college."

"Your engaged, buddy."

"I can still look," Owen replied, and then added, "Jenny said so."

The waitress approached the table. "You guys want another beer, Zack?"

"No, I think we're good. Thanks, Michelle."

As the waitress left, Owen leaned over and said, "I have been coming here for three years and no one here ever calls me by my name." He pointed at Zack. "See, you have the magic when it comes to women."

"Her brother works with me." He shook his head slowly. "No, I'm just destined to be single. I realized that a long time ago and I'm okay with it."

"Don't give me that 'woe is me' crap," Owen said. "Boo hoo. No one loves me so I'm never getting married."

"Thanks for all your support, asshole," Zack shot back, annoyed.

"Then get real. You're a great guy," Owen replied, "and the right girl is just waiting for you." Owen focused on his beer mug, and after a few moments added, "This is going to sound a bit crazy, but when my mom has a difficult question in her life, she gets a… reading."

"A what?"

Putting his hands up in a defensive gesture, he said, "A fortune teller. She swears by them."

Zack shook his head slowly. "I've known you since grade school, yet only now do I realize your family is nuts."

"Come on, Zack. What can it hurt? If she gives you good news, it will put your mind to rest."

"And if it's bad?"

Owen shrugged. "Then you find out how to fix it. Come on, the one my mom uses is on our way home."

"Did you just suddenly come up with this idea, or did you have a little guidance?"

"Okay, okay. My mom was visiting with your mom yesterday…" he paused waiting for a caustic remark from Zack, which didn't come, so he continued, "and they both decided that this particular fortune teller might help solve your problem." Owen shrugged his shoulders. "What the hell? The worst thing that could happen is that nothing happens." He added, "And by the way, your mom goes to fortune tellers, too."

Zack stared at one of large screen TVs for several moments before speaking. "When your mother and my mother agree on something, that scares the hell out of me."

They paid up and left the bar. Three blocks later, they were walking on a street lined with brownstones. In the basement level of one of them, a sign was posted: "Madame Ruddka, The Gypsy Reader:

Fortune's Told, Palms Read."

"This is the one," Owen said, looking at Zack. "So are we good to go?"

"Yeah, what the hell?"

As they passed through the door into a small room, a bell announced their arrival. It was several minutes before the curtain parted in a doorway across the room, and a young lady entered.

"Welcome to Madame Ruddka's," she said with a strong foreign accent. "You have come for the fortune telling, yes?"

The young woman had long, black hair some of which was arranged in braids on the top of her head. She wore a brightly multicolored, pleated dress with a white peasant blouse and gold vest.

Zack took in the extensive dark eye makeup behind the purple-tinted granny glasses, the deep brown eyes surrounded by white facial powder, the dangling silver earrings, and finally the amulets on her arms. Not what I would like to wake up to in the morning, he thought.

"Please, follow me into the spirit chamber," she said.

They entered a larger room with a circular table in the middle and chairs around it. The walls were draped with a black material covered in stars and astrological signs.

"Please to be seated," the woman commanded.

As they pulled their chairs up to the table, Owen tilted his head toward Zack, "He's your subject."

The woman arranged herself and eyed Zack. "I am Aishe, and will be your guide, yes?"

After Zack nodded, she lifted a deck of tarot cards. "What is it that you seek?"

Seeing that Zack was tongue tied, Owen jumped in. "Uh, he's having problems finding his one true love. He is wondering…"

Zack cut him off. "Your sign says you can tell fortunes." He hesitated. "Understand I don't believe any of this but my friend insisted we come." He found himself distracted by the wart on her chin and another on her nose.

Before he could continue, Owen spoke up. "Our mothers are big believers in fortune tellers. They both know Madame Ruddka." He gestured toward Zack. "My friend basically wants to know if and when he will be getting married."

"So you have questions of love?" she said to Zack.

"You might say that," he replied.

Aishe shuffled the cards and then placed them on the table. "Please to put your $30 dollars on the top of the cards, and then make the sign of the cross."

Zack did so. After tucking the money into her dress, she dealt out three tarot cards. Turning the first over, she smiled knowingly. "This first card always tells what we will talk about. This is the lover's card." She turned a second card over and then looked up at Zack.

"This card tells me that you really don't want to find love so you are have been searching in the wrong places."

Zack shrugged his shoulders. "Could be."

She turned the third card over. "This card says the women you have chosen were not destined for long term relationships." She waited a moment and then pulled another card from the deck. After studying it, she glanced up. "Commitment is hard for you so you have avoided relationships."

Zack turned to Owen and rolled his eyes. When he turned back, Aishe was staring at him.

"Please continue," Owen said, trying to get things rolling again.

After a long moment, Aishe looked down and flipped another card. "This is not good," she said.

"What's wrong?" Owen said.

"Zee cards speak of a problem."

Owen looked at Zack and raised his eyebrows. "See, already we're getting good stuff."

"Can you be a little more specific about this 'problem'?" Zack said.

She put down several more cards, flipping them over as she did. "A powerful woman and her daughter have put an evil spell on you such that you will never find real love."

Zack sat back and put up his hands. "Nonsense!"

Aishe glanced up. "Do not blame me. I am only to tell you what the cards say."

Owen saw Zack start to rise, and pulled him down. "So how do we get rid of this spell?"

"Face it, Owen," Zack said firmly, "this whole thing is a mumbo-jumbo farce."

Owen silenced him with a wave of his hand. "Can you help my friend?"

It was several moments before Aishe spoke. "I am not just zee fortune teller, I am also, how you say, a white witch. Yes, the spell I can remove. Also I am giving your friend a potion that will help him identify his true love."

"And how much more will this cost us?" Owen said, reaching for his wallet.

She gathered the cards and stood up. "It will be costing you nothing since I am finished with my reading. Please to go and do not come back."

Immediately, Owen rose and said, "I'm sorry, we didn't mean to insult you. I will pay whatever is needed."

Aisha contemplated Owen and then fixed her eyes on Zack. "Do you desire my help or not?"

Owen kicked Zack under the table, and spoke before Zack could reply. "Of course he wants your assistance. So what do we have to do?"

Turning toward the door at the back of the room, she said over her shoulder, "Remain here. I will be back with zee potion."

Closing the door tight behind her, Aisha moved to the shelves lining one wall. She pulled a heavy, cracked leather bound volume from the shelf. Blowing the dust off, she laid the book on a desk and opened it to the middle. After sifting through a number of pages, she finally saw what she sought. The book was written in Romanian, the language of the Gypsies, and the title of the section she wanted was Love Potions.

"Why can't they publish these things in English?" she mumbled with no sign of an accent.

She was still mad at her mother for making her stay and work the family business on the weekends. As if it wasn't enough that she worked at her real job 5 days a week, but then she had to come here on the weekends. Her mother was Madame Ruddka, who had been doing this sort of thing since she was a young girl, having been taught by her mother.

Madame Ruddka had tried for years to get Aishe more involved with the business, teaching her much of what she knew. Unfortunately, Aishe had other interests that drew her away from the study of fortune telling and witch craft — like socializing, dating, and basically enjoying life. As a result, she had not mastered all the intricacies of making potions or casting spells. Besides, she didn't believe in them anyway. Sure, she had seen people get better with these treatments, but she felt this was probably just a placebo effect. She had read somewhere that one-third of people will have an improvement in their symptoms with a placebo if you present it in a convincing manner. She rationalized that at least one out of three customers would be benefitted, and the others suffered no harm, except to their wallet.

Her mom, though, was an avid believer in the magic of the spells, potions, and elixirs. If Aishe ever mentioned her true feelings, her mother would be shocked and deeply wounded, so she'd kept these thoughts to herself.

Moving her finger down the list of ingredients she would need, she saw a problem. The book required morning dew collected from the pedals of fresh flowers, but she hadn't thought to collect it this morning. What the heck, she decided. Water is water.

After running some tap water into a vial, she then began to add the other ingredients. Several of the notations in Romani were a bit blurred on the ancient page, and difficult to read. In those cases, she guessed at the ingredient or the amount. The last ingredient she had never heard of, but searching through the bottles and jars on the various shelves, she finally found something with a similar name. Adding a pinch of that, she poured the whole mixture into a mortar and ground it into a paste-like substance with a pestle. With a little more "morning dew" out of the tap, she was done.

During that time, Zack was getting more and more impatient, and it was all Owen could do to keep him from walking out. Fortunately, the fortune teller chose that moment to re-enter the room.

"I have for you the potion," she said very regally, holding up a glass vial filled with a greenish liquid.

"Please tell me I just rub that on my skin," Zack said with a horrified expression.

"You are to drink this," Aishe replied.

Zack felt nauseated just looking at it. "And what is this supposed to do?"

"This is an ancient Gypsy mixture, dating back hundreds of years. It is to help one find their eternal love. Once you drink this, just touching the love of your life will make her want to kiss you. Nothing will hold her back. Yet, if you touch any other women, they will have no response."

"That is cool," said Owen. "You mean he can touch or even just brush against a girl, and nothing will happen unless she is the one."

Zack was back to shaking his head. "You're saying that if she is my true love, she will immediately want to kiss me even if we have never met before? And that's how I will know her?"

"Yes. Simple, no?" Aishe said, laying the accent on. "The one who kisses you, is the one you are searching for."

"What about that evil spell on him?" Owen asked.

Aishe dipped her hand into a small bowel of water on a side table, and with her damp fingertips drew a cross on Zack's forehead. She said several unintelligible words, and then stepped back. "The spell is broken. Now drink this and go in search of your destiny."

Zack swallowed the mixture, trying not to taste it and managing to keep his face from making the expression he felt like showing. He handed the vial back to the fortune teller. She resisted the urge to toss the vial in a the trash and instead carefully placed it next to the bowl.

Aishe accompanied the men to the exit door, and ushered them out. Zack started to hesitate, but Aishe gave both him and Owen a nudge to get rid of them. She had places to be and couldn't be late. She locked the door and put out the closed sign.

They walked almost a block in silence before Owen said, "What did that stuff taste like?"

"If you can imagine what shit tastes like, it was worse."

After a few more steps, Owen said. "Well, are we going to try it out?"

Zack halted. "What are you talking about?"

"Let's go see if it works. You know. Go to a bar and see if any women respond to your touch."

"What? You think that my true love is sitting in some bar around here, waiting for me?"

Owen put his arm around Zack's shoulders. "We have to start somewhere. Might as well be here. Besides, that evil spell is gone, so your chances of success have gone way up."

"No, you're not a nut case, you're absolutely out of your mind, and so am I for going along with you."

"All right. Maybe it was a bit crazy, but that chick was hot in a creepy way."

Zack snickered. "I never got past the warts."

"Come on, let's get a drink and forget the whole thing."

They entered the Pig and Whistle, a local Irish establishment, and went straight to the bar.

"Two Guinnesses, please," Owen said.

As Zack settled himself into a bar stool, he noticed that the girl to his right was a stunner. She saw him looking and smiled back at him. It seemed that she was alone, so Zack said, "Hi. I'm Zack."

"And I'm Lonnie," she said holding out her hand.

Zack was shaking hands with her when her eyes seemed to glass over. "You're the one," she whispered.

"I'm not sure what you mean," he replied with surprise.

She slid off her stool, wrapped her arms around his neck, and gave him a long, passionate kiss. Shocked, Zack pulled back and stared at her. As quickly as it came, the glassy eyed look was gone, and was replaced by confusion and then anger.

"Get the hell away from my girlfriend," a loud voice yelled.

Zack glanced at the figure moving down the aisle toward him, and realized that the movies never tell the truth. King Kong wasn't dead. The giant gave him a shove that sent him reeling into the table behind him.

He and the table went over backwards, knocking the two girls seated there onto the floor. Zack stood up, and turned to the girl closest to him. He was pulling her up when he saw that same glassy look appear on her face, followed by a near shout of, "You're the one." Immediately, she grabbed him and locked her lips on to his. He staggered back disentangling himself, only to bump into the waitress that had come over to help clean up. He turned to apologize, and saw the waitress develop that glassy look, and then she said huskily, "You're the one." Her hands were on his neck before he could move, and then came a wet French kiss. Gently shoving her away, he saw the glassy appearance resolve, only to be replaced by absolute anger. She slapped him, and yelled, "You pervert."

To say the least, Zack was stunned.

Owen grabbed him under the arm, and said, "We're out of here, now!"

They were nearly to the front door when Zack ran into a very elderly lady who was just rising from her table. In his rush, he nearly knocked her down, but managed to grab her before she fell.

She glanced up at him, and started to speak, but then that glassy look appeared. "You're the one," she said, and with no hesitation grabbed his head with both hands and kissed him full on the lips.

He managed to pry her away, and saw the glassy look fade, to be replaced by surprise and then a smile. "Thank you," she said.

Owen yanked him out through the front door and it was a block later before they finally stopped.

"What the hell just happened?" Zack said, wiping off his mouth and rubbing his face.

"I would say there is something wrong with that potion," Owen said.

They stared at each other for several moments, and then almost together said, "We need to see the witch."

They arrived at Madame Ruddka's almost at a run, only to find it was closed. Zack pounded on the door for several minutes, but nothing.

"I'm sure they'll be open tomorrow," Owen offered. "Sunday is a big day in the fortune telling business."

"And you know that how?" Zack said. He leaned back up against the door. "I'm screwed."

"What's the problem? You just avoid touching any women until tomorrow and get this spell reversed."

"It's my mom's birthday tonight, and I am supposed to bring the cake, candles, and paper plates for all her friends that are coming."

After a long pause, Owen's face lit up and he said, "Don't worry. I have the solution."

Sitting in an Uber car later that night, Zack held up a surgical mask.

"Now how is this supposed to help me?"

"Simple," Owen replied. "We tell everyone you are coming down with the flu and they should keep their distance."

"Why do I think this idea is as bad as your idea to see the fortune teller?"

"Trust me, bro."

Once they arrived at the hospital, they took the stairs up to Zack's mother's room to avoid any possible interactions on the elevator.

Entering the hospital room, they found a number of people had already arrived.

"Why are you wearing a mask?" his mother said from the bed when she saw him.

"I'm coming down with something and I don't want to infect others," Zack said. With that, the people around him, took several steps back.

Owen immediately took over as a blocker for Zack, politely moving everyone out of their way, until he got Zack into a corner by his mother's bed where he'd wouldn't be accidently jostled by someone.

Owen then held up a cake box and said, "I've got the real reason why everyone is here." He set it on a side table, and then noticed his mother and sister approaching Zack.

"I never get sick," Owen's mother said, "so Zack give me a hug since I haven't seen you in forever."

"And don't forget me," added Owen's sister.

Zack turned to Owen and saw Owen's eyes wider than he'd ever seen them.

Owen leaped through the crowd, and jumped between his mother and Zack. Putting up his hands to stop his mother, he said quickly, "There is always a chance of getting sick, Mom. And at your age, it could be very dangerous."

Zack saw his chance to pay Owen back for the mess he was in. "Oh, I don't think I'm that contagious, Owen. A little hug with your mother and sister isn't that big a deal."

Owen turned and glared at him, but soon the glare was replaced with a sly smile. "In that case, why don't you give your mother a nice embrace first?"

The two of them held their stare for almost a minute before breaking it off. Owen shuffled his mother and sister away, and then opened the cake box. He'd already put ten candles on top, so he went ahead and lit them.

Turning to Zack's mother with the cake, he said with a smile, "I was afraid that if I put the real number of candles on, it might set off the fire alarm."

Zack's mother shook her head and then smiled as she bent forward and blew out all the candles.

"What did you wish for?" an older woman asked.

Just then, the nurse came in. "What a crowd," she said with a grin as she wrangled her way through the mass of people and up to the bedside. "I just wanted to stop in and wish you happy birthday, Gloria," she said.

"My wish is answered, Robin," Gloria said, turning and holding out her arm toward Zack. "I want to introduce you to my son, Zack."

Robin smiled at him, and said, "Your mother has told me so much about you, I feel like I already know you." Raising her eyebrows slightly, she gestured at the mask.

Zack felt like a fool as he stared at her. He felt an immediate attraction, but not because of her looks. Oh, she was nice looking enough with blondish brown hair, a pretty face, and deep blue eyes. A definite 8 in his book. But that wasn't it, he realized. Instead, it was something about her movement and her manner – the way she dealt with his mother, spoke so easily with him, and had seamlessly inserted herself into the party crowd – that made him to want to know her more than just casually. He belatedly realized if she was grading him, he must look like a 1 in her book.

"I think I might be coming down with something and I didn't want to infect anyone," he said.

Robin tilted her head and said, "That's really considerate of you. I wish more people followed your example."

"Robin is single and doesn't have a boyfriend," Zack's mother chimed in. "What a coincidence, Robin. My son's single and doesn't have a girlfriend."

Zack felt his face go red and wanted to disappear, but Robin just laughed it off, patting his mother's hand, and saying, "Gloria, you are definitely the match maker." She turned to Zack. "I'm going on a dinner break in thirty minutes if you'd like to get coffee downstairs?"

In the few seconds it took Zack to get over his surprise, Owen stepped in and said, "That's so nice of you Robin, but Zack really needs to get home and rest."

Before Zack could object, Owen gave him a subtle kick and gestured toward his mask. Zack realized he could completely blow their date if they accidently touched. Better to wait until this was corrected, he decided. "I'd love to get together sometime, but Owen's right."

The next morning Zack headed out early for the fortune teller's shop. When he entered, there was a sign in the waiting area warning that a seance was in progress and it shouldn't be disturbed.

"The hell with that," Zack said, pulling the curtain aside and stepping into the darkened room.

Aishe sat at the small round table with an elderly woman. She looked up at Zack, anger on her face. "Did you not see zee sign?"

"We have a problem," Zack said loudly.

Aishe glared at him. "What problem?"

Zack touched the elderly woman on the shoulder. She turned to look at Zack, and then her eyes went glassy. "You're the one," she said, standing up and giving Zack an intense kiss. When she finished, she stepped back and gave Zack a strong slap. "How dare you," she said and stormed out of the room.

"That problem," Zack said, rubbing the side of his face. He went on to explain his experiences over the last 24 hours.

As he talked, Aishe's eyes got bigger and bigger listening to his adventures. When he finished, she was speechless.

"Well, can you fix it?" Zack said impatiently.

"Ah…" she said, "why don't you come back tomorrow and I will have a potion ready that will correct your problem. Yes?"

"Tomorrow? I need something now!"

"Well, I…" she stuttered. "I need to collect morning dew tomorrow before I can make the new potion."

That night, Aishe poured over the old potion book, trying to find a way to reverse what she'd done. This time she vowed to use the exact ingredients and amounts of whatever potion she made. And this time, she was going to collect the morning dew off the flowers. But when she went outside the next morning, the flowers were dry. She'd slept in too late.

Well, everything else is as close to the book as I can make it, she thought, staring at the concoction. She heard her entrance door open, and then Zack's voice. "Hello. Anyone here?"

Aishe pulled the curtain aside and gestured for Zack to come in. Holding up a small vial with a mustard yellow liquid, she said, "This will make you to normal again."

Zack tossed it down without hesitation. There was a bitter after-taste, but if it was going to work, he didn't care.

"What do I owe you?" he said.

Aishe shook her head. "Only to get better. That would be enough."

Zack left the shop with a new spring in his step. He came to a signal and stopped next to a group of people.

Is this new potion going to work or not, he wondered? Might as well fine out. He reached over and gently brushed against a girl waiting at the signal. She turned around and stared at him. Suddenly her eyes changed, and she said, "You're the one."

Zack pulled back, putting his hands up.

She moved toward him. "You're the one with the computer for sale. Owen showed me your picture. I desperately need a new computer."

After making plans on when they could get together, Zack continued on down the street, purposely brushing against several women but nothing happened. The spell was broken. Life was back to normal.

He was still congratulating himself when he bumped into a homeless man that had suddenly come out of a side alley. "Hey, sorry about that," Zack said.

The man started to reply, but then his eyes went glassy, and he said, "You're the one." With that, he grabbed Zack and gave him a full mouth kiss. Zack shoved him off, and realized that now he had an even worse problem. He started running back toward the fortune teller, afraid she might close for the day before he got there. In his haste, he cut across the middle of the street and, of course, there was a policeman standing right there.

"Hold up, sir," he said as Zack started to move past him.

"Officer, I'm in a bit of a hurry," Zack said.

"Do you realize you were jaywalking?" he said. "We've had too many pedestrian injured around here doing that, so we're ticketing everyone who jaywalks."

Zack knew it was hopeless to plead his case, so he just waited for the policeman to finish writing the ticket. As he handed it to Zack, their hands briefly touched.

"Oh, shit," Zack said, as he watched the policeman get that glassy eyed stare. He was already running when he heard the policeman behind him say, "You're the one." It was a race, but Zack finally eluded him and got back to Aishe's.

Once again the seance warning sign was posted, and once again Zack ignored it. This time Aishe was at the table with an older man. She looked up as Zack entered, a questioning look appearing on her face. He immediately went to the man and tapped him on the shoulder. The gentleman turned, saw Zack, and the glassy stare appeared. He went into the usual ritual, completing it with a shove that staggered Zack back several steps, and then the man charged out the door.

Zack looked at Aishe. "We still have a problem."

Zack visited his mother that night, but his mind was on tomorrow morning when Aishe had promised to have a cure. He was half listening to his mother's complaints about the hospital food when her nurse, Robin, came in.

"Time for your evening vitals," she said, and then saw Zack.

"Hi, Zack," she said smiling. "I see you have your mask off. Everything okay?"

"I'm doing fine." He paused then plunged on. "What's the chances of a cup of coffee tonight with you?"

She finished taking Gloria's blood pressure and then looked over at him. "I have a 15 minute break coming up. Would that work?"

After she left, Gloria said, "You're the one."

Zack whipped his head around. "What did you say?"

"You're the one for her. She's not only a very nice girl, but she's also a nurse and can take care of you when you get sick."

"Just the thing I look for when I meet a woman."

"Well, I won't always be around to take care of you."

"Mom! You don't take care of me now."

Zack met Robin in the employees' cafeteria. Sipping on coffee, they both slowly explored each other's lives. Robin was 28, born and raised in New York City, and attended Columbia University before going to nursing school.

"What decided you on being a nurse?" Zack said.

"When I was young I had a bad respiratory infection and had to be hospitalized. I remember how frightened I was that first day. My nurse came and sat with me for almost 30 minutes, telling me jokes and reading stories. She was like my guardian angel the whole time I was there." She paused. "I decided I wanted to be that guardian angel for other people who are hospitalized."

"That's really cool," Zack said.

"And what do you do?"

"Nothing as noble as you. I'm a lawyer, handling trusts and retirement plans." He paused. "If this will give me any atta-boy points, I guess you could say I'm helping people through the scary world of the IRS."

Robin smiled. "Well, that's worth at least five atta-boy points."

"My mother sure thinks the world of you," Zack said.

"She is a really sweet lady, and always talks about you."

Zack laughed. "Yet despite what she says, you still agreed to have coffee with me?"

"Oh, I've got my mace under the table," she said with a grin.

"This may seem a bit forward, but I figure we are both about the same age," Zack said.

Robin raised an eyebrow.

"I just meant, are you getting a lot of hassle by your parents to get married and have kids?" he asked.

"Oh, only about once or twice a day," she said with a grin.

"Same for me. Every time I see my mom, the word marriage comes up."

"Well, at least she wants you to get married first. My mom just wants grandkids, with marriage a distant second," Robin said, drinking her coffee. She set it down and said, "So how is your search for a wife going?"

Zack shook his head. "I recently asked myself that same question with disastrous results." He thought for a moment. "When I was in college, it was all about a girl's looks. But now that I'm older, it's more about personality, intelligence..."

"And looks," Robin added, which set them both laughing.

"What about you?" Zack said.

"Well, I was engaged, but when we moved in together his real person emerged."

"Like what?"

"He wanted a mother in the form of a wife. Someone to pick up after him, feed him, do his dishes, wash his clothes, and yet he never offered to do anything." She took a sip of coffee. "So one day I had enough, I moved his stuff into the hallway of the apartment building and texted him to come pick it up."

Zack groaned. "Brutal! Remind me not to get on your bad side."

They talked for another five minutes and then Robin said she had to get back to work.

"This has been really nice," Zack said.

"You sound surprised," Robin replied.

"Well, my mom doesn't have the best batting average when it comes to choosing girls."

"Not good looking enough?" Robin said with a smile.

"I never even had the desire to make a second date with any of them."

"So if you hold true to form, I guess this is our first and last date," she said mischievously.

Zack laughed. "And what about you? What is your dating history like?"

"A mirror of yours. Oh, there were occasional second dates, but I haven't found anyone I've been interested in for a long time."

"Then we should just agree not to have a second date," Zack said, seriously. He waited for a moment watching Robin's face, and then added, "Instead, we'll have a happening. I will just happen to be in the same place you are at the same time."

Robin smiled. "Now that just might break the first date curse."

They settled on next Saturday night at Al and Nick's Restaurant, a trendy eatery on the upper west side of Manhattan.

Aishe was up early, and committed to collecting morning dew. This time she found several flowers that were damp and drained off some slightly amber colored fluid. She was heading back inside when she noticed a large black dog lifting his leg on the flowers several doors down. Holding up the collection container, she hoped the fluid inside was only morning dew.

Several hours later, Zack arrived. They exchanged pleasantries and then Aishe offered him her new creation.

"We haven't been very lucky with these mixtures of yours," Zack said, holding up the vial, filled now with an amber fluid.

"Zees time it will work. How do you say? Trust me."

"Well, anything is better than what's happening now," he replied, downing the fluid. He glanced around. "Where is Madame Ruddka? I thought this was her shop?"

"She is on the vacation, and will be back in several days."

Zack left the shop and set off for work. He was hesitant to test the results of the mixture, but knew he had to. When he got to the signal just across the street from his work, there was a group of business men waiting to cross. Gritting his teeth for what might be coming, he chose the smallest man and 'accidently' bumped into him. The man turned quickly and looked at Zack, but there was no glassy stare.

"Sorry about that," Zack said with a strong sense of relief. The craziness was over. Life could resume its normal course.

As he stepped away from the group of men, he bumped into a dog walker that had at least ten dogs. Before he knew it, he was wound up in all the leashes. Gradually, he extricated himself, pushing many of the barking dogs out of the way. Suddenly, they all went quiet and Zack found them staring up at him with that familiar glassy-eyed look.

Oh, hell, he thought. Not again. The dog walker tried to get the dogs moving but they only had eyes for Zack. As he rushed across the street, several of the dogs broke free from the handler and began to chase him. Zack made it into his building, closing the glass doors behind him. The dogs began to howl and scratch at the glass, trying to get in.

At lunch, he snuck out the back and grabbed a cab to Aishe's. By the time he got out of the cab, and reached her door, he had picked up four dogs all howling and leaping on him. Slamming the door behind him, Zack confronted Aishe.

"Now its dogs," he said. "And I don't even have to touch them. If they smell me, they're after me."

Aishe glanced at the whining, barking dogs outside her door.

Zack looked back at the dogs and then at her. She had the beginnings of a smile. "It's not funny," he said. They stared at each other as the dogs began to bark and bray even louder. Try as he might, Zack couldn't help himself, and started to smile. Abruptly, they both began to laugh.

"Well, if nothing else, you've brought some variety into my life," he said. "But this time I am going to wait here until you give me something to correct this."

It was almost an hour later, when Aishe reappeared from the back of the shop.

"Here is zee new mixture we can try," Aishe said. "If it fails, Madame Ruddka will be back tomorrow."

This mix was a dark brown liquid with a taste so foul that Zack almost vomited it back up.

The next morning Aishe found Zack sitting on her door step, covered by birds. He stood, waving the birds away only to have them immediately return.

"Now I know what statues feel like," he said when she opened the door a crack. "It's not that I don't appreciate you, Aishe" he said, "but please tell me that Madame Ruddka is back today."

Aishe opened the door wider and together they managed to get Zack inside sans birds. She brushed off his coat and said, "Madame Ruddka will be here any minute. I've already told her the troubles we have had."

"What happened to your accent?" Zack said.

"It's a long story. I'll tell you later."

A deep voice behind them, said, "Hello, Aishe. Who is this with you?"

Zack spun around and saw an older version of Aishe standing near the curtained entrance to the room.

Aishe smiled. "Zack, this is my mother, Madame Ruddka."

The older woman stepped forward offering her hand. "I have known your mother for years, and now I have the pleasure of meeting the son she always talks about." After they shook hands, she said, "I understand this all started as an attempt to find your true love, is that right?"

"Yeah, something like that," Zack said, feeling embarrassed.

Madame Ruddka nodded. "I gather the idea was if you touched your true love, she would want to kiss you while anyone else would be unaffected."

"Yes, but instead every woman I touched wanted to kiss me."

"I went over with Aishe what she put in her potion and I think I know what happened. Her mixture resulted in the exact opposite effect. The only one who wouldn't want to kiss you when you touched them or they touched you would be your true love." She paused. "Do you remember anyone like that?"

Zack thought back on the last six days. "No, there was no one. Everyone I came in contact with wanted to kiss me." And then it hit him. He turned to Aishe. "Immediately after I drank that first mixture, you pushed Owen and me out of the shop. You touched me and it had no effect on you." And then he realized what he was saying.

Madame Ruddka laughed. "Unbelievable. Who would have guessed?" She rubbed her hands together. "I can't wait to tell your mother, Zack."

He looked over at Aishe, at the dyed black hair and facial warts, and shook his head. "Yeah, who would have guessed? I… I think I need some time to digest all of this." He started toward the door and then turned. "What about my bird problem?"

Madame Ruddka smiled. "The effects of these potions are gone within twenty-four hours. You can just wait it out."

"So that's the story, Mom," Zack said several hours later sitting at his mother's bedside. "If your gypsy fortune teller is to be believed, Madame Ruddka's daughter is the one," he said, still stunned.

"I've known Madame Ruddka for years. I knew you'd like her daughter once you got to know her," his mother said.

"Mom, I'm just not feeling it."

"I think maybe if you spent more time with her. In fact, when you told me you were coming, I invited her to join us."

At that moment, there was a knocking on the door jamb, and into the room stepped Aishe. She walked over to the foot of the bed and stopped. "Zack, I want you to know that I'm not a believer in any of this hocus-pocus, but I can't explain what happened any other way."

"So you think we are star crossed lovers or something like that?" he said.

"I don't know what we are, so let's just see how things play out. But first, I need to get one thing clear."

"Yeah?"

"I hope Aishe isn't the girl of your dreams or you're going to be very disappointed." With that, she went into the bathroom and closed the door.

Zack turned to his mother, but she remained silent. Several minutes later, the bathroom door opened and out stepped Robin, his mother's nurse, holding a black wig and her costume jewelry. The make-up, including warts, was gone.

"What the hell?" Zack said. "Why didn't you tell me who you were when we first met?"

"I was too embarrassed. Here I was, a nurse in mainstream medicine, involved in fortune telling, casting spells, mixing potions. The whole reason I wear the Aishe outfit is so no one will recognize me." She dropped the wig and her jewelry on a chair. "And then, when all the potions went wrong, I definitely wasn't going to unveil myself and look like an idiot."

"Yeah, I can understand that."

"Besides, if it wasn't for my mother I'd never be involved with anything like this. I'm not a believer in potions and fortune telling."

"Well, I think we need to talk about that," Zack said, a smile lighting his face as he moved toward her, "because I'm now a real believer in potions and fortune telling."

* * * * *

My mother and three sisters use to visit a fortune teller periodically. I'm not sure how ardent my sisters were about believing it, but my mother apparently put some stock in what the woman told her. So whenever I pass a sign announcing a fortune teller, I feel this curious desire to go in and hear what they have to say. I blame it on genetics – thanks, Mom – but so far I've been able to avoid their influence. This story gave me the chance to visit them without really visiting them. In order to add some humor, I used an idea from Goethe's ***Sorcerer's Apprentice****, a poem written at the end of the eighteenth century, about an apprentice who creates havoc when he tries to perform magic before he's learned his craft.*

The Midas Touch *was the result of a question I asked myself. What if you could just touch a girl on the shoulder, and her response would* *tell you whether or not she was right for you? There might be a lot of shoulder touching, but it would sure be better than Match.com, Timber, and all the other crazy internet dating services.*

The Promise

Some days it pays to read your horoscope. Today's advice for Virgo's was, "Bad day for travel."

Nikki Law, a Virgo, sitting on a moss covered rock, pulled her coat tighter in an attempt to stop shivering, and assessed her situation. She was at the bottom of a ravine high in the mountains with either a badly sprained or fractured ankle that wouldn't support her weight. The weather was freezing, the snow falling in clumps, and as far as she knew, no one was aware of her location. This was not the get-a-way she had envisioned.

Another quick look at her cellphone merely confirmed that she had no reception. The temperature must have dropped fifteen degrees since she started up the mountain just three hours ago. Pocketing the phone, she glanced around for some place to shelter but there was nothing. Trying to ignore the cold, she let her mind drift back to the series of events that had stranded her.

The high desert roads had been nearly deserted earlier in the day when Nikki had pulled into Ted's Trading Post, with its ancient gas pumps. She would have driven to a newer facility but she desperately needed to use the bathroom. Noting the 'pay inside' sign on the pumps, she'd gone into the antiquated store. After a brief stop in the bathroom, she'd approached the counter.

"Hi," she said. "Here's a credit card for pump 2." As the counter man set her card aside, she asked. "I am running a bit late. Is there a short cut through these mountains instead of going around them on the interstate?"

The man scratched the top of his head, and then said, "Well, there is old highway 168, but it's rarely used in winter since storms can blow in so quickly that you could get stranded up there."

"Are you expecting any storms?"

"Can't say. I don't pay much attention to the news 'cause… it's always bad news," he said with a gap-toothed smile.

Nikki left the store and while waiting for her tank to fill, she called her mother.

"Hi, mom."

"Hello, honey. I'm so excited to see you. Are you bringing Michael?"

Nikki sighed. "Mike and I… we broke off our engagement." She tried to keep the emotion out of her voice. "So I needed to get away. That's why I'm coming home."

"Oh, I'm so sorry, honey. What happened?"

"We'll have time to talk later," she said, not wanting to relive the break-up at this moment.

"Where are you?"

"Right now I'm at someplace called Ted's Outpost getting gas." She glanced at her watch. "From what I can tell I should be home no later than 3 pm. See you then."

The gas pump had just shut off when she heard a voice behind her.

"I heard you asking about highway 168," a man said.

Nikki hung up the pump handle, closed the gas cap, and turned to the source of the voice. The man must have been in his late seventies or early eighties, but his bright smile and tanned face belied his age.

"Ted is store-bound so not someone to give you advice on the roads," he said.

"You think 168 would be reasonable to try?" Nikki asked.

"It's old, but it will save you at least 2 hours."

She noticed the worn but clean clothes overlying his thin frame, and just below his John Deer ball cap, a set of twinkling blue eyes.

"Hell, I remember when they celebrated the opening of that road. Had quite a party," he said with a grin. "Took the town several days to sober up." For a moment, he seemed lost in his memories, then he adjusted his cap brim, and went on. "But over the years, there hasn't been enough money to keep it up. Yet, it's still safe to drive."

"Well, thank you."

"Just take your time and you'll be fine." He began to smile, but then developed a slight frown. "Don't mean to me nosy, but I noticed you're ring finger's empty. I'm surprised some lucky fellow hasn't scooped you up already."

Nikki shrugged, wondering why small town people were always so forward, but there was something about this man that put her at ease. "Just waiting for the right fellow."

The man chuckled. "Doubt you'll wait long. Have a safe drive."

After settling up with the cashier, Nikki pulled out on the highway and headed north. She wanted to reach her mother's house in the late afternoon, but it might not be possible unless she took the short cut. Ah, what the hell, she thought. Let's take it. What could happen?

Highway 168 was definitely in need of repair, with numerous cracks and potholes scattered along the two lane asphalt road. The highway cut back and forth as it snaked up into the mountains. A sign mentioned she was entering a state forest area. As she rose higher and higher above the desert floor, trees began to appear. At first, there was just a scattering of sugar pine and Douglas fir, but gradually the forest became a dense mat of dark green covering the entire hill side.

It was deep in the mountain pass when it happened. Her car made a sputtering, jerking movement and then the engine died. She managed to coast the vehicle to the side of the road before it came to a complete halt. She tried the ignition but the engine failed to respond.

Struggling to keep down her fear of being stranded, she reached for her cellphone. I'll just call a tow truck, she thought. She pulled out her cellphone. No bars.

Okay, no need to panic, she told herself. I'll wait for someone to come by.

But over the next two hours, not another car appeared on either side of the road. The sky darkening with angry looking clouds finally convinced her it was time to take matters into her own hands.

Grabbing her phone, she looked around. "Maybe if I can get higher, I might get some bars," she said out-loud to convince herself.

With an experienced eye, she decided to try the hills nearest her since they were still in sunlight. After years of hiking in the Sierras, she felt no hesitation about a jaunt into the mountains. Opening her car trunk, she changed into hiking shoes, and slipped on a thick jacket since the day was turning cold.

Nikki made her way back and forth through the brush and trees, gradually moving up the hillside. After covering about a half a mile, she stepped out onto a rock outcropping. Lifting her phone, she noticed one bar intermittently. Encouraged, she continued on up. At some spots, it was difficult going, but nothing she couldn't handle. The trees were becoming a bit indistinct, and she realized it was getting darker. Looking up, she saw the threatening clouds now covered the entire sky.

About a mile into the woods, she checked her phone again. This time there was a steady one bar, but attempts to call where unsuccessful. She glanced around. The highway had not been visible for some time, but she wasn't worried. She felt comfortable finding her way back, and worst case she would head downhill and eventually hit the highway. She climbed over several hummocks, and then worked her way up a ridge. She topped out on a knoll, and once again checked her phone. As the light on her phone came on, she realized it was snowing. Not hard, just a gentle downfall. This time she had two bars. She moved slightly and they were gone. Damn, damn!

What to do, she wondered. Keep going up or head back? There was no rescue going back, but going a bit higher might make all the difference. Another half mile, and if I still can't get reception, I'll head back, she concluded.

She continued her climb, and the ridge became bare rock. The snow had made it slick, and just as she realized that, she slipped and her foot went in between two rocks. There was an incredibly painful wrench on her foot, and then she was rolling down the side of the ridge for about twenty feet into a narrow ravine. She tried to stand but the pain was tremendous, and impossible to put weight on it. If the ankle wasn't broken, it was badly sprained she realized.

And now here she was two hours later, freezing cold and alone in the wilderness hoping someone would come along. It was then that she noticed the grey shadows standing on the ridge above her. Someone had come. No, not someone...wolves.

The squawk of the radio broke the stillness of the late afternoon. "Sheriff, come in please."

John Taggart glanced over at the patrol car, and then back at the two bronze grave markers he was kneeling in front of. He came out once a week to clean the markers up, and say a few words. Yanking out another weed, he stared at the marker on the right which read, 'Miriam Taggart. Beloved wife and mother.' The other marker was engraved with, 'Jacob Taggart. Beloved husband and father'. John had arranged for the burials, but his mother had decided on the inscriptions. John might have added more to his father's, like 'his bourbon was bonded, and so was his word' but mom wouldn't allow it. Even she admitted, though, that dad loved his whiskey, and that he'd never made a promise he didn't keep. Except that one time. That promise had been a lovely gesture, but John never believed his father could come through with that particular one.

Mom had her faults too, and hadn't been the easiest woman to live with, but deep down his parents had loved each other, and they had loved him.

"Sheriff, are you there?"

John stood, brushed the dirt off his knees, and went to the patrol car. "Hello, Maddie. What's up?"

"There's a loose dog on the main highway. Two near accidents.

Several people have tried to capture the dog without success."

"I'm on my way," he said.

Driving through town, John passed his old high school. Memories were heavy with that place, not the least of which was Carol Sue Johnson, his high school sweet heart. He shook his head. When he'd come back to visit, he'd discovered that she was even prettier than he remembered, and his feelings for her even stronger than he'd realized. His second night back, they'd gone out and it was as if no time had passed. They laughed until they cried, danced cheek to cheek, and shared a long goodnight kiss. Several nights later, they met for a drink and Carol Sue broke the news. She was getting married to Brad Silver.

"You're kidding, right?"

"No. Brad asked me last night."

"What about us?"

"I haven't seen you for almost 6 years, and then you roll back in town and think we'll just start right back up again," she said with a slight edge in her voice.

"Then what was the other night all about?"

She stared down at her drink, her voice softening, "A glimpse of what we could have had." She looked over at him, tears at the edge of her eyes. "You just came back a few months too late."

One month later, she was married. And 6 months later, the baby arrived.

It had taken several years, but now he could finally see her around town and not get that ache in his chest or the anxiety that went with it. At one time, he'd hoped Brad and Carol Sue might break up but now he realized that wasn't going to happen and truth be told, he didn't want it to. He knew Brad from high school, and he was basically a good guy. And as far as he could determine, Carol Sue was happy. They presently had two kids.

Yes, it had been a mistake to come back because once there, his parents had snagged him with their pleas for help. And dad had made his unrealistic promise. Now both were gone, and here he was with no family and no social life, at least no romantic social life.

After driving through town, he pulled onto the interstate and hit his flashers. As he sped up, he saw thick, black clouds in the darkening sky. Weather report got it wrong again. Looks like it's gonna snow tonight instead of tomorrow, he thought. Bad night to be in the mountains.

It was the end of a long day when John Taggart pulled into the police station lot. They were short one officer so everyone was working longer shifts. Entering the police station, the dispatcher, Maddie, waved John over.

"Got a call from the Sheriff up in Weaverville. Seems a Mrs. Law reported her daughter missing. He wants us to look around down here since the last time her mother spoke with her, she was getting gas out at Ted's."

"How long has she been missing?"

"She was expected home at three, and now she's four hours late. Mom can't raise her on her cellphone which is very unusual." Maddie looked at her notes. "Mom's not the worrying type according to the sheriff, so when Mrs. Law is concerned, so is he."

"Get the info on her car, and tell the highway patrol to keep an eye out for it," John said. "I'll call Ted and see what he knows."

Maddie rolled her eyes. "Good luck with that." She held out a piece of paper. "I've got a faxed copy of her driver's license. Might get better results showing her picture to Ted."

He smiled. "Didn't you and Ted have a fling a while back?"

She let out a snort. "In a matter of speaking. He showed up on my doorstep one night, and I flung him off."

John entered Ted's and moved over to the counter. "Evening, Ted. I'm looking for a missing girl. Supposedly her last known stop was here to get gas."

Ted held up his arms and took a step back. "I'm a born again Christian, Sheriff. Unattached women and me don't mix," he said.

"Now Ted, you just got bullshit all over my boots," John said with a half-grin. "Here, take a look at this picture and see if she looks familiar."

After looking at the fax for several moments, Ted handed it back. "Yeah, she was in here around noon. She asked me if there was a short cut through the mountains so she could get home quicker."

John shook his head. "And you told her about highway 168, right?"

"Ah, hell Sheriff, I was just trying to help her."

"When's the last time you drove that road, Ted."

He thought for a moment. "Must have been 5 years ago. Pretty beat up so I quit using it."

"And neither does anyone else if they can avoid it."

As John was turning to leave, Ted said, "You know I saw her talking to some old guy out by the pumps just before she left."

"Anybody you know?"

"No, but he sure did look familiar."

Returning to his car, John called Maddie at the station. "Ted sent her up 168."

"Sounds like Ted. You do remember we closed that highway late this afternoon because of the approaching storm."

"I'm going to get my search and rescue gear, and then check 168 out. Call me if you hear anything."

In ten minutes, he was home. Blue, a mixed German Shepard, started howling as soon as he came through the door.

"I know, I know," he said, stroking the dog, "I'm late with your dinner." While Blue was eating, John put several plastic baskets containing his search and rescue gear into the trunk of his car. After a few more chores, he waved Blue into the car and they drove off.

The climb up 168 was fairly step, and the road was getting icy even with the small amount of snow that had fallen. His car had 4-wheel drive, and chains if needed, so John wasn't worried. He was half way through the pass, at its highest point, when he saw the blue Corolla. Pulling in behind it, he put on his flashers. A quick once around the car showed it was locked and empty. Using his flashlight, he slowly searched the area between the car and the hillside. Much of the ground was covered with a light dusting of snow, but under a tree that was in a direct line from the car to the hill, he saw tracks coming from the direction of the car and heading up the mountain. They appeared to belong to just one person.

Wearing gloves, he used a Slim-Jim to open the car door. Pushing a lever under the dashboard, the trunk popped open. It contained a partially open suitcase. John saw a pair of muddy pumps set alongside the suitcase.

She probably changed into something more appropriate to climb with, he thought. But why leave the warmth and comfort of the car to wander into the fierceness of the forest and hillside? Did she stop here on purpose or did the car give out? Either way, why wander up into the hills?

John climbed back into the police vehicle and called the station. "Hello, Maddie. I found her car. She's nowhere around, but there are tracks heading into the mountains. We're going to need a search and rescue dog team ASAP."

"Why not just a plain search and rescue group?"

"Because it is getting very cold and the snow is starting to dump. We may have only one chance to save her in this weather, so I want to make it our best." He stared at the small car in front of him. "There is a SARD team over in Hadley. Have the Operations Leader call me right away. Better patch him through to me using your line. Cellphones won't work up here." And then he understood why she'd gone into the hills.

Ten minutes later, Maddie was back on the line. "I'm going to patch a Mr. Lawrence Medford through. He is the OL for the unit."

"Hi, Sheriff. This is Larry Medford. What can I do for you?"

"Missing person's case. 31 year old female. I'm up on highway 168 and it's snowing fairly hard. The woman's car is on the side of the road. I found a single set of tracks leading up the mountain. The way I put it together is that her car broke down. Her cellphone didn't work in this area. No cars came by, so she went up the mountain to see if she could get cellular reception. And now she's lost."

"How long has she been in the mountains?"

"My guess is at least 3-4 hours."

"Conditions?"

"Cold and getting colder. Moderate to heavy snowing with a light wind from the west," John replied.

"I'll get my unit together. We've got 4 dog/handler teams available. Should be there in no more than 2 hours."

John said, "I use to be a dog handler for a rescue unit. I have my dog with me, so I am going to do a 'hasty search' while waiting for you. If nothing else, it will give us a good idea of what the terrain is like."

"That will be a big help, Sheriff."

"I'm at the high point on 168 with my flashers on. You can't miss me."

"Good. We'll set up base camp about 50 yards back so as not to contaminate the incident scene."

Opening his trunk, John lifted the clothes out he would need for the cold weather. After pulling them on, he put on a head lamp, placed a compass in his jacket pocket, a CB radio in the other pocket, and finally a folded map of the area.

Blue was out of the car, and whining to get going.

John pulled a sweater from the woman's suitcase and let Blue smell it. He was a search and rescue dream dog. First, he was a scent tracker — a so-called tracking dog — who could follow a particular individual's tracks or scent on the ground. In this case, it would help confirm which direction she had initially taken. Unfortunately in weather like this, the snow would gradually cover and destroy the tracks and obliterate the ground scent. Luckily, Blue was also an air-scenting dog. These dogs searched for any human scent in the area, whether in the air or on the ground. They were the best in conditions like this for they could detect the scent of any nearby humans.

John snugged the Search and Rescue (SAR) vest around Blue, and he immediately began to pace with anticipation. John led Blue over to the tracks he had found earlier and let him sniff around. "Find!" he said loudly, and with that the dog started up the hill.

John paused and stared up at the inky blackness stretching before him, and wondered if they'd find her, and more importantly would she still be alive.

Nikki had managed to hobble to a large rock where she could sit with her back against an enormous tree stump. Up on top of the ravine, the wolves slunk around peering down at her. She'd thrown a number of rocks, and hit several of them, but they came right back. With the darkness and blankets of falling snow, it was hard to tell, but it seemed like they were moving slowly down into the ravine.

She turned her cellphone light on and flashed it at them but to no avail. What's that old saying about music soothing the savage beast, she remembered. Holding the cellphone out in front of her, she hit play on her rock and roll playlist. The music was loud and raucous, and it startled the animals. But very quickly, they were back and even closer.

One large, weather beaten animal bared its teeth and slid toward her. Nikki drove him off with a well-thrown rock. With the music turned up max, she started yelling trying to intimidate with noise. Her harsh sounds did move them back a few feet but the effect was only transient. They slunk back, obviously hungry.

Suddenly, a bright light illuminated the area. Nikki looked up and saw a dim figure above the ravine.

"You okay, miss?" a male voice said.

"Oh, thank God you're here."

The man moved toward the wolves. "Time to head home, boys," he said. As he approached, the wolves cowered as if frightened, and then the group moved off.

As he climbed down into the ravine, Nikki realized it was the old man from the gas station.

"I got to worrying about you when I heard about the storm," he said. "Drove up here and saw your car on the side of the road. I pulled over and started searching. Thought I'd never find you, but then I heard the music and you yelling."

"Thank God you're here," she said as she started to relax for the first time in hours.

He stopped and looked down at her. "Let's get you back down the mountain. Okay?"

"Easier said than done. I've twisted my ankle and can't put any weight on it."

The old man pondered that for a few moments. "Now that is a problem. Hate to admit it, even to myself, but my back just won't allow me to help support your weight." He glanced around. "Let's try this." He moved about ten feet away and picked up a thick branch. "Use this as a crutch."

The snow was coming down heavily and, with the fear of the wolves abated, Nikki was beginning to really feel the cold. Furthermore, the wind was strengthening with frequent gusts, dropping the wind chill factor rapidly.

"If we were on level ground, maybe I could," she said, her teeth chattering, "but not on this hill."

"I got an idea," the old man said. "I used to hunt all through these hills. Seems to me there is a cave close around here that could offer some shelter."

"Anything is going to be better than freezing out here."

"You stay here, while I…" The old man paused and then chuckled. "Now that was a brainless comment." He brushed snow off his jacket. "Let me search around. I'll be right back."

Nikki watched him fade into the night. Her initial elation at his arrival was slowly eroded by a subtle sense of fear. She was helpless and alone in the middle of nowhere, and who was this old guy really? Could she trust him? Was he a serial killer who preyed on lonely women? Or was he just who he appeared to be — a Good Samaritan? If push came to shove, she could probably whoop his ass. She laughed at the absurdness of that thought. Here I've spent years of kick boxing and practicing self-defense and I'm wondering if I can fend off an 80 year old man with an arthritic back.

"I found it." The old man was back. "The cave is only about 50 yards away. I think you could crawl to it since it's fairly flat ground once you get out of this ravine."

Nikki slid off the rock. "Point the way. I can't last much longer in the open."

It took almost twenty minutes, but she finally made it to the cave. There was a weather worn tarp across the entrance which the old man pulled aside to let her in. While she had been crawling, he had built a fire in the cave and the heat was heaven.

He pointed to several low slung folding chairs set around the fire. "Found these in the back. Get yourself situated in one of them while I look for something for you to drink."

A few minutes later, he was back with an old half-filled bottle of Wild Turkey, along with two tin cups.

"This'll warm you up," he said, handing her a tin cup and starting to pour the whiskey.

"No, really. This fire is doing the job, and I'm not a drinker."

"Sweetie, the fire will warm your outside but you still need something to warm your inside." He gave her a big grin. "And this will do the job. I can vouch for that."

Reluctantly, Nikki allowed him to pour some in her cup and then she took a sip. "Wow! That is strong."

"Just feel that warmth," he said. "Couple more sips and we'll have you dancing down the mountain." He watched her as he took another swallow. "Never like to see people drinking alone," he said and poured himself a drink.

"Where did you find this?" Nikki asked, holding up her cup.

"I always carry a flagon of whiskey in case of snake bite," he replied in his best W. C. Fields' imitation. "And furthermore I always carry a small snake."

After they stopped laughing, he said, "Actually, I think I left this bottle here a number of years ago."

Nikki glanced around. "Why isn't smoke building up in here?"

"The cave has a natural chimney which pulls the smoke away," he said.

Gradually warming up, Nikki said, "Aren't you cold in that light jacket?"

"No, cold never bothers me." He held his cup up. "Especially if I have this to keep me warm."

"I'm taking a wild guess here that you are a local."

The man leaned back in his chair. "Lived all my life down in Newman. Wife died a while back, and now it's just me and my son. Hell, I'd probably be gone myself except for some unfinished business."

They sat silently staring in the fire, and then the old man spoke. "So tell me about yourself. Where you from?"

"I live down near San Francisco, in Sausalito."

"Nice area if you like crowds. I remember you said something about waiting for the right man. Couldn't find one in that mob scene?"

Nikki smiled. "I thought I had, but it didn't work out."

"Why? Was he cheating or something?"

"No, he finally admitted that he didn't want a family, he just wanted a companion." She leaned toward the fire. "He said kids restrict your independence, they're always getting into trouble, and they cost too much to raise."

"Sounds like one selfish son-of-a-bitch," the old man said.

Nikki turned toward him. "I just realized I don't even know your name." She held out her hand. "I'm Nikki Law."

They shook. "Just call me J.T.."

"Your hands are freezing. Don't you want to stick them over the fire?"

"Getting old has its advantages. I don't seem to feel hot or cold." He leaned over and threw another log on the fire.

"What brought you to these parts?" he said.

"I was heading home to see my mom. She lives up in Weaverville."

The old man slowly nodded. "So you're originally from around here?"

"Yeah, but it was just too quiet, too boring, so when I was old enough, I headed for San Francisco."

"How's that working out?"

"Well, it costs me an arm and a leg to live there just so I can get stuck in traffic each morning driving to a job I don't like, and date a jerk that I just broke up with." She held out her cup. "Mind if I have a bit more of that?"

"Of course not," he said, picking up the bottle and pouring her some more. He took a drink from his own cup. "Maybe it's time to homestead elsewhere?"

"I've been contemplating that, but I can't think of any other big city I'd want to live in. Los Angeles is way too crowded and just too crazy. Seattle has terrible weather as does Portland."

"Not to mention Portland's filled with them Greenpeace, tree huggers," the man added sarcastically. He scratched his beard and then said, "How about a smaller municipality, say like Newman?"

"After all these years in San Francisco, I'm not sure I could ever be a small town girl again."

The old man stared in the fire, and then looked over at her. "Well, what if that small town held the man you were looking for?"

She laughed. "If I can't find that man in a large city, what makes you think I could find him in this small town? No offense meant."

"No offense taken." The old man smiled, "But I think I might know the man you're looking for."

Blue had immediately lost the trail scent once they ventured up the hill in the open area between the trees. This was likely due to the snow accumulating on the trail. Now he was searching the air for any scent of humans in the area. He had been trained to ignore animal scents.

They didn't do a grid search. That would be done by the dog teams when they arrived. Their job was the 'hasty search' — scout the area and get to know the topography so the dog teams would have an idea what they were up against and could plan accordingly.

The head lamp allowed John to make good time as they moved up the hill. He noted that the wind was blowing from his right to his left, which meant that any scent to his left would be blown away from them. The higher they went, the stronger the wind and the colder the air. Several times he slipped on wet, icy rocks. He periodically gave Blue commands if he started to stray one way or the other. It took over an hour but they finally reached the apex of the hill. No sign of Nikki on the way up or at the top. He liked to use the person's name when he thought about the object of the search. It made it more personal, and as such, strengthened his commitment to find them.

He sat down to catch his breath, and while doing so, called his dispatch with the CB radio.

"Maddie, this is John. See if you can get Mrs. Law on the line so I can get more information about her daughter."

"Will do, Sheriff."

The more they knew about Nikki, the better chance they would have to find her.

John was nearly down the mountainside when his radio buzzed.

"Hello, Sheriff. I have Mrs. Law on the line. Go ahead Mrs. Law."

There was a lot of background static, but the woman's voice was still fairly clear.

"Mrs. Law, this is John Taggart. I'm the sheriff of Newman, and will be involved with the search for your daughter." He quickly brought her up to speed, and then started asking questions.

"Tell me about your daughter. Is she healthy? Any experience in the outdoors? That sort of thing."

"Very healthy. She goes to the gym three days a week, and has run several 10Ks. Her father use to take her camping in the Sierras almost every year until he died three years ago."

"Her personal life has been going well lately?"

"Well, she told me today that she and her fiancé broke up. She was coming up here to mend." She paused, and then added, "But I'm actually glad they ended it. He was a narcissistic jerk, and didn't deserve her."

John had to smile. Mothers were all the same, constantly watching over their babies even when full grown.

"Please find my daughter, sheriff." There was a pause and then, "Is there anything I can do to help?"

"Just stay by your phone. We will call with any updates."

The snow was now coming down so heavily that it was hard to see more than ten feet in any direction. Periodically John had to pull out his GPS to make sure he was heading in the right direction. At one point, he thought he smelled a whiff of wood smoke, but it was gone so quickly he wasn't sure he hadn't imagined it.

When he finally reached the highway, the snow fall was lighter. To his surprise, his police cruiser was only about 30 feet away. Thank God for GPS and search dogs to get you home, he thought, reaching down to pet Blue.

In the distance, he saw lights and realized that the SARD teams had arrived.

Larry Medford was a short, stocky man with a full beard streaked with gray. He had a casual, yet authoritative air about him. John had never worked with him before but knew his reputation as a no-nonsense operational leader. Larry introduced him to the four dog handlers who were involved in setting up a large tent and getting the lights going with a generator. A folding table and chairs were added to the scene, and immediately after that coffee was set to brew.

John rolled open a large topographical map of the area on the table. As they all leaned over it, he went over what he knew of the area in general, and what he had discovered during his hasty search.

"This is going to be a tough. The snow up there is dumping which may eliminate any scents in the area." He looked around the group. "Visibility is so poor that you really have to depend on your GPS to guide you."

"Thank you, Sheriff," Medford said. "Fortunately, we've worked in heavy snow conditions before." He glanced around at the group. "Since time is essential, let's map out the sectors I want each team to search, and then get you guys on your way."

John turned around at the noise of a car pulling up. Medford said, "That's two more of my volunteers that will help man this base camp and the radio."

It was thirty minutes later when John watched the last of the SARD teams take off. The night was frigid cold, with moderate snowfall, and pitch black since there was no moon. Not an ideal setting to find someone lost in this terrain, John thought. He reached down and stroked Blue whom he'd leashed up to prevent him from following the SARD teams. Once again, he thought of that hint of wood smoke he noticed earlier.

Nikki tried not to laugh. "You have a man for me?" she said, incredulously. "I've spent years looking for the right guy, and now in a cave in the middle of nowhere, you think you've found him?"

The old man stared at her for a long moment. "What? You think that the only man worth having must live in a big city." He slowly shook his head. "The man I'm thinking of would be right for you in any sized city." He paused. "He's my son."

Nikki immediately felt bad about her negative response. She did not want to offend this man who had risked all to save her life. "Tell me about him," she said softly.

The man picked up a stick and stirred the fire before answering. "He's a good man. Has a paying job. Respected by everyone. I've heard him described as good-looking by some, although others might disagree. Played on the basketball team for the high school and was a star if I say so myself." He tossed another piece of wood on the fire, and then looked over at Nikki. "Need a refill?"

"No. Anymore of that and I'm won't be able to walk even with a good ankle."

"I know he wants children so you wouldn't have to worry about that. And he loves small towns so you could avoid all the crowds and hassles of living in a big city." He leaned back and grinned. "Yep, he would be perfect for you. His name is Michael."

John was in the base tent listening to the radio conversations going on with the SARD teams. So far no one had found anything, and there wasn't a single alert signal from any of the dogs. With the snow getting deeper, the handlers were finding it hard tracking through the heavy powder.

Medford glanced at John. "Not sure how long we can keep this up without exhausting our teams. I'm getting more and more worried this is no longer a rescue mission but rather a recovery mission."

"Her mother assured me she was at home in the mountains. So there is a good chance she found shelter and is waiting out the storm before coming down."

"What if she is injured, and can't get to shelter? Stuck outside in this storm, the odds are ten to one she wouldn't survive the night."

The crackle of the radio interrupted further discussion. "Base, this is team 2. We are heading back. My dog pulled a muscle trying to get through a snow drift, and now is limping." He gave the coordinates of where he had stopped the search, and signed off.

"There is another SARDs group in Riverton three hours away. I'm going to alert them about what's going on. If we still have nothing in an hour or so, I'll ask them to join us," Medford said.

John stroked Blue and wondered about Medford's comment. "When I was up there earlier, I thought I caught a whiff of wood smoke. Not sure it was real or just an overactive imagination."

Medford turned from the radio. "At this point, we'll take any clues to her location. But she'd have to be sheltered. This snow would put out any fire in the open."

"There's a cave up there that some of the local hunters use if they stay overnight. I wonder if she might have stumbled on to that. It could definitely be a source of wood smoke."

"Do you know where it is?"

"Vaguely, but I'm pretty sure I can find it."

Medford thought for a moment. "Let me call one of the SARD teams in to go with you."

"They have enough to do without going on a wild goose chase with me," John said. He held up his CB radio. "I'll keep you informed."

Ten minutes later, Blue and John set out. He hadn't mentioned it to Medford but he'd been in the cave several times when hunting with his dad, but the last time was more than seven years ago, which is why he'd only just remembered its existence.

John recalled the old line — "It ain't a fit night for man nor beast." — and thought it very apropos to now. It was well below freezing, the snow was stacking up in huge drifts making it difficult to maneuver up the hillside, and visibility, with the lack of a moon and the heavy snow fall, was terrible. Using his GPS, his faint memory of the cave location, and a strong dose of prayer, he pushed up the hill. Twice he had to backtrack to go around obstacles. Once he fell into a snow pile and had difficulty getting out.

Several times Medford called to see if he was all right and to confirm his location.

After what seemed like an eternity, he found the cave or it found him. The smoke smell, and the light leaking out around the tarp at the entrance snagged his attention. He stood for a moment in front of the cave opening to catch his breath, and while doing so brushed the snow off Blue. Pulling back the tarp, he stopped in mid stride at the scene in front of him.

A young woman sat in a folding chair, jacket snug around her, holding her hands out toward a moderate sized wood fire. There was another chair next to her that was empty. The woman glanced up casually, and then her expression changed to surprise.

"Who are you?" she said, straightening up.

"I'm John Taggart, sheriff of Newman. And I'm hoping you are Nikki Law."

She leaned to one side trying to see around him. "Where's the old man? He said he was going to fetch you?"

"There's someone else with you?" John asked with concern.

"Yes, an old man who found me and led me to this cave." She thought for a moment. "I think his name is... T.J.."

John stepped closer to the fire to warm up, while Blue moved over to Nikki. He ran his nose over her, and then licked her face.

"Blue, leave the lady alone," John said, pulling off his gloves. "Tell me more about this T.J.."

Nikki reached out and ran her hand over Blue's thick fur. "If you didn't run into him, how did you find me?"

"There is a whole search team that's been looking for you. I remembered this cave and thought I'd take a chance that you might be here." It was then that he noticed her right foot had the shoe off, and was elevated on a rock. "What happened to your foot?"

She looked at it. "Either I fractured my ankle, or it's a major sprain. I can't put any weight on it." She paused. "I had to crawl to get here."

Once more she regarded the cave entrance. "God, I hope T.J. is okay."

"How long ago did he leave?"

"Just a couple of minutes before you showed up."

"Are you sure it wasn't longer because I didn't see anyone outside when I approached. In fact, if he'd just left, I should have seen tracks in front of the cave but I didn't."

"That is weird." She thought for a moment. "Maybe it was longer ago, but I don't think so."

"I'm going to call base camp and let them know I've found you. But before I do, what do you know about this T.J. fellow? We may have to start searching for him."

Nikki relayed her experiences with the old man, starting with meeting him at Ted's Trading Post, and then through everything that happened on the mountain.

John was silent as he took all this in, and then said, "He told you that he saw your car, and parked his behind yours?"

Nikki nodded.

"Your car was the only one on either side of the road when I arrived, and that was more than four hours ago."

"So then how did he get up here?" Nikki said slowly. "There is no way he could have walked all the way from that gas station."

"You're sure he was the same man?"

"Absolutely." She thought for a moment. "He told me he had a son named… Michael. That's it. Michael."

"An old man with a son named Michael." John shook his head. "Not very helpful."

"Wait," she said, snapping her fingers. "The old guy also said his son was a star basketball player."

Pulling out his CB radio, John called the base. Medford answered immediately. "We were getting a bit worried about you, Sheriff."

"Well I've got good news. I found her in the cave I mentioned and she's safe. The problem, though, is she has a severe ankle injury and will have to be brought out on a stretcher."

Medford was quiet, and then said, "Let me call the SARD teams in and then I'll send up some people with a rescue sled to bring her out. This may take a while. Are you guys okay with that?"

"No problem. We're in a cave with a fire going. Let me give you the GPS coordinates. Oh, one other thing. Keep an eye out for an old man named T.J.." John went on to further explain, finishing with, "He appears to know this mountains quite well, and so I don't think he's lost." After a beat, he added, "In fact, I'm not sure what to think about him."

After completing the call, John sat down in the other folding chair. "I spoke with your mother. She's the one that got this whole search going."

"Oh, poor mom. She must really be worried," Nikki said. She looked over at John, and saw something in his expression. "Okay, so what else did she tell you?"

John smiled. "Well, she did mention you'd recently broken up with a boyfriend that she wasn't very fond of."

"I'm sure her description of him was a bit more colorful," Nikki said.

"A bit."

"He wasn't really that bad," Nikki said, "just not what I wanted. Unfortunately, it took me four years to figure that out."

They both turned their attention to the fire, and for a while the only sound was the wind and the crackling of the burning wood. John cast a quick look at her, enjoying the way the camp fire cast reddish tints in her dark hair.

Still fixated on the fire, Nikki said, "I want to thank you for coming out in weather like this." She swivelled toward him. "I have friends that wouldn't even go out in a light rain to search for me."

"No thanks needed. Just part of the job," John replied.

"You sound as stiff as Jack Webb from the old *Dragnet* series: 'All we want are the facts, ma'am'," She grinned. "I'm sure you had a million better things to do. Be with your family? Go out with friends? Maybe just go to bed early?"

He shrugged and leaned back in his chair. "That all sounds good, but the truth is I'm single, have no family, and the social scene here is seriously lacking." And where did all that come from, he thought, startled at his openness.

"Don't feel bad. San Francisco has a great social life, but it gets old quickly if you're alone." She stared at him. "I'm surprised you're single." Immediately she covered her mouth. "Oh, I'm sorry. I think that's the whiskey speaking."

John half smiled. "You mean that I'm such a great catch you can't believe someone hasn't reeled me in already?"

"Not exactly," she said, "although I'm sure you are a… great catch."

"If you were Pinocchio, your nose would've just grown a foot," he said grinning.

She laughed. "No, it's just that in my experience most people living in small towns get married right out of high school."

"And you've had experience in small towns?"

"Lived in Weaverville until I finished junior college. And all my friends were married within a few years of graduating high school." She threw a piece of wood into the fire.

Moving his chair closer to the fire, John thought of Carol Sue. "Well, I haven't always lived here. I left right after high school for college, and after that joined the Army, ending up in the military police. When I came back, my high school sweetheart was engaged."

"What made you stay?"

"My parents. They were getting old and needed help around the house. The town was looking for a sheriff so I applied. Now they've both gone, and I sometimes wonder why I remain."

"Well, I'm living in the big city and I wonder why I remain."

They were quiet for a bit, and then John said, "Sounds like we're coming to the same crossroad but from different directions." He smiled at her. "Maybe we should compare notes sometime."

They stared into each other's eyes, and slowly a smile spread across Nikki's face. "I'd like that."

John noticed the tin cup on the floor and a thought occurred. "For someone to know the whereabouts of this cave, I should know him. Describe him again?"

"Old, but able to get around. Thin with bright blue eyes. Dressed in worn Levis, an old down-jacket, and an ancient ball cap. Claimed he had a bad back. Does that help?"

John shook his head.

The CB radio crackled and Medford's voice said, "Come in, Sheriff."

Grabbing the radio, John replied, "What's up?"

"My boys tell me they're nearly there, so you might keep a lookout for them."

John stood up. "You just rest while I make some arrangements." He pulled the tarp aside to emit more light to help the rescue party locate them. In a few minutes, he heard voices.

"Over here," he yelled.

It was several hours later, and Nikki was now in John's police car. Once they got off the mountain, the SARD teams would be going in a different direction, so it had made sense to have the sheriff take her to the Newman hospital rather than the SARD team. Surprisingly, Nikki's car immediately started up when they tried it, so one of the search volunteers offered to drive it down.

They were nearly off the mountain when Nikki said, "I just remembered the old guy's name. It wasn't T.J., it was J.T.."

John glanced over at her. "Are you sure of that?"

"Definitely."

John drove for a while in silence, then asked, "Was J.T. missing the small finger on his left hand?"

Nikki thought for a moment. "Yes, he was. How did you know?"

They hit the main highway, and started toward Newman. Once in town, John made several turns, and then pulled up to a metal archway.

"I want to show you something before I take you to the hospital." He drove through the arch, made two right turns, and then pulled up to a grassy knoll. Opening his door, he came around to Nikki's side. Grabbing a flashlight from the glove compartment, he leaned in to pick her up, but she said, "Just give me a shoulder to lean on and I can hobble over, if we're not going too far."

He helped her go a short distance from the car, and then eased her down on the grass. Pulling his flashlight out, he shined it on a picture that was set in a gravestone. "Is that your J.T.?"

Nikki stared at the picture, at first nodding, and then abruptly shaking her head. "That can't be. He was on the mountain. He saved my life. This can't be the same man."

"Everyone called him J.T. Since he's dead, I never connected him with the man in the woods."

She ran her hand over the gravestone. "His last name is Taggart." She glanced up at him. "He was your father?"

"Yes, and my full name is Jack Michael Taggert. When I was young people started calling me John, but he always called me Michael."

"And you were a basketball star?"

"The star part is debatable, but I did play," he said.

She sat back on the grass. "I don't understand any of this."

"Well, you're not alone." He dropped down next to her. "I have a theory but it doesn't explain all of it, and... it adds a lot more questions."

"If it explains even part of this, let me hear it."

"My father was known for keeping his promises. He never broke a one until he made his last promise to me, just before he died."

Nikki raise her hands in a question like gesture. "And that has something to do with all of this?"

"Well, I think he was trying to carry out that last promise."

"Which was?"

"He promised me if I stayed in Newman, he'd find me a woman to marry."

* * * * *

Somehow, and I really don't remember how, I got interested in search and rescue dogs. After reading about them, I decided to write a story about their use in the search and rescue process. The fact that these dogs could be scent tracking – reading a scent from the ground – and/or air scenting – taking it out of the air – I found fascinating. Now all I needed was a rescue to put them to work.

I believe my wife and I were kicking around astrological forecasts one day when I read a forecast for Virgo – "bad day to travel" – and slowly the story fell into place.

Two Bits Worth of Magic

You can't always get what you want
But if you try sometimes you might find
You get what you need.

Rolling Stones

It was like no other Christmas I'd ever had.

Bundled up against the cold, I was heading back to my dorm room on the University of Nevada at Las Vegas campus to continue my lonely Christmas holiday vigil. The school was essentially deserted, except for the basketball team of which I was a member. Our schedule only allowed a few days off before the holiday basketball tournament which was not enough time for me to fly back and see my family, even if I could afford it. Most of my team members, though, lived closer and were long gone. This would be my third Christmas holiday alone, and I was dreading it. The holiday decorations are impressive, but not when there is no one to share them with.

Since the school cafeteria was closed, our coach had set up meal arrangements with an all-you-can-eat restaurant just off the Vegas strip. The quality of the food matched the price, and so my stomach was still trying to adjust to some of my gourmet selections as I stroll-ed home.

In the glare of bright neon signs and Christmas lights strung on various buildings, I noticed a girl pulling a wheeled suitcase, walking about a half a block in front of me. Her clothes reflected the cold — sweater, leggings, and Uggs. The cracked and rutted sidewalks gave her an awkward stride which wasn't helped by the suitcase trailing behind her. Stumbling along, her toe caught on something and she pitched forward, right into a man who had suddenly emerged from a doorway to her right. She struck him hard, knocking him sprawling into the gutter, while she fell back onto the sidewalk.

Two thick-necked hulks came out of the same doorway and shouted at the man in the gutter. I made out a few words, "Bum" and "Don't come back." One of them noticed the girl and helped her up. He was brushing off her sweater when she suddenly yanked away. He laughed, said something to his partner, and they both laughed. He pulled a card from his coat and stuffed it in her hand, and then both men strode back into the building.

Illuminated by the neon lights of Jack's Bar and Casino, I saw the young girl bend over and try to help the man in the gutter stand up. She was still engaged in this tug of war when I arrived.

"Come on," she pleaded, "try and get up."

The man attempted to rise, only to fall back with a groan. "My ankle's broken!"

It was her turn to groan as she sank down onto her suitcase, and buried her face in her hands.

Since anything would be preferable to the nothingness I had planned for the evening, especially anything with legs as shapely as hers, I stepped over. "Can I help?"

She looked up and it became a Polaroid moment. Even with her overuse of makeup, she was a head-turner. Dark brown eyes, freckles lightly sprinkled across her cheeks, and chestnut blond hair piled up and held by a clip. I had been right. She was young, probably just out of high school.

"This has been a day from hell, and now this," she said as she flung her arm out toward the man in the gutter. "I've broken his ankle," she said.

"Why don't I take a look at him?"

She glanced up expectantly. "Are you a doctor?"

"No, but I've had a lot of experience with ankle injuries." I didn't mention it was all on the basketball courts.

I moved to the man in the gutter who had been strangely quiet. He was laying flat on his back, staring up at the night sky. In the flashing neon lights, I noticed his clothing budget was worse than mine. He had a stained white shirt, a filth-covered suit, shaggy beard, and collar-length greasy, grey hair. Squatting down at his feet, the odor of the long unwashed drifted up amidst fumes of cheap alcohol. Not sure if he'd heard us talking I said, "I'm just going to check your ankle, all right?"

His eyes gradually focused on me and he nodded. I flexed his ankle and he let out a moan. It was already swelling, but nothing felt out of place.

"I think it's just a sprain," I said to him, "but you'll need to go to the emergency room for x-rays to be sure. At the very least, you are going to need crutches for the next week or so."

"No hospital," he said. "No money."

The girl dropped her head back in her hands and sighed. I was wondering who to comfort first when a gleaming black limousine slowed and stopped right next to us. The driver's door opened and a well tailored man in a dark suit and a chauffeur's cap climbed out. He eyed us speculatively and then strode to the man on the ground.

"What's your name, sir?" he said.

It was the derelict's turn to stare. He finally responded with just a touch of pride. "Jones. Remington Jones."

"Well, Mr. Jones, since it is the Christmas season, my employer has a gift for you."

Jones raised himself up on his elbows. "A gift?" He paused. "How about money? That would be a good gift."

"Exactly his thought." The chauffeur reached inside jacket and pulled out a small, thin, leather wallet "Here," he said, handing it to Jones.

Jones was starting to open it when one of dark tinted windows in the limousine slid down and a deep voice echoed from inside. "Use the gift wisely, my friend."

By then the chauffeur was back in the car and in a moment it sped off.

"What did he give you?" I asked.

Jones finished unzipping the wallet and looked inside. He snickered. "A fortune." He threw the wallet to me. "Here you count it."

I flipped it open and saw a single quarter sitting in a plastic insert. Nothing else, just a quarter.

The girl had gotten up and was looking over my shoulder. "Why would he give you just a quarter? " she asked. "Oh, maybe it's the first money he ever made and it brought him luck, so he's giving it to you."

"Maybe he's just a cheap son of a bitch with a bad sense of humor," Jones snarled.

I moved toward Jones. "Whatever the reason, it doesn't change the plan. We need to get you to an emergency room. I wouldn't worry about expenses. They will bill you later." And good luck collecting, I thought.

I handed him back the leather wallet. "Let me help you up." I got behind him and pulled him up to his feet. Moving to his side, I put my arm around his waist so he could lean on me and keep his weight off his injured ankle. I glanced at the girl. "I think we missed the introductions. I'm Nick Fallon."

She half smiled. "I'm Robin Sutter."

"Well, Robin, can you flag us down a cab?"

Before she could move, Jones spoke. "Who the hell is getting into a cab? Not me. I told you, no hospital! At least not while I still have money to gamble with." He held up the wallet. "Two bits is two bits."

"Oh, come on," I said. "What can you do with a quarter?"

Jones pointed at Robin. "Maybe the little lady is right. Maybe this was the guy's lucky quarter." He paused. "And what have I got to lose… except this fortune."

He had it bad. My psych professor had done one whole lecture on the addiction of gambling. It was as bad as alcohol or cocaine. People would bet everything they owned and more. Marriages were wreck-ed, businesses failed, relationships lost, hearts broken but nothing mattered except the next wager. And they would bet on anything, at anytime. It wasn't about winning or losing, it was about the adrenaline high of betting. Something else the same professor taught me. You don't try to get an alcoholic to agree to a rehab program "if they were a quart shy." In other words, if they still needed another drink. Well, Jones was a quarter shy of going to the hospital.

"All right, we play the quarter in a slot machine, then its ER time." I glanced at Robin who nodded her agreement.

"Okay, but not at this place," he said pointing toward Jack's. "I'm persona non grata there."

Two buildings up was the Vegas Nugget, a twin of Jack's. There was a tall, sparkling metal Christmas tree out front radiating commercialism. "Fine," I replied. We started moving, me supporting him on one side while he hopped on his good foot. This wasn't going to work. I turned to Robin who had fallen in behind us.

"Think you could lend another shoulder for him to lean on. With both of us giving support, we can get this done a lot easier." I saw her reticence. "I can handle your suitcase. After we drop him at the hospital, I'll help you get to wherever you're going."

She flashed a tentative smile. "Okay."

"And where were you going?" I asked.

"I was heading for the Gold Dust Casino. I have a job arranged there for the holidays."

With us acting as his crutches, Jones made it into the Nugget and up to the nearest slot machine. In the background, I could faintly hear Christmas carols.

Jones pulled the quarter out of the wallet and immediately flung it to the ground.

"What the hell," he yelled rubbing his hands together.

"What's wrong?" I said.

"That thing gave me a shock."

We all stared at the quarter as it rolled around finally stopping at

Robin's feet. She took a step back and looked over at me. I pointed at the quarter and gestured for her to pick it up. Hesitantly at first, she bent over and gingerly touched the quarter with her index finger. "Ouch," she cried jumping back. "It gave me a shock too."

I shook my head. "Oh, come on. You are both full of static electricity. Let me try." I stretched my fingers out and touched it. Zap! A bolt of electricity hit my hand. "Whoa," I said. The two of them nodded at me.

"Yeah, the little bastard is alive," Jones said.

Feeling chagrined with my own reaction, I bent back over and grabbed the quarter determined to hang on no matter what. Nothing happened. After a moment, I extended it to Jones.

He touched it carefully, and then grabbed it. "Let's get this show going." He dropped the quarter into the slot machine and pulled the handle. We watched the wheels spin round and round. First one wheel stopped on "Jackpot," then the second on "Jackpot." The third wheel rolled to a stop — "Jackpot." There was a collective breath hold as we waited for the fourth wheel to stop. When it did, our screams were drowned in the flashing lights and sirens that erupted. Quarters poured from the machine. Jones extended his hands out trying to catch them but had no chance as a river of silver flowed onto the floor. In all my life, I'd never seen so many quarters.

Jones glanced at the quarters in his hands and the pile on the floor, then at me. "We are not going to the ER tonight, kid. This is the start of a winning streak and I'm — no we — are going to ride it to the end!"

Something had happened to Jones. He was no longer the silent, defeated derelict we'd pulled out of the gutter. He stood taller, he moved smoother, he spoke with confidence, and his whole demeanor radiated action. And then I realized what had brought him back to life — his addiction. He was feeding it again.

He hobbled to the next machine while Robin and I picked up the quarters. We were still bent over when the lights and sirens went off again. Jones was ready this time and placed a cardboard bucket under the mouth of the machine. By the time Robin and I added our quarters to the bucket, it was full.

"Take that to the cashier and get chips," Jones said.

"No. Let's cash out and go to the ER. Now you have some money to pay them."

"Oh, no. This isn't money. This is a start. Before the night is over, I'm going to buy the ER."

I should have been bowled over with the excitement and the thrill of it all, but I was too much in shock. What had I gotten myself into, I wondered? Walking to the cashier window with its Christmas card decorations, I got $250 in chips. When I returned to Jones, Robin was gone.

"Where's the girl?" I asked.

He pointed over his shoulder. She was sitting on a stool fifteen feet away from the machines. "She's too young to play."

"She's not playing."

"I know that, but security doesn't even want her near the machines so they put her over there." He eased off his stool onto his one good leg. "Help me to the roulette table."

We made our way to the table and people opened up a spot for Jones what with his smell and attire. I saw the dealer roll his eyes when he saw us, then he barked out, "Place your bets."

Jones placed all $250 on the table. "Pick a number," he said to me.

"Are you crazy?"

"No! So pick one, now!"

"Red three."

The dealer's eyes swept the table. "All bets down."

Jones pushed the chips out. "Red three."

As the dealer spun the wheel, we all watched, fascinated by the silver ball. Round and round it went, jumping from number to number. This was too much for me so I closed my eyes and waited.

The sound of the bouncing ball suddenly ceased and I heard the dealer cry out, "Red three!"

First a quarter, then $250, and now almost $8000! I couldn't believe it.

"How would you like your winnings?" the dealer said.

Jones waved at Robin. "When's your birthday, honey?"

She yelled back. "October 13th."

Jones swung back to the dealer. "Let it all ride on black thirteen."

A tall man in a dark blue suit came up behind the dealer and eased him aside. "I'm sorry, sir, but that is above our betting limit."

"Gotcha worried, huh?" Jones said.

The man responded with a humorless smile. "I don't make the rules, sir."

"What's your betting limit?"

"Four thousand."

"You guys are on the cheap side." He thought for a moment. "All right. Leave $4000 on the table and give the rest back to me."

The tall man nodded. "Your name, sir?"

He eyed the tall man. "Remington Jones. And yours?"

He smiled back at Remington, this time with some humor. "Elton," he said then turned to the dealer. "Max, I will handle this." He surveyed the crowd that had gathered, eager to see if Jones could continue his streak. "For this one spin," he said loudly, "only Mr. Jones will be playing."

"Are you ready, Mr. Jones?" With that, Elton spun the wheel then dropped the silver ball.

My concentration was so intent on the leaping, caroming silver ball that the casino could have burned down around me and I wouldn't have noticed. Finally, the ball found a home and the wheel slowed down.

The crowd leaned forward while I held my breath. "Thirteen black," the dealer called out. "Congratulations, Mr. Jones. How would you like your winnings?"

Jones beckoned him over. "We'll take it in one hundred dollar bills. Keep a thousand for yourself, Elton," Jones said. "In return, help my friend here collect the money, get us a limo, and make a call for me."

"The tip isn't necessary," Elton said softly.

"I know that. I just like the way you do business."

"Who would you like me to call?"

"Call Marv Jackson at the Venetian. Tell him Remington Jones is in town with $100,000 to burn. I'll be there in twenty minutes. I want the red carpet out, his biggest suite, and someone who can supply me with a change of clothes and a haircut."

Fifteen minutes later, we were out front when a long white limo pulled up. Jones was in a wheelchair supplied by the casino and I helped him into the car.

"Good luck, Mr. Jones," I said starting to close the door.

"Nick, Robin, don't even think of leaving. We're all in this together. Now, climb in and let's get rolling. This is going to be a night to remember."

The red carpet was definitely out. No less than three bellmen whisked us up to the top floor into an Olympian pool size living room. The enormous picture windows gave us an unobstructed view of the lights of Las Vegas. The bell captain pointed out the three large bedrooms, each with a king size bed and its own private bathroom. We were still taking the tour when four men arrived; two were tailors and the other two hairstylists.

Jones gestured to the tailors. "I'll make this easy. I want a dark blue suit for tomorrow, but for tonight I need a top of the line tux."

He pointed to Robin. "For the young lady, we need an elegant red evening dress, and don't worry about the cost. Oh, and another tux for my young friend." He waved his hand toward the phone. "Nick, this is going to be thirsty business. Call room service for hors d'oeuvres and two bottles of Dom Perignon. Make sure they're very chilled. Nothing worse than warm Dom."

He swung his attention to the stylists. "I need a haircut and a shave. And for the young lady, as beautiful as she is, work some of your magic on her."

Robin's mouth hung open and she turned to me like a deer-caught-in-the-headlights. I knew how she felt. Who was this guy, Jones? A few hours ago he'd been like a small deflated balloon lying in the gutter. Now he was a huge, multicolor hot air balloon soaring above Las Vegas.

Showered and shaved, Jones was sitting in the living room getting his haircut when I came out of the bedroom. Robin was sitting near him with the stylist doing God knows what to her long blond hair.

"So Robin," Jones said, "What brought you to Vegas?"

"I guess you could say my family."

"You have family here?"

"No, my parents have a small farm north of here." She hesitated a moment. "My dad was injured six months ago while driving his tractors and needs some corrective surgery. I had been working in town to help pay for it, but business was so slow that the store had to let me go. I finally managed to get a job in housekeeping at a casino here for the holidays. I was hoping, that in time, I could find an even better paying position."

Nodding slowly, Jones said, "And what kind of position would that be?"

"Oh, maybe as a model or a dancer in one of the casino shows."

"Do you have experience in either of those fields?"

"Not modeling, but I was a dancer in several school plays."

Jones gave me a look and I knew what he was thinking. Girls like Robin usually ended up in a harsher line of work in this town.

"Any thoughts about going to college?" he asked.

"My high school boyfriend for four years got a football scholarship to San Diego State University. He told me that he had bigger plans than spending his life in our hick town. He never looked back when he left." She glanced at both of us and then looked down. "Well, I wanted to show him that I had aspirations just as grand as his. I was going to work for a year and use the money for college." She paused. "But with my dad sick, my plans will have to wait."

"What about you, Nick?" Jones said. "How did you end up here?"

"School. I got a basketball scholarship, and came out here."

"Where is home?"

"Florida."

"Why aren't you home for the holidays?"

I explained about our limited time off from basketball, and my families' lack of money so they couldn't fly here or me back there.

"Well, I'm just glad you both came along when you did. I was pretty much tapped out on life. " He stretched his arms out, encompassing the suite. "And now this." He glanced at the two of us. "I owe you guys."

An hour later, Jones and I were in our tuxedos waiting for Robin. When she emerged from her room, I was tongue-tied.

"Pick your jaw off the floor, Nick, and hand her that glass of champagne," Jones said, lifting his glass for a toast while smiling at her. "Here's to gorgeous women, and tonight, Robin, you are at the top of that list."

"And here is just a little something to complete your Christmas outfit," Jones said, handing her a fluffy white and red Santa cap.

She put it on, and turned to us for comments. "Christmas has never looked so beautiful," Jones said. "Wouldn't you agree, Nick?"

Speechless, I could only stare, eventually nodding my agreement.

Champagne was our drink and it flowed. We were whisked from casino to casino in a black stretch limo. Much of the night was a blur. Craps, roulette, poker, slot machines — we did it all. Jones never lost. The most outlandish bets, the craziest odds, and yet he always won.

In contrast, Robin and I rarely had a winning hand. Yet we loved it all — the glitz, the noise, the people, the celebrity treatment — as we went from one establishment to the next.

At one point while driving between locations, I opened the sunroof so Robin and I could stand up. With our elbows perched on the roof, we watched the lights flash by, and with the wind in our faces toasted the milling crowds on the sidewalks. The town had Christmas decorations everywhere, including fake snow and icicles, which made the ride that much sweeter.

She leaned in against me. "I am having such a blast. I only wish I didn't feel so guilty when I think about my dad."

I poured some more champagne into her glass. "Tonight we only worry about ourselves. Tomorrow will come soon enough."

The word had passed throughout the strip. Whenever we hit another casino, there would be several men in the inevitable dark suits following us around. Jones explained they were worried that he had some gimmick that was allowing him to win. No one would believe that his incredible winning streak could merely be luck. And neither could I. That quarter had something to do with all of this. But if that was the case, how come he kept winning, yet Robin and I usually lost. We had all touched the quarter, all gotten the electric shock, and yet he was the only winner. It's not like Robin couldn't have used the money for her family, or I couldn't have spent it flying my family out for Christmas.

The casinos would let Jones win a certain amount then politely but firmly ask him to leave. They had no idea how he continued to win, but they figured it couldn't be legal so they would escort us out, very smoothly of course.

Robin and I started wearing down about four in the morning. Tired and hungry, we excused ourselves and found a restaurant open in the casino. We were waiting for our order when Jones appeared, now with a cane, and followed by his dark suited shadows.

He settled carefully into a chair next to me. "Man, what a night! I just cannot lose." He shook his head. "What the hell is going on?"

Robin looked up. "It's the quarter, Mr. Jones. It brought you luck."

"No, this isn't luck. Luck is when you beat the odds more often than you lose. No, this is more than luck. It's spooky." He glanced around the room. "Watch this. Nick, I bet you twenty dollars that the waitress carrying those two plates is going to slip and drop them."

We all turned to look. Sure enough, she hadn't walked ten feet when she stumbled and the plates went on the floor.

"Well, what do you think of that," Jones asked? "That is not luck."

"I think that was our food," I replied, shaking my head.

"For someone who loves to gamble and is now winning at everything," Robin said, "I can't understand why you aren't more excited."

Jones leaned forward in his chair, glancing back and forth at each of us. "The reason I gamble is the risk, the adventure, the suspense of what's going to happen when I pull that handle, throw those dice, or flip those cards. It is not about the winning, it's about the excitement." He shook his head. "Where the hell is the excitement, when I never lose?"

We all pondered on that, and then Robin said, "Merry Christmas, Mr. Jones," and slide the leather wallet across the table to him.

"What's this?"

"It's the quarter that you were given. I found it on the floor when you won that first jackpot. It has a red mark on it that is very distinctive."

"That can't be. It would have stayed in the machine."

"Well, it didn't, so Merry Christmas."

Jones grabbed the wallet and stared at it for a long time. He was still fixated on it when our food belatedly arrived. He said nothing, just stared off into the distance, as Robin and I ate. I was finishing my hamburger, when he stood up. "We have work to do, kids. Finish up and meet me at the entrance. I have a stop to make." He slipped the wallet in his pocket. "Wish me luck," he said and then grimaced. "Guess I don't need that, do I?" With that, he reached for his cane and limped off.

It was forty-five minutes later when he finally appeared at the casino entrance and climbed into the limo with us.

Something had happened. The tenseness around his eyes was gone, and when he eased into the limo, his smile was genuine and lit the interior with its warmth. After instructing the driver where to go, he settled back into his seat.

"Something I need to tell you kids about myself," he said with a half-smile. "You found me as a bum in the street, but I wasn't always like that. I started a tech company twenty years ago and discovered that I had a natural affinity for business. The result was that I made a lot of money. But with the passing of time, business lost its challenge and I turned to gambling. At first it was just with friends over poker or ball games. Quickly it moved to more serious betting. I was steadily draining the company's money. My wife and my lawyer, who is also my best friend, stepped in and cut off my access to company funds. It saved the company but it was too late for me. I was in the grip of the addiction and nothing seemed to help. I tried gamblers anonymous, hypnotists, psychiatrists — nothing worked. I decided to come to Vegas and try to make a living through gambling. You saw the results. I have lived in the gutter for the last six months and even that couldn't stop me. My wife, my kids, my friends have all given up on me. And to tell you the truth, I had given up on myself." He held the leather wallet up. "Then this came into my life."

I cringed. Even at my age I knew that if there ever was a chance of him giving up his addiction, the quarter had ruined it.

"The last half hour I spent on the phone with my wife. We hadn't spoken in months but I discovered she had never stopped praying for me... and never stopped loving me. I told her my gambling days were over and explained why. And I told her I was coming home. This Christmas is going to be a joyous one for both of us." He frowned slightly as he shook his head. "If you can't lose, all the allurement, all the thrill of gambling is gone. And with that, the need to gamble is gone since the outcome is never in doubt." He looked at both of us and then smiled. "Now I can really go home."

"That's wonderful," Robin said.

"More notable, the two of you have made me realize how essential family and friends are to our existence. Nothing I could ever win is more important."

Turning to Robin, he said, "When I first met you tonight, what was the most pressing desire you had?"

Robin thought a moment. "To get to the Gold Dust casino and start my job."

"Well, I hate to disappoint you, but you won't be needing that job."

"But my father…"

Jones lifted his hand to cut her off. "He is going to be taken care of. I spoke with my lawyer and he will make sure your father is seen by the best doctors available. All of his medical care will be covered as well as any debts on your family farm."

Robin leaped across the narrow interior space and threw her arms around Jones's neck. "Oh, thank you, thank you," she said, the tears streaming down her face.

"No, thank you. In the midst of all your own troubles, you took the time to help a bum in the gutter and it saved my life." He paused, then added, "You always seem to put other peoples' needs before your own. Well, now it's time we think about your needs."

Robin moved back to her seat, wiping her eyes.

"Did I mention that the other reason you don't need a job is that you now have a full tuition to the college of your choice. Everything and I mean everything will be paid for. The only condition is you do not go to San Diego State University. That ex-boyfriend is a jerk!"

Robin let out a yelp and leaped on Jones again, only this time it was my turn to get misty eyed.

"Any idea where you might want to go?" Jones asked as Robin moved back to her seat.

Robin shyly glanced at me, and said, "I am leaning toward the University of Nevada at Las Vegas."

Jones chuckled and turned to me, "You might want to stay in college a few more years, Nick." Leaning back in his seat, he cleared his throat and continued, "I want to thank you also, Nick. I'd still be on the street if you hadn't invested your time in me. And I'm sure having Robin around played no role in your commitment." Embarrassed, I peeked quickly at Robin who smiled back.

"Thank you from the bottom of my heart." Jones stuck his hand out and we shook. His grip was firm and strong. He blinked several times and I realized there were three sets of wet eyes in that car.

Settling back in his seat, Jones said, "So Nick, what was the most pressing wish you had just before we met?"

"Oh, I just wanted to get back to my apartment." I said as casually as possible.

"Good. Now, how about the truth?"

After a moment's hesitation, I admitted, "I wanted to be with my family for Christmas."

"I thought so. Well, tomorrow they will find that for the rest of your college years they have free round-trip tickets to Las Vegas as often as they want."

I was speechless.

"But I don't think that was really the wish you had when we first saw you," he said, staring intently at me

"No, it wasn't," I admitted. "I didn't want to spend another Christmas alone."

Jones laughed and the sweep of his arm took in everything around us. "I don't think that you spent this Christmas alone."

"Mr. Jones," Robin said, "what was it you wanted when we found you on the street?"

"Good question. I wanted to gamble… and I wanted to win." He held the leather wallet up. "It took me a long time before I finally figured this gift out. Remember the guy in the limo. He said, 'Use it wisely', not 'Spend it wisely'."

Jones opened the case and pulled the quarter out. "Remember we all got the shock from this quarter, but I was the only one winning at the casinos. That was the key. The quarter was doing something but it was different for each of us, yet it had to have a common thread." He smiled. "What I wanted was to gamble, but what I needed was to stop." He pointed to me. "You wanted your parents out here, but what you needed was company for the holidays," he paused, "and you got us," he added winking at Robin.

Robin chimed in. "And what I wanted was to start working, but what I needed was help for my family."

Now I saw it, and so did Robin.

"This quarter doesn't bring you what you want," I said.

"It brings you what you need," Robin added.

Jones smiled and nodded his head. "Exactly."

The driver lowered the connecting window. "We are at the destination you requested, sir."

Robin and I peeked through the tinted windows. It was a small, bright white building with a lighted cross on the top. Strings of Christmas lights decorated several of the surrounding trees as well as the building. There was a line of homeless appearing people stretched out from a side door, apparently waiting for food.

"I've had a lot of early morning breakfasts here," Jones said wistfully. He leaned forward, spoke to the driver, and then handed him the wallet. The driver climbed out and walked over to a man dressed in black standing near the back of the line. The driver handed the case to the man and after a moment pointed back at the limo.

Jones smiled, rubbing his hands together in anticipation. "This is going to be good." He rolled the window down and leaned out. "Use the gift wisely, Father."

* * * * *

The original inspiration for this story was a comment made by a sports radio host. He mentioned that when he played basketball at University of Nevada at Las Vegas, the players were stuck at the college practicing during the Christmas holidays. Since the college cafeteria was closed, the coach had arranged for the team to get their food at an all-you-can-eat restaurant down on the strip. I pictured this young college student walking back to campus from the restaurant and I wondered what adventures he might fall into on a Christmas Eve in Vegas. The possibilities seemed endless.

My grandmother left me, of all things, a 25-cent slot machine which is still very functional. So slot machines and a quarter found a place into the story.

I argued with my wife on how many people would know what "two bits" meant. When I was growing up, a quarter was always called "two bits" which definitely ages me since I haven't heard that term in decades.

Lastly, in stories where people fine some magical device, the object usually grants them the wish they want. Instead, I decided to make it the wish they need and see where that led me. The result was a glorious ride through Vegas.

Reindeer Don't Fly

The harsh jangle of the telephone shattered the early morning stillness of Robert Marley's bedroom. Quickly, he reached for the phone, hoping to stop its shrill ring before it woke his wife. Then he remembered he was sharing his bed alone.

"Yeah?" he croaked.

"Dr. Marley, this is Janice in the Emergency Room," a female voice said.

Perfect, Marley thought. Just what I need. He glanced at the illuminated bedside clock: Three AM. He'd been asleep for exactly thirty minutes. This would make the third time he'd gone into the hospital to admit a patient from the Emergency Room.

"What have you got," he said, trying not to yawn.

"Let me have Dr. Keller speak to you," the nurse said, giggling. "And Merry Christmas."

Uh, oh, Marley said to himself. When a nurse jumps off the phone that fast to get the doctor, he knew something was wrong.

"Hey, Bob. It's Jack Keller. I'm sorry to wake you again, but I've got another patient that needs to be admitted."

"What's his problem?"

"A nice old man with severe stomach pain. I think it's his gallbladder."

"Jack, is there something you're not telling me."

Marley heard a stifled chuckle. "Why don't you come in and see for yourself. And, oh, Bob?"

"What?"

"Merry Christmas from the E.R." Just before the connection was broken, Marley heard a chorus of laughs in the background.

What was that all about, he wondered as he swung out of bed. The cold hit him immediately. Man, I can't remember a winter as cold as this, he thought.

For a week now, the temperatures had been below freezing. Three feet of new snow had nearly paralyzed the city. The only vehicles moving were four-wheel drive, and even those were skidding.

Walking down the hall toward the bathroom, he found himself shivering. Whether it was due to the cold or just the lonely feeling of an empty house, he wasn't sure. The door to his sons' room stood open, but their usual snoring sounds were absent. And so were they. Marley's wife had taken them and his daughter to her sister's house fifty miles away. The ache of their leaving was intense and he tried to push it out of his mind. He stopped at their "wall of memories." There were a myriad of pictures — the children laughing, wrestling, snow skiing, birthday parties, playing baseball. He and his wife sailing on their honeymoon. Marley standing alongside the YMCA basketball team he had coached last year. His son, Travis, standing a head taller than his teammates.

He turned away and went into the bathroom.

Bundled in his down jacket and fleece-lined boots, Marley flung open the front door and jogged through the snow to his Chevy Suburban.

Once inside, his breath steamed up the windows. In his heavy wool mittens, he fumbled with the key, finally getting it into the ignition. Fortunately, the engine started on the first try. Marley immediately switched the heater to high.

As he pulled away from the five foot high snow berm, he wondered what he was going to find in the emergency room that everyone thought was so humorous.

Sue Marley lay in the dark, starring at the ceiling. Occasionally the lights from a passing car reflected off its white surface, briefly illuminating the small room and its many occupants. The next time it happened, she leaned over and checked to see if her six year old twins, Parker and Spenser, were both covered by the down comforter. Spenser had a tendency to pull it off Parker.

The quick flash of light revealed them both nicely positioned. Stretched out next to them was their eleven-year-old brother, Travis, his long lanky form covered by multiple blankets. And next to Sue lay her seven year old — going on twelve — daughter, Tyler. All were warm and asleep. Sue lay back in the bed, one less worry off her mind.

What a way to spend the Christmas holidays, she thought, camping out at my sister's. How did it ever come to this?

She loved Bob. They'd had a wonderful twelve years together. Oh, they'd had their disagreements, but never anything like this. In truth, the situation was comical, but still it was threatening to ruin Christmas.

She couldn't even talk with her sister about it. How could she explain that she didn't want her kids to spend the holidays with their father because he had "pretended long enough" and this was the year he was going to tell them there was no Santa Claus. And this expose was based, he'd explained two nights ago to her, on his long held knowledge that "reindeer don't fly."

It took Bob Marley almost thirty-five minutes to reach the E.R. His home was up in the mountains that ringed the east side of the city and the road down was treacherous in the icy conditions.

When he arrived, the doctors' parking stood empty except for the Jeep that Marley knew belonged to Doctor Keller in the E.R. He turned off the engine, pulled his collar up, and lumbered to the E.R. entrance.

Not surprisingly, the Emergency Room was nearly empty. The two night nurses, upon seeing Marley, both grinned hugely. "Your patient is in room 3, Dr. Marley," one of them said. "I hope you brought your Christmas wish list."

Marley half-smiled, although he had no idea what she meant. He shuffled into exam room 3.

"Hi, I'm Dr. — ," the words caught in his throat as he starred at the occupant of the bed.

Marley had seen a lot of old men with white beards in the E.R., but he had never seen one dressed like Santa Claus.

"Excuse me," Marley said, "I'll be right back."

Marley found Dr. Keller sleeping in one of the exam rooms.

"Wake up, Jack," he said, shaking Keller's shoulder.

Keller opened his eyes, saw Marley, and immediately began to smile. "Did you ask him for a ride in his sled," he said.

"What's going on, Jack?"

Keller sat up, rubbing the sleep from his eyes. "The guy's a nice old bird, just a little crazy."

"What gives with the Santa outfit?"

"One of the nurses recognized him. He works every year at the Macy's Department Store as Santa Claus. She's taken her kids to see him for several years."

"Why's he wearing his Santa getup to the E.R.?"

Keller shrugged his shoulders. "How do I know? Maybe those are the warmest clothes he owns."

Marley went back into exam room 3. "Hi, I'm Dr. Marley. The E.R. doctor asked me to examine you."

The man smiled and held out his hand. "Nice to meet you, Dr. Marley. I'm -" and he paused for just a second, "Chris Smith." He gestured around the room. "I'm sorry to put everyone to such bother, but I'm feeling fine now so I think I'll be on my way."

"Whoa, just a minute there," Marley said, gently pushing him back on the bed. "Why don't I ask you a few questions, examine you, and then we can decide if you should go home. Okay?"

"Dr. Marley, I'm in quite a rush. I only came in because I was in such terrible pain I couldn't continue to work. But now, I'm much better."

"I can't force you to stay, Mr. Smith, but -"

At that moment, Mr. Smith let out a cry and dropped back on the bed. Clutching his stomach, he rolled around moaning in pain. Marley quickly called one of the nurses. Together they undressed Mr. Smith down to his red underwear as he continued to cry out in pain. While the nurse placed his clothes in a plastic bag, Marley asked a number of questions and then carefully examined Mr. Smith. After he finished, he said, "I'm sorry Mr. Smith but you apparently have a very sick gallbladder that needs to come out."

Mr. Smith glanced over, his face grimacing with pain. "Do you mean surgery?"

"Yes, I'm afraid so."

"How long will I be in the hospital?"

"Well, it's now five in the morning Christmas eve. With a little bit of luck, we can have you out Christmas day or the following day."

Mr. Smith shook his head vigorously. "No! No! That just won't do. I have to be out of the hospital this afternoon at the very latest."

Marley patted Mr. Smith's hand. "That's just not possible. You'll probably either be in surgery then or sleeping in the recovery room."

"Can't you just give me some pain pills? I could come back the day after Christmas and you could operate on me then."

"Your gallbladder is getting sicker by the moment. If we wait until then, it may be too late to save you."

"I don't care," Mr. Smith said. "I must leave." He levered himself up in bed, slide his legs over the side, and tried to stand. The pain was too much and he nearly fell to the ground. All that saved him was Marley's arms around his waist.

"Do you believe me now? You're too ill to leave the hospital." Marley said helping him back into bed. He left the room and started making arrangements to get Mr. Smith admitted to the hospital and set up for surgery. A little later he saw the nurse take the portable phone into

Mr. Smith's room.

After Marley finished the admitting orders, he called a surgeon and explained the problem.

"Definitely sounds like he's going to need surgery. Hopefully, we can do it through a scope," Dr. Banner the surgeon replied. "It's five AM. How soon can we get him into an operating room?"

"The first available room won't be until two this afternoon," Marley said.

"That's fine. I'll see him later this morning. In the meantime, put him on pain medication and antibiotics."

Marley hung up and went to give Mr. Smith the news. He didn't take it well.

"Oh, my heavens. You must get me into surgery sooner. I have to be out of the hospital by this evening. Everything depends on it."

After a long sleepless night, Marley was out of patience. "Look, Mr. Smith. You are not going home today. Probably not even tomorrow. So get use to the idea. The department store will just have to find another Santa Claus."

Mr. Smith shook his head. "Is that what you think this is all about, Dr. Marley? My job at Macy's?" He laughed bitterly. "No, this is a much more important job."

"What is so urgent about your work that you'd leave the hospital on Christmas Eve, risking your life to get it done?"

Mr. Smith beckoned Marley to come closer. "You must promise to tell no one," he said softly. "Do you promise?"

He's crazy, thought Marley, but I'll humor him. "Sure, you've got my word."

"You ask what job I have that's so important?" he whispered. "I'm Santa Claus."

"Yeah, at Macy's."

"No, I live at the North Pole. I am the real Santa Claus."

Marley was speechless. Mr. Smith was crazier than he'd thought.

"So you can imagine what will happen if I'm not free to go on my appointed rounds this evening." Mr. Smith shuddered. "A Christmas without Santa Claus. What a terrifying thought."

Maybe he's delusional from his illness, Marley wondered. "If you are the real Santa, then why are you working at Macy's year after year as their Santa?"

"The answer should be obvious, Dr. Marley. If I don't have the children come and tell me what they want for Christmas, how will I know what toys are popular? Which one's we need to make more of or less of. All the information I gather from them goes right back to my workshop at the North Pole."

More than crazy, Marley concluded. "So how did you end up here, Santa?"

Mr. Smith glanced hurriedly around. "Please, Dr. Marley. Don't use my real name. Someone might hear you."

"Oh, yeah. I forgot," he said sarcastically. "Sorry, Mr. Smith."

"The reason I'm here is that I became ill just as I was leaving for home."

"Home? As in the North Pole?"

"But of course."

"Exactly how were you going to get there? The airport has been shut down for two days." Marley threw up his hands. "No, wait. Don't tell me. You were going to fly there in your sled. Right?"

Mr. Smith half-smiled. "You don't believe me, do you Dr. Marley?"

"I'm sorry Mr. Smith, but no I don't."

"Well, that's okay. Many adults seem to lose their belief in me which is fine because my job is to bring Christmas to the children."

"Well, my job is to get you well," Marley said. "Then you can go live whatever fantasy you want."

"You seem angry with me. Have I done something to upset you?" Mr.

Smith asked.

"Now that you mention it, yes. You and your kind have made up this cock and bull story about a little fat man and his eight tiny reindeer -"

"Actually, nine reindeer with Rudolph," Mr. Smith said interrupting him.

"Of course, how could I forget? And you foster this myth onto our kids, year after year. If some poor father tries to convince them you aren't real, then he's in the dog house."

"Ah," Mr. Smith said slowly nodding. "And you are that poor father. Now I see." He paused a moment. "When did you stop believing in me, Dr. Marley?"

Marley took a deep breath. Why am I even discussing this with him? The last thing this old man needs is me beating up on his fantasies. But there was something about the man that forced him to go on. "When I was nine years old, there was a toy I wanted so badly that it was all I could think about. I didn't tell anyone that I wanted it, not even my parents. Instead, I sent a letter to Santa. Christmas morning I raced downstairs and guess what? The present wasn't there. That's when I decided it was all a myth."

"On the basis of not receiving one toy, you gave up your belief in me? What if you'd prayed to God for something and didn't get it? Would you give up your belief in God?" Mr. Smith stroked his beard. "There must have been something else. Some other reason you stopped believing."

"That same year, I read in an encyclopedia that reindeer don't fly. I knew, therefore, there was no way they could fly your sled around."

"And that's why you gave up your belief in me. I've heard of a lot of reasons but that's a first." He closed his eyes for a moment, apparently deep in thought. "I don't suppose you believe in magic?"

"Magic is just the art of illusion," Marley replied.

"Yet you believe in miracles, such as the story that Jesus, whose birth we celebrate tomorrow, rose from the dead and ascended into heaven. Is that a delusion? Some more trickery?"

Marley didn't answer.

"So maybe there are things you don't understand," Mr. Smith said, "yet still believe in."

"Whatever," Marley said. "So what's your point?"

"My point is that much of what I do involves a kind of magic."

"So you're a magician?"

"Oh, no. I'm just an ordinary man. It's the things around me that are magic. Those are what allow me to be Santa Claus."

"I don't follow you."

"Everything around me has magical powers. My sled, my reindeer, my toy shop. Which reminds me, where did they put my clothes?" He looked around worriedly.

Marley walked over to the corner of the room and picked up a heavy plastic bag. "There all in here."

"Thank God." Suddenly, he was overcome with pain, clutching his stomach, rolling about on the bed. Fortunately, the spasm quickly passed.

"Dr. Marley," he said through clenched teeth. "You must do me a favor. A life or death kind of favor. I'll grant any Christmas wish that's in my power if you'll do this one thing for me."

"What is it?" Marley asked apprehensively.

"If I'm still confined in the hospital this afternoon, you must take my clothes and deliver them to an associate of mine. I can't stress the urgency and importance of this task."

"Or there won't be any Christmas. Is that it?"

Mr. Smith slowly shook his head, giving Marley a sad smile. "You don't understand Christmas. It's not about me bringing presents. It's not about your relatives sending you gifts or you buying something for them. That's not the real meaning of Christmas."

"Don't let Macy's here that."

"Christmas is celebrating the birth of Christ. The birth of love, joy, and salvation for all of us. It's about caring and giving. Caring about your fellow neighbor and giving to them. Giving your love, your time, your concern. And it's a time to be close to your family. The trees, the bright lights, the ornaments, and even me, we're all secondary to the true meaning of Christmas."

Marley found himself wanting to hear more, wanting to just sit and listen to this…this crazy man. And then he realized how he sounded. Quickly he stood, clearing his voice. "I have to go see the rest of my patients. I'll peek in later."

"What about the favor I asked?"

"You want me to drop off your clothes. Well, I'm not going to drive to the North Pole if that's what you want."

Mr. Smith smiled. "No, no. You just have to drop them a short ways outside of town. Please, Dr. Marley. Without your promise to help me, I couldn't possibly go to surgery. I'd have to deliver them myself."

Best not to upset him, Marley thought. After surgery, he won't even remember he asked. "Sure. Just write out the directions and I'll drop them off."

"In return, I'll keep my part of the bargain and fulfill whatever gift you want for Christmas."

"You can't get me what I want for Christmas," Marley said.

"You'd be surprised at the range of gifts I've had to get," Mr. Smith said.

"I'd like my family to be with me Christmas morning."

"Where are they now?"

"They are at my wife's sister's house in Springfield."

"What are they doing over there?" Mr. Smith asked.

"I was going to tell the children that reindeer don't fly so they could stop believing in Santa Claus."

"Well, aren't you the Christmas Scrooge?" Mr. Smith rubbed his chin for a while. "This is going to be a very tough gift, indeed."

"Hey, don't worry about it," Marley said. "Ever since my ninth Christmas, I've never expected anything from you." Besides, he thought, I don't want this nice old guy fretting about a present for me when he needs to concentrate on getting well.

Marley left the exam room and went to the doctor's lounge. He showered, shaved, and changed into some clean clothes. The next six hours were spent seeing patients in the hospital and admitting two more. For some reason, he couldn't get Mr. Smith out of his mind. There was just something about him. Something, something — he didn't even want to think it — something magical. He'd called surgery several times and each time had been reassured that all was well. Finally, at three o'clock, he was done. He could go home and enjoy Christmas Eve.

Not much to enjoy with no one at the house, he thought. Maybe I should drive over to Springfield and surprise Sue and the kids. No. He was too tired to make the drive and what would he say? Gee, sorry I was wrong. Reindeer do fly.

He was just leaving the hospital when his name was paged. "Dr. Marley. Dr. Marley. Come to the surgical recovery room."

Mr. Smith! He's had a complication. I should never have taken someone else's word. I should have checked on him myself, he thought as he raced to the recovery room.

"Mr. Smith is fine, Dr. Marley," the recovery nurse said when Marley arrived breathless. She pointed to the bed in the far corner and Marley saw him sleeping comfortably.

"So why the call?"

"Before he went to surgery, he made us promise to give this bag of clothes to you. He said you'd know what to do with it."

She handed Marley a large white plastic bag containing the Santa outfit. A white envelope was stapled to the bag.

The snow was coming down hard when Marley walked to his car. A strong wind blew through his heavy clothes and froze him to the bone. By the time he had the engine started, he thought he'd never get warm again. While he was waiting for the motor to heat up, he tore open the envelope.

Dear Dr. Marley,

Thank you again for doing me this most important favor. I have drawn a map of where you need to go to drop off my belongings. Please be punctual. You must be there no later than five o'clock. One of my business partners, Mr. Small, will be there to meet you.

I'm sorry about not getting you the Hopalong Cassidy Holster and Gun Set you wanted on your ninth Christmas, but we only had so many, and they'd already been promised to other children by the time I got your letter.

Merry Christmas,

Chris Smith

P.S. Whatever you do, please be very careful with my clothes.

Marley sat staring at the letter. How did he know what I wanted for my ninth Christmas? I don't remember telling him that. But I must of, or how else would he have know? Marley thought of the other way he would know and decided to stop thinking about it. Besides, he was too tired to remember what he'd told Mr. Smith.

He glanced back down at the letter. Deliver it to a Mr. Small? If I had to make up a name for an elf, I hope I could be more creative.

He pulled the map out of the envelope and checked Mr. Smith's directions.

Great! The drop-off spot was almost twenty miles out of town in a nearly deserted canyon area. Even with four-wheel drive, he'd have trouble getting through all the snow piled up on the highway. Maybe he'd be lucky and the roads would have been recently plowed.

He switched on the radio to check the weather as he drove out of the doctor's parking lot. Even thought the city plow had just been through, the streets were already covered with several inches of snow.

The tone of the radio announcer's voice caught his attention. "A severe winter storm is rapidly moving into the area. Several feet of new snow is expected. Along with the freezing cold, the accompanying winds should bring the temperatures far below zero. The national weather bureau is advising everyone to stay indoors for the next twenty-four hours. Do not go outside unless it is an absolute emergency."

Marley shouted sarcastically at the radio, "I have to drop off Santa's clothes to one of his elves. Is that emergency enough?"

He drove for another fifteen minutes, several times nearly skidding off the road. How did I ever get talked into this? I must be as crazy as that old man. If someone had told me I'd be out driving in the worst storm of the century to deliver Santa's belongings I'd have put them in the looney bin.

Up ahead, he saw the turn off for the road to his house. A little voice whispered in his ear, "You could be home in twenty minutes. A nice fire, some soft music, a hot meal."

"And an empty, lonely house," Marley said out loud as he drove past the turnoff.

The next thirty minutes included some of the worst driving conditions that Marley had ever faced, and he'd driven in a lot of bad storms. Even the windshield wipers couldn't clear the snow fast enough, so he'd had to stop several times to wipe the windshield by hand. Each time he got back into the car, it had taken him nearly five minutes to warm up. After a while, he quit thinking about why he was doing this and just concentrated on reaching the drop-off point.

He turned onto Forest Canyon Road and finally he had some luck. It had been recently plowed. Even so, there was already nearly a foot of new snow on the roadway but Marley's Suburban easily handled it. He stopped and checked the map again.

He was supposed to meet Mr. Small at mile marker twelve. Marley had just seen mile marker six in his headlights. He'd switched them on earlier because the storm had brought an early darkness. He counted the markers in his head as he passed them.

Seven.

Eight.

Nine, he apparently missed because the next marker he saw was ten.

Eleven.

And then his luck ran out. He hit the brakes hard but the car just keep moving, sliding on black ice right toward a huge avalanche blocking the road. Marley's car slammed into the snow pile and everything went black.

He was stunned for a moment with the force of the impact and a feeling like someone had slapped him in the face. He found himself pinned to the seat, unable to move, and then realized that his air bag had deployed. It was pushing him back into the seat. With his left hand, he reached over and tried to open the door. The latch released but the door refused to open. Something was pressing on it from the outside. He inched his right hand up into his jacket, eased a ball point pen out, and then jabbed it into the bag. It took several tries, but finally the bag collapsed.

Removing the flashlight from the glove compartment, he shone it through the windows. His car had gone a fair distance into the snow bank, burying it almost up to the front doors. With the crash, the engine had gone out. He turned the key and it immediately started.

Thank God, he said. And he meant it.

He put the car into reverse and gave it some gas. Nothing happened. He gave it a little more gas. Still nothing. He finally pressed the gas pedal to the floor. Absolutely no movement, just the spinning of his wheels. For the next five minutes, he tried every trick he knew to get the car free but it wouldn't budge.

He hit the steering wheel with his hand. Darn it. Why didn't I just go home? This is a mission of pure insanity. He glanced over at the clothes' bag. The more he looked at it, the more he wanted to get rid of it.

All right. Let's get organized, he thought. I've got plenty of gas in the car. With the engine on, I can run the heater to keep warm until someone finds me. All night if I have to. He had a small survival kit in the back with food and water so that wouldn't be a problem. Besides, he reasoned, the snow plow should be back, at least by morning. He checked his watch. Four-forty.

The words in Mr. Smith's letter flooded into his mind: "You must be no later than five o'clock."

Then he heard that little voice in his ear again. "You could still make it. It couldn't be more than a half a mile to marker twelve."

"Weren't you the one that wanted to go home? Well, forget it, I'm not going outside." He said this loudly, hoping that would silence the little voice.

"You've come this far already," the voice said. "What's another half a mile?"

"Are you crazy? Didn't you hear the weatherman on the radio? I could die out there."

"You can't walk a half a mile?" The voice answered. "You jog six miles three times a week. Besides, what if that old man was telling the truth? What if he really is...?"

"Stop it. I don't want to hear it. You win. But I'm only doing it because... because I would do anything to get my family back home. I don't believe a thing that old man said. And if good old Mr. Small isn't standing by that mile marker, I'm not waiting for him. You got that." Marley remembered that one of the first signs of losing your mind was supposed to be talking to yourself. No, he decided, the first sign is letting some crazy old man convince you to drop off his underwear. The front door was blocked by the snow and wouldn't open. He tossed the bag into the back seat and climbed over after it. The rear door open easily and Marley stepped out into the wind whipped, swirling snow. The cold was far worse than he'd anticipated, much worse. He buttoned his coat up to his neck, threw the bag of clothes on his shoulder, and headed into the storm.

By the time he crossed the avalanche, which couldn't have been more than fifty yards, he was exhausted. The snow was so soft that he sank to his mid-thigh with each step. But that was nothing compared to the cold. It was everywhere, coming through every possible opening in his clothes, not to mention his exposed face and ears. His lips were so numb that he couldn't even cuss when he stumbled and fell for the fifth time.

I'm going to freeze to death out here, he thought. At the very least, I'm going to get frost bite on my face and ears. I have to turn back.

It was at this point that he reached the road on the other side of the avalanche. The snow there was only about two feet deep. Still slow going, yet much easier than before. But the cold still continued to eat him up, draining all his energy.

He stopped and looked back in the direction of his car. All he could see was a curtain of falling snow. I must have been crazy to think I could survive this cold dressed like I am, he thought. I'm going to have to go back. There's nothing else I can do. I gave it my best try.

Faintly, over the sound of the howling wind, he heard that same little voice in his ear. "There's a way you can still go on."

"And exactly what would that be," Marley mumbled.

"Put on the old man's clothes," the voice replied. "They'll keep you warm and it would be a lot easier to wear them than carry them."

If Marley's stiff, frozen face had allowed it, he would have smiled. For once the voice had a good idea. He reached into the bag and pulled out the bright red coat and pulled it on over his own. Immediately, he felt warmer. Next, he slipped the pants on over his own trousers. Warmer still.

He lifted the bag up and looked to see what remained. Heavy black leather boots. A pair of thick gloves. One red woolen hat with white trim.

The pants and coat had added a lot of warmth, but still his hands, face, and feet were numb and painful. He plopped down in the snow and exchanged his wet boots for the black ones in the bag. Within seconds, his feet began to thaw out. He slipped his mittens off, and put on the thick leather gloves. Lastly, he pulled the woolen hat on over his head.

For the first time, since he'd left the hospital, he felt warm. Actually cozy might be a better term. He picked up his discarded clothes and tossed them in the bag.

No wonder Mr. Smith had worn these clothes to the emergency room, he said to himself. They really were warm. He'd have to ask him where he purchased them so he could get a similar set. Only not in red, he concluded with a smile. He wondered what his friends, or even his own family, would think of him if they could see him now.

He began walking again, only this time it seemed so much easier. The boots seem to glide through the snow and he never stumbled. I'm getting my second wind, he thought. Just needed a little rest.

The wind charged around him, the snow fell so heavily he couldn't see more than a few feet, and the cold snapped branches off the nearby trees, yet Marley felt as comfortable as if he were sitting in his easy chair in front of the fireplace.

In the midst of this, he had a sudden clear thought. He knew exactly what each of his children wanted for Christmas. Things that they had never told him. Things, in fact, that he'd never even heard of.

And then he began to know exactly what his sister's children wanted. And what his sister-in-law's children wanted.

This is weird, he thought. I must be hallucinating. The cold, the lack of sleep, the stress of Sue and the children leaving. It's all starting to hit me now.

But still the Christmas wishes of every child he knew, even children he didn't know, bombarded his mind, pushing everything else out.

Now he was really worried. He tore off the woolen cap, hoping the sudden exposure to the cold would clear his mind. Immediately, the Christmas wishes stopped.

With a sigh of relief, he pulled the cap back on. Within a minute, the Christmas wishes of children around the world were buzzing through his mind.

What is going on here, he ask himself?

Now, he really was worried. He yanked the cap off and his mind went quiet again. Cautiously, he replaced the cap and sure enough, within seconds, the Christmas wish lists were back.

I'd rather be cold, he decided, and pulled the cap off, jamming it into his jacket pocket.

Up ahead, he could barely make out the twelve mile marker sticking up through the snow. When he reached the marker, he looked around. There was no one in sight. No Mr. Small. No Mr. Big. No one at all. He checked his watch. Four-fifty meaning only ten minutes had elapsed since he left his car! That was impossible! It had taken him at least fifteen minutes just to cross the avalanche and put on Smith's clothes. He knew at least twenty-five minutes had passed since getting out of the car.

He leaned against the mile marker. So what do I do now, he wondered? Leave the clothes here? Wait for someone to show up? I guess I'd better take them off. It'll look a little funny if I'm wearing the clothes I'm supposed to drop off. He suddenly remembered the P.S. in Mr. Smith's letter: Please be careful with my clothes

Yeah, I'd better get them off before someone shows up. He was struggling to get the gloves off, which seemed to have a mind of their own, when he heard his name called out behind him. He spun around, ready with excuses for wearing the clothes. He wasn't sure what surprised him more. The little man dressed in his winter best or the reindeer he was riding.

"Is this Sue Marley?" the deep voice said on the phone.

"Yes," Sue wondered who would be calling at seven thirty on Christmas morning.

"This is Sheriff Johnson. I'm looking for your husband. Do you know where he might be?"

"Home or at the hospital. Why?"

"Well, we checked both of those places and he's not there."

A sudden fierce apprehension gripped Sue Marley. "What's going on, Sheriff? What's the matter?"

"Now, don't get yourself alarmed. I'm sure it's nothing to worry about. We found you husband's car out on Forest Canyon Road. He'd plowed into an avalanche that was blocking the road. The car was so buried that it couldn't be driven out. There was no sign that he was injured, although his air bag did deploy."

"But you haven't found my husband?"

"That's why I'm calling. Hoping maybe you'd heard from him."

"No," Sue said. "I haven't spoken to him in several days. Maybe someone came by and gave him a ride somewhere."

"That's quite possible. What bother's me, though, is that the car's engine was still running. I would have thought he'd turn it off unless he was planning to come right back."

You mean unless something stopped him from coming back, Sue thought to herself. "You searched the surrounding area?"

"As best we could, considering the weather. One of my men thought he found some vague tracks heading up over the avalanche, toward Forest Canyon but they faded out. Would your husband have had any reason to go up Forest Canyon?"

"No reason that I know of. But, he's a doctor. Maybe someone was sick and asked him to make a house call?"

"There's no one living back up the Canyon, except at the Ranger Station. But that's been closed this last week, due to the weather."

"Please find my husband, Sheriff."

"We'll do all we can, Mrs. Marley. But I should warn you, if he went up Forest Canyon, in this brutal weather, I am real worried.

"Wake up all you sleepyheads. Time to find out if you've been naughty or nice."

Marley groaned, rolled over to the side of his bed, and snapped off the radio. Man, he was exhausted. He felt like he just run a marathon, then lifted weights for six hours. Just the simple act of turning off the radio had caused a momentary cramp in his forearm.

The clock radio read ten o'clock. Boy, I haven't slept this late for years. Then, remembering what day it was, he added, I've never slept this late Christmas morning. I'd better get up and see what Sue and the kids are doing.

He yanked the covers back, swung his legs over the side of the bed, and sat up. The stillness in the house reminded him that he was alone, and he felt an emptiness in his chest.

Well, what had he expected? Sue had made it very clear she wasn't coming back until after Christmas.

Outside the window, the storm had stopped and the sun was breaking through in patches. He put his bathrobe on and opened the room door.

Once again, he got a stab of pain in his forearm just turning the door knob. Both wrists and forearms felt like he had been exercising the heck out of them. The only time they'd been that sore was many years ago when Marley had been a kid visiting his uncle's ranch. His uncle had hitched his two mules up to a wagon and let Marley drive the wagon around to help with the chores. His forearms had felt like that the next day also.

He stepped out of the bedroom, walked through the hallway, and was halfway down the stairs when he abruptly halted.

In the center of the living room was the most beautiful tree he'd ever seen. Spread out beneath it was a huge pile of wrapped presents.

Where did that come from, he wondered? I didn't put up any tree, much less buy all these presents. Maybe it was Sue.

He ran down the rest of the stairs, calling out her name, looking through the kitchen and den. The house was still empty.

Sadly, he walked back to the tree. A tag on one of the presents caught his eye. "For Robert from Santa." He bent down and lifted the package up. He shook it once but it made no sound.

Without warning, he felt a sudden surge pass through him. All the excitement of getting up at the crack of dawn and racing into the living room to see what Santa had brought flooded back into his mind. And he was nine years old, breathing in the scent of the Douglas fir his mother had so carefully decorated, hearing the fire crackle in the brick hearth, hoping against hope that this was his special present. He tore part of the wrapping off, and his breath caught in his throat. Through eyes blurred by tears, he read the label: The Hopalong Cassidy Holster and Gun Set.

On spaghetti-like legs, he stepped back and dropped into his easy chair. All sorts of thoughts flooded into his mind. Now he remembered the dream he'd had last night. A dream of flying over towns and cities and oceans. Of presents, and decorations. Of eating more cookies and milk than he knew ever existed. A dream where time moved so slowly it almost stood still. It had seemed so real last night but this morning he knew it all to be a dream. But what a beautiful dream.

He set his present down and looked at all the other unopened gifts. What good were they if the family wasn't here? Christmas really had nothing to do with presents. It was family and friends. Goodwill to all men. All those things he use to think were so trite, yet now they seemed so right.

With a sigh, he laid his head back on the cushion of the chair and closed his eyes. Using his imagination, he could almost hear Sue's car pull up in the driveway. Hear the slamming of the car doors. Now he could imagine their footsteps echoing on the wooden porch. Next they would open the front door and he would hear — .

"Robert, oh Robert you're safe. Thank, God."

"Daddy, daddy," several other voices yelled.

Marley popped up and there was Sue and the children standing in the front doorway. Just then, the children spied the tree.

"Santa's been here," they yelled, racing for the presents.

"Yes, he has," Marley said, "and he's brought presents for all of us."

He turned to Sue and they hugged each other for a long time. They turned and, still holding each other, watched the children open their gifts.

"Robert," Sue said gently, "This is so nice of you to get a tree and presents for the kids." She paused. "I've been thinking about what you said, about the fact that reindeer don't fly."

Robert threw back his head and laughed. "Isn't that the craziest notion that reindeer can fly? What dunderhead ever thought that up?" He squeezed her tightly. "I'm going to make sure my family knows the truth."

She looked up at him, a frown on her face. "The truth?" she asked.

"Of course the truth. I can't have my children spreading falsehoods like that. Reindeer don't fly, they leap. They can leap ten feet or ten miles, whatever is needed. But they definitely don't fly."

He wasn't sure how he knew this, but he was sure that it was true.

* * * * *

I wrote this many years ago for my children, now all grown, some married, and one expecting our first grandchild. When I first read this to them, I realized they were too young to fully understand it, but we all enjoyed it and still do.

My original inspiration was from Clement Clarke Moore who in 1823 wrote the poem, "Twas the Night Before Christmas," for his children. I asked myself why couldn't I write a Christmas story for my children? And thus this story was born. Even though I wrote it so many years ago, I still get a bit misty-eyed reading it again. Christmas is such an incredible time when people let their caring, loving side appear, while opening their hearts to their fellow man.

But I laugh at telling you all this because you are Hungry Romantics, and you already know and live the meaning of Christmas every day.

Stories for the Hungry Romantic

Four Wheels and a Daughter

By Tyler Moran

"I don't know why your mother is having such a problem teaching you to drive," I said as I sat in the car with my daughter. "It's not that stressful."

"Dad, I can drive!" she replied exasperatedly. "But Mom makes me so nervous with her loud comments, and her white-knuckle-grip on the dashboard, that I lose it."

"Well, that's why we are out here today; so I can give you some pointers. Help you through the infant stages, so to speak, of driving." I looked over at the gem of my heart. "First lesson, don't hold the steering wheel like that. Put your hands at 3 o'clock and 9 o'clock position." I paused. "Do you know why?"

She shrugged her cute little shoulders. "Mom told me that's the best position to flip off bad drivers."

"What did you say?!" I half-yelled in disbelief.

"Just joking, Dad…" She smirked.

"Keep your eyes on the road," I retorted. It seemed my wife was teaching lessons far passed the introductory stages of driving. "Okay. We are coming to an intersection. Do we stop 10 feet before the crosswalk, just at the crosswalk, or in the crosswalk?"

"Duhhhh," she said, rolling her eyes.

"If you're driving with me, then we're going to discuss all the potential problems that may develop. After all, what's the Boy Scout motto?"

"I wouldn't know Dad; I was a Girl Scout."

"Err, right... Well it's 'Always Be Prepared'! Or something like that..." I took a sip out of the water bottle I was holding. "So let's do a few pretend scenarios that could happen in this intersection."

"Whatever." She sighed in sync to another eye roll.

"Keep your eyes on the road," I reminded her. "Think of approaching an intersection like approaching a relationship. Anything can happen. You may race into it without mishap, or you may stop, look both ways, and still get blindsided." I lowered my window slightly. "That reminds me of when I started dating your mother..."

"Let me guess," she interrupted, "you proceeded cautiously and still got blindsided?"

"Oh, Ha-ha! Funny, honey... Actually, I raced into it and ended up with four mishaps! One of whom is a very sarcastic daughter." I took another sip from my water bottle. "In truth, I did proceed cautiously, but I failed to follow my English teacher's favor rule..."

"I before e except after c?" She slipped in.

"No. It was 'To be precise is to be concise'."

My daughter's chin dropped to her chest. "Can we make this story more concise?"

"I cautiously asked your mother what she thought of marriage," I replied. "That was not a precise sentence since I definitely was not proposing. What I was asking was her view on marriage."

"But her answer was very precise," my daughter replied. "She said yes, and you were engaged." She shook her head. "I have heard this story before."

"The point is that when some future boyfriend asks you what you think of premarital sex, you will be precise and concise so there is no misunderstanding, and say 'No'."

She shook her head and brushed a lock of hair back from her face. "Can we get back to driving?"

"All right. Let's make a right hand turn. First, we need to change into the right lane. How do you do that?"

"I use my mirror and look back to make sure the lane is clear."

"Let's see it," I smiled. "Nicely done! I just don't know what your mother's problem is." I stated again. "It's just patience and common sense."

I pointed to the steering wheel. "You didn't use your turn indicator. That's not a problem now since there are no cars, but you always need to let the people around you know what you are doing. Think of it as calling home and letting us know where you are going. That, like your turn indicator, seems to be something you fail to do."

"Driving Dad. Stick to the driving."

I pointed ahead of us. "Yellow light coming up. Do we try and beat it?"

"No, we never race a yellow light." She shook her head firmly. "We only race trains to the crossing."

I sighed. "Sweetheart, I'm just trying to make sure we cover all potential situations. I would never forgive myself if something were to happen to you and it was because I failed to adequately prepare you." A thought flittered through my mind. "It's the same thing with premarital sex..."

"Dad! You already made that point." She shot me a withering glare. "This is about me getting my license next year. Stop trying to make it a lecture on boyfriends and dating!"

"Eyes back on the road!" I said again. "And speaking of boyfriends, you need to remind yours not, and I repeat 'not' to call our house after 9 P.M. And I don't care what the reason."

"None of my friends call after nine. They are too afraid." She said plainly.

"In regards to boyfriends, fear of your father is a good thing!"

My daughter hit the horn. Honk! Honk! "Dad! Can we please get back to my driving?!"

"What do you think we've been doing?" I responded. "Your driving and your life are intimately related. Your philosophy of life may well determine how you handle your car. Do you know why?"

She slumped forward and banged her head on the steering wheel.

I threw up my hands "Okay, okay, I'll stop. But don't blame me when you look back over your life and see it littered with broken relationships and smashed cars." I nodded sagely.

"Speaking of cars...Are you going to buy me one for my birthday, Dad?" She pursed her lips and blew a kiss in my direction.

"Of course I am, Sweetheart!"

She gave a yelp of surprised excitement.

"I'm just not sure which birthday it will be!" I chuckled at my wit.

She sank in her seat. "Then what car will be mine? I'm supposed to drive the old white truck?" Her face darkened.

"I drove that 'old white truck' for ten years and had no complaints."

She rolled her eyes. "Well, let's see. You can't turn off the heater, smoke is always belching out the back, the seats have no springs left, the tape player eats tapes, there is only one speaker working, and the best part is it smells like a cross between old sweat socks and dog vomit.

I smiled, "A perfect car for a first-time driver!"

"Oh yuck," she disagreed.

"Think of it like some of the boys who you hang out with at school. On the outside they look like hell – nose rings, earrings, tattoos, spiked hair, baggy clothing, inane conversations-yet you seem to find some endearing qualities under all that. So too the car. Looks bad on the outside, but has it ever broken down? Ever not gotten us home?"

She remained silent, staring straight ahead.

"Sometimes a flashy sports car isn't the vehicle you want permanently in your garage," I concluded.

It was a moment before she spoke. "You're right, Dad."

I nodded. I'd finally won a point with my daughter.

"If I had that beat up truck," she continued, "I would keep it permanently in the garage so it would never be seen. I'd park my BMW convertible out in the driveway."

Another battle lost. Oh well, just as long as I don't lose the war. I pointed ahead. "There's a cop and we're going too fast. What do you do?"

"Slam on the brakes!" she cried, hitting the brake pedal.

"Now that was really subtle. You sure wouldn't attract attention laying down skid marks for twenty yards."

I glanced back over my shoulder. "He's turning around. And he's switched on his lights." I stared at her. "So what now?"

She pointed to the glove compartment. "Ditch the drugs!"

I dropped my water bottle, spilling it all over my lap. Over my exclamations of disgust, I heard her laughter. "Funny, funny," I said, brushing off the water. "Pull over and let's see how funny you are with this cop."

"Here he comes." I said. "Roll down your window and be polite," I paused. "Pretend he's a potential boyfriend."

"I know what to do, Dad. I've heard Mom deal with traffic cops a million times."

"What are you talking about?" I asked quizzically. "Your mother has never had a ticket."

She gave me one of her patented are-you-really-that-stupid looks, and it was a moment before I could recover.

"Well, the idea is not to talk your way out of a ticket, but rather not to do something that will result in a ticket in the first place." And I will be speaking to your mother about the same concept, I told myself.

"Hello, Officer," she began. "I know I was driving too fast, but it wasn't my fault. I'm just learning to drive and my father told me to go faster because I was holding up traffic. Then when he saw you, he told me to slam on the brakes. He also said when you walked over, I should flirt with you, like you were a potential boyfriend, so that I could talk my way out of the ticket." She looked over at me and smiled. "Isn't that right, Father dear?"

"I think that's enough driving instruction for today, Daughter dear."

"What do you mean enough?" she exclaimed. "We haven't even left the driveway yet!"

I climbed out and headed toward the house.

"Come back you coward!" she called as I slipped away.

* * * * *

This was written by my daughter as an assignment in high school, and I loved it. I never saw the ending coming. I think the story easily displays her humor, her knife-slicing wit, and her writing talent. With all of those virtues, she has tried a number of jobs, including writing for a TV news station, singer in a band, song writer, and now has just finished her second year in law school and loves it. Hopefully, she will take up writing as a side venture in the future since she is a natural.

SETON
PUBLISHING

Made in the USA
San Bernardino, CA
18 September 2018